Neglected Visions

Neglected Visions

Edited by

BARRY N. MALZBERG,

MARTIN HARRY GREENBERG

and

JOSEPH D. OLANDER

DOUBLEDAY & COMPANY, INC.

GARDEN CITY, NEW YORK

1979

All of the characters in this book
are fictitious, and any resemblance
to actual persons, living or dead,
is purely coincidental.

ISBN: 0-385-14613-2
Library of Congress Catalog Card Number 78-22797
Copyright © 1979 by Barry N. Malzberg, Martin Harry Greenberg and
Joseph D. Olander
All Rights Reserved
Printed in the United States of America
First Edition

Contents

Introduction to *Neglected Visions*

Of all branches of contemporary literature, science fiction has probably done the best job of keeping its best work alive, but this is perhaps a matter of less negligence rather than more attention. One need not be bitter about this. Popular or, for that matter, high culture* turns over nowadays rather rapidly, and Americans have never been noted for their sense of history; too great a sense of history, some analysts have noted, might create an excess of remorse. So the caravan moves on.

The fact is, however, that many of science fiction's acknowledged masterpieces or even good second-rate work manage to stay around *if they have been done by writers of major reputation within the field*. Sturgeon's *More Than Human* (1953) has never really been out of print, Bester's *The Demolished Man* (1952) comes back in a new edition every few years, ten collections of Bradbury are on sale at this very moment, Walter Miller's *A Canticle for Leibowitz* (1959) is in a twelfth printing. And Tom Godwin's 1954 short story "The Cold Equations," a distinguished work by a writer who produced no other story of impact and only one minor novel, has appeared in at least forty anthologies in this country. The optimistic facet of the negative fact that the readership of science fiction turns over 90 percent every four years is that the audience is constantly replenished by those who can approach the major work for the first time.

The *negative* facet of that negative fact, however, is that the caravan does indeed move on and some important work and important writers are left behind. This anthology is an attempt not only to restore to the science fiction audiences some short fiction of lasting value but to restore the reputations of nine writers who for various reasons did not achieve in the time of their greatest productivity the recognition which they deserved and which went to writers no more talented. Some of these writers remain active at a lessened level to this day, others have not published for years, and one of them has been dead for a decade and a half. The true and terrible complete history of science fiction, if it is ever written, will take no less ac-

* And television, angst, and the American high school are rapidly obliterating any useful distinctions.

count of them than of the fifty or so who have struggled to critical recognition within the field. The true and terrible history of science fiction, in fact (I have no plans to write it, by the way; I am no objective historian), will have to point out, in judiciousness, that many of these writers had larger intrinsic gifts and did work of more lasting value than some of our household names.

Why are the nine writers in this book relatively forgotten, then? Why in some cases will this be their first restoration to print in many years? Well, writing, more than any other branch of the so-called creative arts, is a highly individualistic business devoid of easy generalities, and any easy statement will fail to apply to all or even half of them. Some—Abernathy, Phillips—never published novels in the field, and novels not only coalesce a reputation but, unless one is Ray Bradbury, are central to its creation. Others—Clifton, Wallace, Anvil, Garrett—did, but at a level incontestably below their work as short-story writers. Neville did publish novels that were as good as his magazine work and as good as much of what was being done at the time but failed through circumstance or luck. And then again, science fiction, like poetry, seems able to accommodate only a given number of writers of reputation at a certain time; the audience can absorb no more. A concentenation of reasons, as they like to say in the graduate seminars. It would be more constructive to concentrate on what these writers gave rather than on why what they had to give was not accepted to the fullest. The work, as the contents of this anthology will make clear, makes its own statement and will survive.

Of necessity, a book dedicating to restoring to print the work and reputations of undervalued writers of science fiction can be only a partial testimony. There is a *lot* of such work and such writers, and it is our hope that this will be the first of a sequence of such volumes, mostly concentrating on the decade of the 1950s when science fiction, however hesitantly, began to be more than a circumstantial literature, began to become an art form. In the meantime, duty necessitates that we cite some writers whom we would gladly have put into NEGLECTED VISIONS had we but had world enough and time, writers whose work should be sought out and reprinted and who in their time made a major contribution to this difficult literature: Raymond F. Jones, Winston K. Marks, T. L. Sherred, Eric Frank Russell, Laurence M. Janifer, Jim Harmon, Raymond E. Banks, Evelyn E. Smith, Chad Oliver, Daniel F. Galouye, Stephen Barr, Roger Phillips Graham, Mildred Clingerman, Ralph Williams, Margaret St. Clair, Charles Harness . . . any list of this sort by definition cannot be inclusive. If science fiction has twenty writers who are overvalued, it has two hundred who are undervalued. The performing arts is a tricky business.

In any event, here is a modest attempt to bring back to print some good stories and good writers. It would be pretentious (and superfluous) to go much further than that; sufficient to say that the work which follows is as good as or better than the best work available anywhere and there is a hell of a lot more of it, from these and other writers, where this came from.

B.N.M.
March 1978: New Jersey

Neglected Visions

Mark Clifton (1906–63) turned to science fiction only in the last decade of his life, his retirement as an industrial psychologist having apparently been forced by ill health. Clifton's first story, "What Have I Done?," appeared in *Astounding* in 1952 and within three years, through about forty appearances, mostly in that magazine, he made an impression upon the field of great dimension; it is hard for younger readers to take on faith now but I am asking that they do so the fact that for a brief period Mark Clifton was, in the narrow compass of the field at the time, the most influential and controversial short-story writer within the magazines. His career essentially peaked with the 1954 publication, in *ASF*, of *They'd Rather Be Right*, a computer novel in collaboration with Frank Riley that won the second Hugo award in its category, and through the remainder of the fifties his production gradually slowed. Two late novels, *Eight Keys to Eden* (1960) and *When They Come from Space* (1962), made no addition to his reputation, and in 1963 Clifton, a bachelor with no living relatives, made the mistake of dying untimely and intestate.

The fact that no one controlled the copyrights to Clifton's work or could apparently give permission for reprinting meant that for many years anthologists avoided his stories—the possibility of someone appearing with a copy of an anthology screaming *Unauthorized use, I own the copyright, I'm suing* is the anthologist's and publisher's nightmare. By the time the newly organized (1965) Science Fiction Writers of America got to work on the problem with a few devoted friends of Clifton and put some order into the situation, he had been dead for half a decade and his important work was another decade behind that. He simply fell out of print and is almost totally unknown to the audience for science fiction that came to the field after 1960 (which is about 90 percent of it).

This is unfortunate. I consider Mark Clifton to be the most unjustly forgotten of all science fiction writers, and the idea for this anthology originally came from my feeling that some vehicle had to be created to reintroduce his work. Clifton's weaknesses were clear: (a) not schooled or sophisticated in fiction technique, he was by absolute literary standards rather clumsy; (b) he was perhaps too responsive to the editorial whim of his primary editor, John W. Campbell, who in the mid-1950s for many reasons had become obsessed with a science fiction that explored the areas of extrasensory perception and abilities. If Clifton's primary market had instead been obsessed by stories of alien biology, there is the suspicion that Clifton might have written a lot of alien-biology stories.

Those are the *sum* of Clifton's weaknesses and they are human rather than creative flaws, the weaknesses of any of us who try to survive within the framework of the genre markets, realizing that ambition must be subordinate to slant. Clifton's strengths were manifold and easier to state: he had extraordinary perception; his years spent in the evaluation of human personality for short-run technocratic purposes had given him a cynical insight into bureaucratic structure, hierarchical motivation, and individual survival; and in their own way his stories, with their sly and ironic subtext, caught the mood of the 1950s as well as any other writer's inside or outside science fiction. Within his limitations he wrote honestly, painfully, and with great perception, and he was in a never-ending struggle to improve his work, which by 1955, when this story was written, had attained a great deal of professionalism.

"Clerical Error," a brilliantly bewildering story, is, in my evaluation, a masterpiece up to its hasty and unjust ending, which was obviously written for Clifton to sell it to *Astounding,* the top-paying market of its time. (Campbell was a willful editor.) Up until that ending the story in its detachment, irony, and insight that goes beyond pity or remorse stands not only as a stunning indictment of contemporary psychiatric practice (an indictment even more valid two decades later), but as an indictment of all the prejudices by which Campbell ran his magazine. Mark Clifton *sneaked* this one by. As one who has done a little sneakery myself, I bow to the master. May he rest in peace and glory.

B.N.M.

Clerical Error

by MARK CLIFTON

The case of David Storm came to the attention of Dr. K. Heidrich Kingston when Dr. Ernest Moss, psychiatrist in charge of the Q Security wing of the government workers' mental hospital, recommended lobotomy. The recommendation was on the lead-off sheet in Storm's medical history file. It was expressed more in the terms of a declaration of intention than a request for permission.

"I had a little trouble in getting this complete file, doctor," Miss Verity said, as she laid it on his desk. "The fact is Dr. Moss simply brought in the recommendation and asked me to put your initials on it so he could go ahead. I told him that I was still just your secretary, and hadn't replaced you yet as Division Administrator."

Kingston visualized her aloof, almost unfriendly eyes and the faint sarcasm of her clipped speech as she respectfully told off Dr. Moss in the way an old time nurse learns to put doctors in their place, unmistakable but not quite insubordinate. He knew Miss Verity well; she had been with him for twenty years; they understood one another. His lips twitched with a wry grin of appreciation. He looked up at her as she stood beside his desk, waiting for his reaction.

"I gather he's testing the strength of my order that I must personally approve all lobotomies," Kingston commented dryly.

"I'm quite certain the staff already knows your basic opposition to the principle of lobotomy, doctor," she answered him formally. "You made it quite clear in an article you wrote several years ago, May 1958, to be exact, wherein you stated—"

"Yes, yes, I know," he interrupted, and quoted himself from the article, " 'The human brain is more than a mere machine to be disconnected if the attending psychiatrist just doesn't happen to like the way it operates.' I still feel that way, Miss Verity."

"I'm not questioning your medical or moral judgment, doctor," she answered, with a note of faint reproof, "merely your tactical. At the time you alienated a very large block of the profession, and they haven't forgotten it. Psychiatrists are particularly touchy about any public question of their omnipotent right and rightness. In view of our climb to power, that was a tactical error. I also feel the issuance of this order, so soon after taking over the administration of this department, was a bit premature. Dr. Moss said he was not accustomed to being treated like an intern. He merely expressed what the whole staff is thinking, of course."

"So he's the patsy the staff is using to test my authority," Kingston mused. "He is in complete charge of the Q. S. wing. None of the rest of us, not even I, have the proper Security clearances to go into that wing, because we might hear the poor demented fellows mumbling secrets which are too important for us to know."

"You'll have to admit they've set a rather neat trap, doctor," Miss Verity said. A master of tactics, herself, she could admire an excellent stroke of the opposition. "Without a chance to see the patient and make a personal study, you can't very well override the recommendations of the psychiatrist in charge. You'd be the laughingstock of the entire profession if you tried it. You can't see the patient because I haven't been able to get Q. S. clearance for you, yet. And you can't ignore the Security program, because that's a sacred cow which no one dares question."

It was a clear summation, but Kingston knew she was also reproving him for having laid himself open to such a trap. She had advised against the order and he had insisted upon it anyway.

He pushed himself back from his desk and got to his feet. He was not a big man, but he gave the impression of solid strength as he walked over to the window of his office. He looked out through the window and down the avenue toward various governmental office buildings which lined the street as far as he could see. His features were strong and serene, and, with his shock of prematurely white hair, gave him the characteristic look of a governmental administrator.

"I've not been in this government job very long," he said, as much to the occupants of the buildings down the street as to her, "but I've learned one thing already. When you don't want to face up to the consequences of a bad decision, you just promise to make an investigation." He turned around and faced his secretary. "Tell Dr. Moss," he said, "that I'll make an investigation of the . . . who is it? . . . the David Storm case."

Miss Verity looked as if she wanted to say something more, then clamped her thin lips shut. But at the door, leading out to her own office, she changed her mind.

"Doctor," she said with a mixture of exasperation and curiosity, "suppose you do find a way to make effective intercession in the David Storm case? After all, he's nobody. He's just another case. Suppose you are able to get another psychiatrist assigned to the case. Suppose Dr. Moss is wrong about him being an incurable, and you really get a cure. What have you gained?"

"I've got to start somewhere, Miss Verity," Kingston said gently, without resentment. "Have you had a recent look at the sharply rising incident of disturbance among these young scientists in government work, Miss Verity? The curing of Storm, if that could happen, might be only incidental, true—but it would be a start. I've got some suspicions about what's causing this rising incident. The Storm case may help to resolve them, or dismiss them. It's considerably more than merely making my orders stick. I've got to start somewhere. It might as well be with Storm."

"Very well, doctor," she answered, barely opening her lips. Obviously this was not the way she would have handled it. Even a cursory glance through the Storm file had shown her he was a person of no consequence. Even if Dr. Kingston succeeded, there was no tactical or publicity value to be gained from it. If Storm were a big-name scientist, then the issue would be different. A cause célèbre could be made of it. But as it was, well, facing facts squarely, who would care? One way or the other?

The case history on David Storm was characteristic of Dr. Moss. It was the meticulous work of a thorough technician who had mastered the primary level of detachment. It recorded the various treatments and therapies which Dr. Moss had tried. It reported sundry rambling conversations, incoherent rantings and complaints of David Storm.

And it lacked comprehension.

Kingston, as he plowed through the dossier, felt the frustrated irritation, almost despair, of the creative administrator who must depend upon technicians who lack any basic feeling for the work they do. The work was all technically correct, but in the way a routine machinist would grind a piece of metal to the precise measurements of the specs.

"How does one go about criticizing a man for his total lack of any creative intuition?" Kingston mumbled angrily at the report. "He leaves no loopholes for technical criticism, and, in his frame of thinking, if you tried to go beyond that you'd merely be picking on vague generalities."

The work was all technically correct. There wasn't even a clerical error in it.

A vague idea, nothing more than a slight feeling of a hunch, stirred in Kingston's mind. In some of the arts you could say to a man, "Well, yes, you've mastered all the technicalities, but, man, you're just not an artist." But he couldn't tell Dr. Moss he wasn't a doctor, because Dr. Moss had a diploma which said he was. Men with minds of clerks could only understand error on a clerical level.

He tried to make the idea more vivid in his mind, but it refused to jell. It simply remained a commentary. The case history told a complete story, but David Storm never emerged from it as a human being. He remained nothing more than a case history. Kingston could get no feeling of the substance of the man. The report might as well have dealt with lengths of steel or gallons of chemical.

In a sort of self-defense, Kingston called in Miss Verity, away from her complex of administrative duties, and resorted to a practice they had established together, years before.

He had started his technique with simple gestalt exercises in empathy; such as the deliberate psychosomatic stimulation of pain in one's own arm to better understand the pain in some other person's broken arm. Through the years it had been possible to progress to the higher gestalt empathies of personality identification with a patient. Like other dark areas of the unknown in sciences, there had been many ludicrous mistakes, some danger, and discouragement amounting to despair. But in the long run he had found a technique for a significant increase in his effectiveness as a psychiatrist.

The expression on Miss Verity's face, when she sat down at the side of his desk with her notebook, was interesting. They were both big wheels now, he and she, and she resented taking time out from her control over hundreds of lesser wheels. Yet she was a part of the pattern of empathy. Her hard and unyielding core of practicality, realism, provided a background to contrast, in sharp relief, to the patterns of madness. Obscurely, she derived a pleasure from this contrast; and a nostalgic pleasure, also, from a return to the old days when he had been a young and struggling psychiatrist and she, his nurse, had believed in him enough to stick by him. Kingston wondered if Miss Verity really knew what she did want out of life. He pushed the speculation aside and began his dictation.

As a student, David Storm represented the all too common phenomenon of a young man who takes up the study of a science because it is the socially accepted thing to do, rather than because he had the basic instincts of the true scientist.

Kingston felt himself slipping away into the familiar sensation syndrome of true empathy with his subject. As always, he had to play a dual role. It was insufficient to enter into the other person's mind and senses, feel and see as he felt and saw. No, at the same time he must also reconstruct the individual's life pattern to show the conflicts inherent in that framework which would later lead him into such frustrations as to mature into psychosis.

In the Storm case this was particularly important. A great deal more than just an obscure patient was at stake. By building up a typical framework of conflict, using Storm as merely the focal point, he might be better able to understand this trend which was proving so dangerous to young men in science. And since our total culture had become irrevocably tied to progress in science, he might be better able to prevent a blight from destroying that culture.

His own office furniture faded away. He was there; Miss Verity was there; the precise and empty notes of Dr. Moss were there in front of him; but, to him, these things became shadows, and in the way a motion picture or television screen takes over the senses of reality, he went back to the college classrooms where David Storm had received instruction.

It was fortunate that the real fire of science did not burn in any of his college instructors, either. Instead, they were also the all too common phenomenon of small souls who had grasped frantically at a few "proved" facts, and had clung to these with the desperate tenacity of drowning men in seas of chaos. "You cannot cheat science," these instructors were fond of saying with much didactic positiveness. "If you will follow the procedures we give you, exactly, your experiment will work. That is proof we are right!"

"If it works, it must be right" was so obviously true to Storm that he simply could not have thought of any reason or way to doubt it. He graduated without ever having been handed the most necessary tool in all science, skepticism, much less instructed in its dangers and its wise uses. For there are true-believer fanatics to be found in science, also.

Under normal conditions, Storm would have found some mediocre and unimportant niche he deserved. For some young graduates in science the routine technician's job in a laboratory or shop is simply an opening wedge, a foot on the first rung of his ladder. For David Storm's kind, that same job is a haven, a lifetime of small but secure wage. Under such conditions the conflicts, leading to psychosis, would not have occurred.

But these are not normal times. We have science allied to big government, and controlled by individuals who have neither the instincts nor the knowledge of what science really is. This has given birth to a Security program which places more value upon a stainless past and an innocuous mind than upon real talent and ability. It was the socially acceptable and the secure thing for Storm to seek work in government-controlled research. With his record of complete and unquestioning conformity, it was as inevitable as sunrise that he should be favored.

It was as normal as gravity that his Security ratings should increase into the higher echelons of secrecy as he continued to prove complaisant, and, therefore, trustworthy. The young man with a true instinct for science is a doubter, a dissenter, and, therefore, a trouble maker. He, therefore, cannot be trusted with real importance. Under this condition, it was as natural as rain that when a time came for someone to head up a research section, Storm was the only man available.

It was after this promotion into the ranks of the Q. S. men that the falsity of the whole framework began to make itself felt. He had proved to be a good second man, who always did what he was told, who followed instructions faithfully and to the letter. But now he found himself in a position where there were no ready-made instructions for him to follow.

Kingston took up the Moss report and turned some pages to find the exact reference he wanted. Miss Verity remained passively poised, ready to speed into her shorthand notes again. Kingston found the sheet he wanted and resumed his dictation.

Storm got no satisfaction from his section administrator. "You're the expert," his boss told him. "You're supposed to *tell* us the answers, not *ask* us for them." His tentative questions of other research men got him no satisfaction. Either they were in the same boat as he, and as confused, or they weren't talking to this new breed who called himself a research scientist.

But one old fellow did talk, a little. He asked Storm, with disdain, if he expected the universe to furnish him with printed instructions on how it was put together. He commented, acidly, that in his opinion we were handing the fate of our civilization to a bunch of cookbook technicians.

Storm was furious, of course. He debated with himself as to whether he should, as a good loyal citizen, report the old fellow to the loyalty board. But he didn't. Something stopped him, something quite horrible—a thought all his own. This man was a world-famous scientist. He had once been a professor of science at a great university. Storm had been trained to believe what professors said. What if this one were right?

The doubts that our wise men have already found all the necessary right answers, which should have disturbed him by the time he was a sophomore in high school, began now to trouble him. The questions he should have begun to ask by the time he was a freshman in college began to seep through the tiny cracks that were opening in his tight little framework of inadequate certainties.

Kingston looked up from the report in his hands; thought for a moment; flipped a few pages of the dossier; failed to find what he wanted; turned back a couple of pages; and skimmed down the closely written record of Storm's demented ravings. "Oh yes, here it is," he said, when he found the reference.

It was about that time that Storm began to think about something else he would have preferred to forget. It had been one of those beer-drinking and pipe-smoking bull sessions which act as a sort of teething ring upon which college men exercise their gums in preparation for idea maturity. The guy who was dominating the talking already had a reputation for being a radical; and Storm had listened with the censor's self-assurance that it was all right for *him* to listen so he would be better able to protect others, with inferior minds and weaker wills, from such exposures.

"The great danger to our culture," this fellow was holding forth, "doesn't come from the nuclear bomb, the guided missile, germ warfare, or even internal subversion. Granted there's reason why our culture should endure, there's a much greater danger, and one, apparently, quite unexpected.

"Let's take our diplomatic attitudes and moves as a cross section of the best thinking our culture, as a whole, can produce. For surely here, at this critical level, the finest minds, skilled in the science of statecraft, are at work. And there is no question but that our best is no higher than a grammar-school level. A kid draws a line with his toe across the sidewalk and dares, double dares, his challenger to step across it. 'My father can lick your father' is not removed, in substance, from 'My air force can lick your air force.' What is our Security program but the childish chanting of 'I've got a secret! I've got a secret!'? Add to that the tendency to assemble a gang so that one can feel safer when he talks tough, the tendency to indiscriminate name calling, the inability to think in other terms than 'good guys' and 'bad guys.' Here you have the classical picture of the grammar-school level of thinking—and an exact parallel with our diplomacy.

"Now, sure, it's true that one kid of grammar-school mental age can pretty well hold his own with another of his own kind and strength. But here's the real danger. He doesn't stand a chance if he comes up against a mature adult. What if our opponent, whoever he may be, should grow up before we do? There's the real danger!"

Storm had considered the diatribe ridiculous at the time and agreed with some of the other fellows that the guy should be locked up, or at least kicked off the campus. But now he began to wonder about certain aspects which he had simply overlooked before. "Consider the evidence, gentlemen," one of his instructors had repeated, like a parrot, at each stage of some experiment. Only now it occurred to Storm that the old boy had invariably selected, with considerable care, the particular evidence he wanted them to consider.

With equal care our statecraft had presented us with the evidence that over there, in the enemy territory, science was forced to follow the party line or get itself purged. And the party line was totally false and wrong. Therefore their notions of science must be equally wrong. And you can't cheat science. If a thing is wrong it won't work. Yet the evidence also showed that they, too, had successful nuclear fission, guided missiles, and all the rest.

This led Storm into another cycle of questions. What parts of the evidence could a man elect to believe, and what interpretations of that evidence might he dispute and still remain a totally loyal citizen, still retain his right to highest Security confidence? This posed another problem, for he was still accustomed to turning to higher authority for instruction. But of whom could he ask such questions as these? Not his associates, for they were as wary of him as he of them. In such an atmosphere where it becomes habitual for a man to guard his tongue against any and all slips, there is an automatic complex of suspicions built up to freeze out all real exchange of ideas.

Every problem has a solution. He found the only solution open to him. He went on asking such questions of himself. But, as usual, the solution to one problem merely opened the door to a host of greater ones. The very act of admitting, openly acknowledging, such questions to himself, and knowing he dared not ask them of anyone else, filled him with an overpowering sense of furtive shame and guilt. It was an axiom of the Security framework that you were either totally loyal, or you were potentially a subversive. Had he any right to keep his Security ratings when these doubts were a turmoil in his mind?

Through the months, especially during the nights, as he lay in miserable sleeplessness, he pondered these obvious flaws in his own nature, turning them over and over like a squirrel in a cage. Then, one night, there came a whole series of questions that were even more terrifying.

What if it were not he, but the culture, which contained the basic flaw? Who, in or out of science, is so immutably right that he can pass judgment on what man is meant to know and what he may never question? If we are not to ask questions beyond accepted dogma, be it textbook or statecraft, from where is man's further knowledge and advancement to come? What if these questions which filled him with such maddening doubts were the very ones most necessary to answer? Indeed, what if our very survival depended upon just such questions and answers? Would he then be giving his utmost in loyalty if he did *not* ask them?

The walls of his too narrow framework of thinking had broken away, and he felt himself drowning in a flood of dilemmas he was unprepared to solve. When a man, in a dream, finds his life in deadly peril an automatic function takes over—the man wakes up. There is also an automatic function which takes over when the problems of reality become a deadly peril.

Storm withdrew from reality.

Kingston was silent for a moment, then his consciousness returned to the surroundings of his office, and the desk in front of him. He looked over at Miss Verity.

"Well, now," he said. "I think we begin to understand our young man a little better."

"But are you sure his conflict is typical?" Miss Verity asked.

"Consider the evidence," Kingston said with deliberate irony. "Science can progress, even exist, only where there is free exchange of ideas, and minds completely open to variant ideas. When by law, or social custom, we forbid this, we stop scientific development. Consider the evidence!" he said again. "There is already a great deal of it to show that our science is beginning to go around in circles, developing the details of the frameworks already acceptable, but not reaching out to reveal new and totally unexpected frameworks."

"I'll type this up, in case you want to review it," Miss Verity answered dryly. She did not go along with him, at all, in these flights of fancy. Certainly she saw no tactical advantage to be gained from taking such attitudes. On the contrary, if he didn't learn to curb his tongue better, all she had worked so hard to gain for the both of them could be threatened.

Kingston watched her reactions with an inward smile. It apparently had never occurred to her that his ability in gestalt empathy could be directed toward her.

There might be quite a simple solution to the Storm matter. Too many government administrators and personnel had come to regard an act under general Security regulations to be a dictum straight from Heaven. It was possible that Storm's section had already written him off as a total loss in their minds, and no one had taken the trouble to get him declassified. Kingston felt he should explore that possibility first.

He made an appointment to see Logan Maxfield, Chief Administrator of the section where Storm had worked.

His first glance, when he walked into Maxfield's office, put a damper on his confidence. Here was a man who was more of a politician than a scientist, probably a capable enough administrator within his given boundaries, but the strained cautiousness of his greeting told Kingston he would not take any unusual risks to his own safety and reputation. He belonged to that large and ever growing class of job holders in government whose safety lies in preserving the status quo, who would desperately police and defend things as they are, for any change might be a threat.

It would take unusual tactics to jar him out of his secure rightness in attitude. Kingston was prepared to employ unusual tactics.

"Storm had been electrocuted," he said quietly, "with a charge just barely short of that used on murderers. Not once, of course, but again and again. Then, also, we've stunned him over and over with hypos jabbed down through his skull into his brain. We've sent him to numerous bone-crushing and muscle-tearing spasms with drugs. But," he sighed heavily, "he's obstinate. He refuses to be cured by these healing therapies."

Maxfield's face turned a shade whiter, and his eyes fixed uncertainly on his pudgy hands lying on top of his desk. He looked over toward his special water cooler, as if he longed for a drink, but he did not get out of his chair. A silence grew. It was obvious he felt called upon to make some comment. He tried to make it jocular, man to man.

"Of course I don't know anything about the science of psychiatry, doctor," he said at last, "but in the physical sciences we feel that methods which don't work may not be entirely scientific."

"Man," Kingston exploded with heavy irony, "you imply that psychiatry isn't an exact science? Of course it is a science! Why, man, we have all sorts of intricate laboratories, and arrays of nice shiny tools, and flashing lights on electronic screens, and mechanical pencils drawing jagged lines on revolving drums of paper, and charts and graphs, and statistics. And theory? Why, man, we've got more theory than you ever dreamed of in physical science! Of course it's a science. Any rational man has to agree that the psychiatrist is a scientist. We ought to know. We are the ones who define rationality!"

Maxfield could apparently find no answer to that bit of reasoning. Along with many others he saw no particular fallacy in defining a thing in terms of itself.

"What do you want me to do?" he asked finally.

"Here's the problem," Kingston answered, in the tone of one administrator to another. "It is unethical for one doctor to question the techniques of another doctor, so let's put it this way. Suppose you had a mathematician in your department who took up a sledge hammer and deliberately wrecked his calculating machines because they would not answer a question *he did not know how to ask*. Then failing to get the answer, suppose he recommended just disconnecting what was left of the machines and abandoning them. What would you do?"

"I think I'd get myself another mathematician," Maxfield said with a sickly attempt at lightness.

"Well, now that's a problem, too," Kingston answered easily. "I'm not questioning the methods of Dr. Moss, and obviously his attitudes are the right ones, because he's the only available psychiatrist who had been cleared to treat all these fellows you keep sending over to us under Q. S. secrecy. But there's a way out of that," he said with the attitude of a salesman on television who will now let you in on the panacea for all your troubles. "If you lifted the Security on Storm, then we could move him to another ward and try a different kind of therapy. We might even find a man who did know how to ask the question which would get the right answer."

"Absolutely impossible," Maxfield said with finality.

"Now look at it this way," Kingston said in a tone of reasonableness. "If Storm just chose to quit his job, you'd have to declassify him, wouldn't you?"

"That's different," Maxfield said. "There are proper procedures for that."

"I know," Kingston said, a little wearily. "The parting interview to impress him with the need for continued secrecy, the terrible weight of knowing that bolt number seventy-two in motor XYZ has a three eighths thread instead of a five eighths. So why can't you consider that Storm has left his job and declassify him in absentia. Then we could remove him to an ordinary ward and give him what may be a more effective treatment. I really don't think he can endure very much more of his present therapy."

Kingston leaned back in his chair and spoke in a tone of speculation.

"There's a theory that this treatment isn't really torture, Mr. Maxfield, because an insane person doesn't know what is happening to him. But I'm afraid that theory is fallacious. I believe the so-called insane person does know what is happening, and feels all the exquisite torture we use in trying to drive the devils out of his soul."

"Absolutely impossible," Maxfield repeated. "Although you are not a Q. S. man"—this with a certain smugness—"I'll tell you this much." He leaned forward and placed his fingertips together in his most impressive air of administrative deliberation. "We have reason to believe that David Storm was on the trail of something big. *Big,* Dr. Kingston. So big, indeed, that perhaps the very survival of the nation depends upon it!"

He hesitated a few seconds, to let the gravity of his statement sink in. Then he unlocked a desk drawer and took out a file folder.

"I had this file sent in when you made the appointment to see me," he explained. "As you no doubt know, we must have inspectors who are constantly observing our scientists, although unseen, themselves. Here is a sentence from one of our most trusted inspectors. 'Subject repeats over and over, under great emotional stress, to himself, aloud, that our very survival depends upon his finding the answers to a series of questions!' There, Dr. Kingston, does that sound like no more than the knowledge of a three eighths thread on a bolt? No, doctor," he answered his own rhetoric, "this can only mean something of monumental significance—with the fate of a world, our world, hanging in the balance. Now you see why we couldn't take chances with declassifying him!"

Kingston was on the verge of telling him what the pattern of Storm's questions really was, then better judgment prevailed. First the Security board would become more than a little alarmed that he, a non-Q. S. man, had already learned what was on Storm's mind, and pass some more silly rules trying to put a man's mind in solitary confinement. Second, Maxfield was convinced these questions must be concerned with some super gadget, and wouldn't believe his revealment of their true nature. And anyway, what business does a scientist have, asking such questions? Any sympathy he might have gained for Storm would be lost. Serves the fellow right for not sticking strictly to his slide rules and Bunsen burners!

"Mr. Maxfield," Kingston said gravely, patiently. "It is our experience that a disturbed patient often considers something entirely trivial to be of world-shaking importance. The momentous question Storm feels he must solve may be no more than some nonsensical conundrum—such as why does a chicken cross the road. It may mean nothing whatever."

"And then again it may," Maxfield answered. "We can't take the chance. You must remember, doctor, this statement was overheard and recorded while Storm was still a sane man."

"Before he was committed, you mean," Kingston corrected softly.

"At any rate, it must have been something quite terrible to drive a man insane, just the thought of it," Maxfield argued.

"I'll not deny that possibility," Kingston agreed seriously. "The questions could have terrified him, and the rest of us, too, if we really stopped to think about them. Wouldn't it be worth the risk of say my own doubtful loyalty to make a genuine effort to find out what they were, and deal with them, instead of torturing him to drive them out of his mind?"

"I'm not sure I know what you mean," Maxfield faltered. This doctor seemed to have the most callous way of describing beneficial therapies!

"Mr. Maxfield," Kingston said with an air of candor, "I'll let you in on a trade secret. Up until now psychiatry has fitted all the descriptions applicable to a cult, and few indeed applicable to a science. We try to tailor the mind to fit the theory. But some of us, even in the field of psychiatry, are beginning to ask questions—the first dawn of any science. Do you know anything about psychosomatic medicine?"

"Very little, just an idea of what it means," Maxfield answered cautiously.

"Enough," Kingston conceded. "You know that the human body-mind may take on very real symptoms and pains of an illness as overt objection to an untenable environment. Now we are starting to ask the question: Can it be possible that our so-called cures, brought about through electro and drug shock, are a type of psychosomatic response to unendurable torture?

"I see a mind frantically darting from framework to framework, pursued inexorably by the vengeful psychiatrist with the implements of torture in his hands—the mind desperately trying to find a framework which the psychiatrist will approve and so slacken the torture. We have called that a return to sanity. But is it really anything more than a psychosomatic escape from an impossible situation? A compounded withdrawal from withdrawal?

"As I say, a few of us are beginning to ask ourselves these questions. But most continue to practice the cult rituals which can be duplicated point by point, item by item, with the rites of a savage witch doctor attemping to drive out devils from some poor unfortunate of the tribe."

From the stricken look on Maxfield's face, there was no doubt he had finally scored. The man stood up as if to indicate he could take no more. He was distressed by the problem, so distressed, in fact, that he obviously wished this psychiatrist would leave his office and just forget the whole thing.

"I . . . I want to be reasonable, doctor," he faltered through trembling lips. "I want to do the right thing." Then his face cleared. He saw a way out. "I'll tell you what I can do. I'll make another investigation of the matter!"

"Thank you, Mr. Maxfield," Kingston said gravely, without showing the bitterness of his defeat. "I thought that is what you might do."

When he got back to his office, Kingston learned that Dr. Moss had not been content merely to lay a neat little professional trap. His indignation over being thwarted in his intention to perform a lobotomy on Storm had apparently got the better of his judgment. In a rage, he had insisted upon a meeting with a loyalty board at top level. In the avid atmosphere of Government by Informers, they had shown themselves eager to hear what he might say against his superior.

But a private review of the Storm file reminded them of those mysterious and fearful questions in his deranged mind, questions which might forever be lost through lobotomy. So they advised Moss that Dr. Kingston's opposition was purely a medical matter, and did not necessarily constitute subversion.

In the report of this meeting which lay on his desk, some clerk along the way had underscored the word "necessarily" as if, gently, to remind him to watch his step in the future.

"God save our country from the clerical mind," he murmured. And then the solution to his problem began to unfold for him. His first step in putting his plan into operation had all the appearances of being a very stupid move. It was the first of a series of equally obvious stupidities, which, in total, might add up to a solution. For stupid people are perpetually on guard against cleverness, but will fall in with and further a pattern of stupidity as if they had a natural affinity for it.

His first move was to send Dr. Moss out to the West Coast to make a survey of mental hospitals in that area.

"This memorandum certainly surprised me," Dr. Moss said curiously, as he came through Kingston's office door, waving the paper in his hand. He seated himself rather tentatively on the edge of a chair, and looked piercingly across the desk, to see if he could fathom the ulterior motives behind the move. "It is true that my section is in good order, and my patients can be adequately cared for by the attendants for a couple of weeks or so. But that you should ask me to make the survey of West Coast conditions for you—"

He let the statement trail off into the air, demanding an explanation.

"Why not you?" Kingston asked, as if surprised by the question.

"I . . . ah . . . feared our little differences in the . . . ah . . . Storm matter might prejudice you against me," Moss said, with the attitude of a man laying his cards on the table. Kingston surmised there were cards not laid out for inspection also. The move had two obvious implications. It could be a bribe, a sort of promotion, to regain Moss' good will. Or, more subtly, it could be a threat—"You see I can transfer you out of my way, any time I may want to."

"Oh, the Storm matter," Kingston said with some astonishment. "Frankly, doctor, I hadn't connected up the two. I've been most impressed with your attention to detail, and the fine points of organization. It seemed to me you were the most logical one on the staff to spot any operational flaws out there. The fact that you can confidently leave your section in the care of your attendants is proof of that."

Moss gave a slight smirk at this praise, and said nothing.

"Now I'd be a rather poor executive administrator if I let a minor difference of professional opinion stand in the way of the total efficient organization, wouldn't I?" Kingston asked, with an amiable smile.

"Dr. Kingston," Moss began, and hesitated. Then he decided to be frank. "I . . . ah . . . the staff has felt that your appointment to this position was purely political. I begin to see it might also have been because of your ability, and your capacity to rise above small differences of . . . ah . . . opinion."

Kingston let that pass. If he happened to rise a little in the estimation of his staff through these maneuvers, that would be simply a side benefit.

"Now you're sure I'm not interrupting a course of vital treatment of your patients, Dr. Moss?" he asked.

"Most of my patients are totally and completely incurable, doctor," Moss said with finality. "Not that I don't keep trying. I do try. I try everything known to the science of psychiatry to get them thinking rationally again. But let's face it. Most of them will progress—or regress—equally well with simple human care. I fear my orderlies, guards, nurses regard me as something of a tyrant," he said with obvious satisfaction. "And it isn't likely that in the space of a couple of weeks they'll let down during my absence. You needn't worry, I'll set up the proper measures."

Kingston breathed a small sigh of relief as the man left his office. That would get Dr. Moss off the scene for a while.

Equally important, but not so easily accomplished, he must get Miss Verity away at the same time. And Miss Verity was anything but stupid.

"Has it occurred to you, Miss Verity," he asked with the grin of a man who has a nice surprise up his sleeve, "that this month you will have been with me for twenty-five years?" It was probably a foolish question. Miss Verity would know the years, months, days, hours. Not for any special reason, except that she always knew everything down to the last decimal. The stern lines of her martinet face did not relax, but her pale blue eyes showed a flicker of pleasure that he would remember.

"It has been my pleasure to serve you, doctor," she said formally. That formality between them had never been relaxed, and probably never would be since both of them wanted it. It was not an unusual relationship either in medicine or industry—as if the man should never become too apparent through the image of the executive, lest both parties lose confidence and falter.

"We've come a long way in a quarter of a century," he said reminiscently, "from that little two-room office in Seattle. And if it weren't for you, we might still be there." Rigidly he suppressed any tone which would betray any implication that he might have been happier remaining obscure.

"Oh no, doctor," she said instantly. "A man with your ability—"

"Ability is not enough," he cut in. "Ability has to be combined with ambition. I didn't have the ambition. I simply wanted to learn, to go on learning perpetually, I suppose. You know how it was before you came with me. Patients didn't pay me. I didn't check to see what their bank account or social position was before I took them on. I was getting the reputation for being a poor man's psychiatrist, before you took charge of my office and changed all that."

"That's true," she agreed candidly, with a small secret smile. "But I looked at it this way: You were . . . you are . . . a great man dedicated to the service of humanity. I felt it would do no harm for the Right People to know about it. You can cure a disturbed rich man as easily as you can cure a poor one. And as long as your job was to listen to secrets, they might as well be important secrets—those of industrialists, statesmen, people who really matter."

She looked about the well appointed office, and out of the window toward the great governmental buildings rising in view, as if to survey the concrete results of his policies in managing his affairs. Kingston wondered how much of her ambition had been for him, and how much for herself. In the strange hierarchy of castes among government workers, she was certainly not without stature.

That remark about secrets. He knew her ability to rationalize. He wondered how much of his phenomenal rise, and his position now, was due to polite and delicate pressures she had applied in the right places.

"So now I want to do something I've put off too long," he said, letting the grin come back on his face. "I want you to take a month's vacation, all expenses paid."

She half arose out of her chair, then settled back into it again. He had never seen her so perturbed.

"I couldn't do that," she said with a rising tone of incredulity. "There are too many things of importance. We've just barely got things organized since taking over this position. You . . . you . . . why a dozen times a day there are things coming up you wouldn't know how to handle. You . . . I don't mean to sound disrespectful, doctor, but . . . well . . . you make mistakes. A great man, such as you, well, you live in another world, and without somebody to shield you, constantly—"

She broke off and smiled at him placatingly. All at once she was a tyrant mother with an adored son who has made an independent decision; a wife with a well-broken husband who has unexpectedly asserted a remnant of the manhood he once had; a career secretary who believes her boss to be a fool—a woman whose Security depended upon her indispensability.

Then her face calmed. Her expression was easily readable. The accepted more of our culture is that men exist for the benefit of women. But they can be stubborn creatures at times. The often repeated lessons in the female magazines was that they can be driven where you want them to go only so long as they think they are leading the way there. She must go cautiously.

"Right now, particularly, I shouldn't leave," she said with more composure. "I'm trying, very hard, to get you cleared for a Q. S. As you know, the Justice Department has a rather complete file folder on anybody in the country of any consequence. They have gone back through your life. They have interviewed numerous patients you have treated. I am trying to convince the Loyalty Board that a psychiatrist must, at times, make statements to his patients which he may not necessarily believe. I am trying to convince them that the statements of neurotic and psychotic patients are not necessarily an indication of a man's loyalty to his country.

"Then, too," she continued with faint reproach, "you've made public statements questioning the basic foundations upon which modern psychology is built. You've questioned the value of considering everyone who doesn't blend in with the average norm as being aberrated."

"I still question that," he said firmly.

"I know, I know," she said impatiently. "But do you have to say such things—in public?"

"Well, now, Miss Verity," he said reasonably, "if a scientist must shape his opinions to suit the standards of the Loyalty Board or Justice Department before he is allowed to serve his country—"

"They don't say you are disloyal, doctor," she said impatiently. "They just say: Why take a chance? I'm campaigning to get the right Important People to vouch for you."

"I think the work of setting up organization has been a very great strain on you," he answered with the attitude of a doctor toward a patient. "And there's a great deal more to be done. I want to make many changes. I think you should have some rest before we undertake it."

There had been more, much more. But in the end he had won a partial victory. She consented to a week's vacation. He had to be satisfied with that. If Storm were really badly demented, he could certainly make little progress in that time. But on the other hand, he would have accomplished his main purpose. He would have seen Storm, talked with him, contaminated him through letting him talk to a non-Q. S. man.

Miss Verity departed for a week's vacation with her brothers and sisters and their families—all of whom she detested.

Kingston did not try to push his plan too fast. He had a certain document in mind, and nothing must be done to call any special attention to it.

It was the following day after the simultaneous departure of Dr. Moss and Miss Verity, in the afternoon, that he sat at his desk and signed a stack of documents in front of him.

Because of Miss Verity's martinet tactics in gearing up the department to prompt handling of all matters, the paper which interested him above all others should be in this stack.

While he signed one routine authorization after another, he grew conscious that his mind had been going back over the maneuvers and interviews he had taken thus far in the Storm case. The emotional impatience at their blind slavery to proper and safe procedure rekindled in him, and he found himself signing at a furious rate. Deliberately he slowed himself down. In event someone should begin wondering at a series of coincidences at some later date, his signature must betray no unusual mood.

It was vital to the success of his plan that the document go through proper channels for execution as a completely routine matter. So vital that, even here, alone in the privacy of his office, he would not permit himself to riff down through the stack to see if the paper which really mattered had cleared the typing section.

He felt his hand shaking slightly at the thought he might have miscalculated the mentality of the typists, that someone might have noticed the wild discrepancy and pulled the work sheet he had written out for further question.

Just how far could a man bank on the pattern of stupidity? If the document were prematurely discovered, his only hope to escape serious consequences with the Loyalty Board was to claim a simple clerical error—the designation of the wrong form number at the top of the work sheet. He could probably win, before or after the event, because it would be obvious to anyone that a ridiculous clerical error was the only possible explanation.

A psychiatrist simply does not commit himself to be confined as an insane person.

He laid down his pen, to compose himself until all traces of any muscular waver would disappear from his signature. He tried to reassure himself that nothing could have gone wrong. The girls who filled in the spaces of the forms were only routine typists. They had the clerical mind. They checked the number on the form with the number on the work sheet. They dealt with dozens and hundreds of forms, numerically stored in supply cabinets. Probably they didn't even read the printed words on such forms—merely filled in blank spaces. If the numbered items of the work sheet corresponded with the numbered blanks on the forms, that was all they needed to go ahead.

That was also the frame of mind of those who would carry out the instructions on the documents. Make sure the proper signature authorizes the act, and do it. If the action is wrong it is the signer's neck, not theirs. They simply did what they were told. And it was doubtful that such a vast machine as government could function if it were otherwise, if every clerk took it upon himself to question the wisdom of each move of the higher echelons.

Of course, under normal procedures, someone did check the documents before they were placed on his desk to sign. There again, if the signer took the time to check the accuracy of how the spaces were filled in, government would never get done. There had to be a checker, and in the case of his department that was a job Miss Verity had kept for herself. Her eagle eye would have caught the error immediately, and in contempt with such incompetence she would have bounced into the typing pool with fire in her eye to find out who would do such a stupid thing as this.

He had his answer ready, of course, just in case anybody did discover the mistake. He had closed out his apartment, where he lived alone, and booked a suite in a hotel. The work sheet was an order to have his things transferred to his new room number. The scribbled information was the same, and, obviously, he had simply designated the wrong form number.

But Miss Verity was away on her vacation, and there wasn't anybody to catch the mistake.

He lifted his eyes from the signature space on the paper in front of him at the rapidly dwindling stack. The document was next on top.

There it was, neatly typed, bearing no special marks to segregate it from other routine matters, and thereby call attention to it. There were no typing errors, no erasures, nothing to indicate that the typist might have been startled at what she was typing. Nothing to indicate it had been anything more than a piece of paper for her to thread into her machine, fill in, and thread out again with assembly-line regularity.

He lifted the paper off the stack and placed it in front of himself, in position for signature. He sighed, a deep and gasping sigh, almost a groan. Then he grinned in self-derision. Was he already regretting his wild action, an action not yet taken?

All right then, tear up the document. Forget about David Storm and his problem. Forget about trying to buck the system. Miss Verity was quite right. Storm was a nobody. As compared with the other events of the world, it didn't matter whether Storm got cured, or had his intellect disconnected through lobotomy, or just rotted there in his cell because he had asked some impertinent questions of the culture in which he lived.

Never mind that the trap into which Storm had fallen was symbolic of the trap which was miring down modern science in the same manner. By freeing the symbol, he would in no way be moving to free all science from its dilemma.

He pushed himself back, away from his desk, and got to his feet.

He walked over to the window and looked down the avenue of government buildings. Skyscrapers of offices, as far as his eye could reach. How many of them held men whose state of mind matched his own? How many men quietly, desperately wanted to do a good job, but were already beaten by the pattern for frustration, the inability to take independent action?

There was one of the more curious of the psychological curiosities. In private an individual may confess to highly intelligent sympathies, but when he gets on a board or a panel or a committee, he has not the courage to stand up against what he thinks to be the mass temper or mores.

Courage, that was the element lacking. The courage to fight for progress, enlightenment, against the belief that one's neighbors may not think the same way. The courage to fight over the issue, for the sake of the issue, rather than for the votes one's action is calculated to win.

And in that sense David Storm was not unimportant. Kingston confessed to himself, standing there in front of the window, that he had begun this gambit in a sort of petty defiance—defiance of the efforts of Moss and the rest of his staff to thwart his instructions, defiance of Miss Verity's efforts to make him into an important figurehead, defiance of the whole ridiculous dilemma that the Loyalty program had become.

He wondered if he had ever really intended to go through with his plan. Hadn't he kept the reservation, in the back of his mind, that as long as he hadn't signed the order, as long as it wasn't released for implementation, he could withdraw? Why make such an issue over such a triviality as this Storm fellow?

Yet wasn't that the essence? Wasn't that the question every true scientist had to ask himself every day? To buck the accepted and the acceptable, or to swing with it and rush with the tide of man toward oblivion?

In the popular books courage was always embodied in a well-muscled, handsome, well-intentioned, and rather stupid young man. But what about that wispy little unhandsome fellow, behind the thick glasses perhaps, who, against ridicule, calumny, misunderstanding, poverty, ignorance, kept on with his intent to find an aspect of truth?

Resolutely he walked over to his desk, picked up his pen again, and signed the document. There! He was insane! The document said so! And the document was signed by the Chief Administrator of Psychiatric Division, Bureau of Science Co-ordination. That should be enough authority for anybody!

He tossed it into the outgoing basket, where it would be picked up by the mail clerk and routed for further handling. Rapidly now, he continued signing other papers, tossing them into the same basket, covering the vital one so that it was down in the middle of the stack, unlikely to call special attention to itself.

They came for him at six o'clock the next morning. That was what the order had stipulated, that they make the pickup at this early hour. Two of them walked into his room, through the door which he had left unlocked, and immediately separated so that they could come at him from either side. Two burly young men who had a job to do, and who knew how to do that job. He couldn't remember having seen either of them before, and there was no look of recognition on their faces either.

"What is the meaning of this intrusion?" he said loudly, in alarm. His intonation sounded like something from a rather bad melodrama. "How dare you walk into my room!" He sat up in bed and pulled the covers up around his neck.

"There, there, Buster," one of them said soothingly. "Take it easy now. We're not going to hurt you." With a lithe grace they moved into position. One of them stood near the foot of his bed, the other came up to the head, and with a swirling motion, almost too quick to follow, slipped his hands under Kingston's armpits.

"Time to get up, Buster," the man said, and propelled him upward and outward. The covers fell away from him, and he found himself standing on his feet, without quite knowing how he got there. The second man was already eying his clothes, which he had hung over a chair the night before. They were beautifully trained, he'd have to give Moss that much credit. It spoke well for the routine administration of the Q. S. wing if all the attendants were as experienced in being firm, yet gentle. It wasn't that psychiatry was intentionally sadistic, just mistaken in its idea of treatment.

"What is the meaning of this?" he spluttered again. "Do you know who I am?" He tried to draw himself up proudly, but found it somewhat difficult with his head being slipped through a singlet undershirt.

"Sure, sure, your majesty," one of them said soothingly. "Sure we know."

"I am not 'your majesty,'" Kingston said bitingly. "I am Dr. K. Heidrich Kingston!"

"Oh, pardon me," the fellow said apologetically, and flipped Kingston's feet into the air just long enough for his helper to slip trousers onto his legs. "I'm pleased to meet you."

"Kingston!" the other fellow said in an awed voice. "That's the big shot, the wheel, himself."

"Well," the first one said, as he slipped suspenders over the shoulders, "at least he's not Napoleon." From somewhere underneath his uniform jacket he suddenly whipped out a canvas garment, a shapeless thing Kingston might not have recognized as a strait jacket if he hadn't been experienced. "You gonna co-operate, Dr. Kingston, or will we have to put this on you?"

"Oh, he's not so bad," the other fellow said. "This must be his up cycle. You're not going to give us any trouble at all, are you, Dr. Kingston? You're going to go over to the hospital with us nicely, aren't you?" It was a statement, a soothing persuasive statement, not a question. "They need you over at the hospital, Dr. Kingston. That's why we came for you."

He looked at them suspiciously, craftily. Then he smoothed his face into arrogant lines of overweening ego.

"Of course," he said firmly. "Let's go to the hospital. They'll soon tell you over there who I am!"

"Sure they will, Dr. Kingston," the first attendant said. "We don't doubt it for a minute."

"Let's go," the other one said.

They walked him out the door, in perfect timing. They seemed relaxed, but their fingertips on his arms where they held him were tense, ready for an expected explosion of insane violence. They'd been all through this before, many times, and their faces seemed to say that you can always expect the unexpected. Why, he might even surprise them and go all the way to his cell without trying to murder six people in the process. It just depended on how long his up cycle lasted, and what period of the phase he was in when they came for him. Probably that was the real reason why the real Dr. Kingston had specified this early hour; probably knew when this nut was in and out of his phases.

"Wonder what it's like to be such a big shot that some poor dope goes nuts thinking he's you?" one of them asked the other as they took him out of the apartment house door and down the steps to the ambulance waiting at the curb.

"I don't think I'd like to find out," the other answered.

"I tell you for the last time, I am Dr. Kingston!" Kingston insisted and allowed the right amount of exasperation to mingle with a note of fear.

"I hope it's the last time, doctor," the first one said. "It gets kinda tiresome telling you that we already know who you are. You don't have to keep telling us, you know. We believe you."

The way they got him into the body of the ambulance couldn't exactly be called a pull and a push. At one instant they were standing on either side of him at the back door, and in the next instant one of them was in front of him and the other behind him—and there they were, all sitting in a row inside the ambulance. The driver didn't even look back at him.

He kept silent all the way over to the hospital buildings. He had made his point. He had offered the reactions of a normal man caught up in a mistake, but certain it would all get straightened out without making a fuss about it. They had responded to the reactions of an insane man, and they hoped they could get him all straightened out and nicely deposited in his cell before he began to kick up a fuss about it. It just depended on the framework from which you viewed it, and he neither wanted to overdo nor underplay his part to jar them out of their frame with discrepancies.

But the vital check point was yet to come. There was nothing in the commitment form about his being a Q. S. man, but he had assigned David Storm's cell number in the Q. S. wing. He'd had to check a half dozen hotels before he'd found one with an open room of the same number, so that the clerical error would stand up all the way down the line.

The guards of the Q. S. wing were pretty stuffy about keeping non-Q. S. men out. He might still fail in the first phase of his solution to the problem, to provide David Storm with a doctor, one who might be able to help him.

The attendants wasted no time with red tape. The document didn't call for pre-examinations, or quarantine, or anything. It just said put him into room number 1782. So they went through a side door and by-passed all the usual routines. They were good boys who always did what the coach said. And the document, signed by the Chief Coach, himself, Dr. Kingston, said put the patient in cell 1782. They were doing what they were told.

Would the two guards at the entrance of the Q. S. wing be equally good boys?"

"You're taking me to my office, I assume," he said as they were walking down the corridor toward the cell wing.

"Sure, doctor," one of them said. "Nice warm cozy office. Just for you."

They turned a corner, and the two guards got up from chairs where they had been sitting at a hallway desk. One of the attendants pulled out the document from his inner jacket pocket and handed it to the guard.

"Got another customer for you," he said laconically. "For *office* number 1782." He winked broadly.

"That's cell's . . . er . . . office's already occupied," the guard said instantly. "Must be a mistake."

"Maybe they're starting to double them up, now," the attendant said. "You wanna go up to the Big Chief's office and tell him he's made a mistake? He signed it, you know."

"I don't know what you men are up to!" Kingston burst out. "This whole thing is a mistake. I tell you I am Dr. Kingston. I'll have all your jobs for this . . . this . . . this practical joke! You are not taking me any farther! I refuse to go any farther!"

He laid them out for five minutes, calling upon strings of profanity, heard again and again from the lips of uncontrolled minds, that would make an old time mariner blush for shame. The four of them looked at him at first with admiration, then with disgust.

"You'd better get him into his cell," one of the guards mumbled to the attendants. "Before he really blows his stack."

"Yeah," the attendant agreed. "Looks like he's going into phase two, and we have not as yet got phase one typed. No telling what phase three might be like."

The guards stepped back. The attendants took him on down the hall of the Q. S. wing.

All the way up the elevator, to the seventeenth floor, and down the hall to the doorway of Storm's cell, Kingston kept wondering if any of them had ever heard of the Uncle Remus story of Bre'r Rabbit and the Briar Patch. "Oh don't throw me in the briar patch, Bre'r Fox. Don't throw me in the briar patch!"

Stupid people resist clever moves but willingly carry out stupid patterns. These guards and attendants were keyed to keeping out anyone who tried to get in—but if someone tried to keep out, obviously he must be forced to go in.

There hadn't even been a question about a lack of Q. S. rating on the form. His vitriolic diatribe had driven it out of their minds for a moment, and if they happened to check it before they stamped the order completed, well, the damage would already have been done.

He would have talked with David Storm.

But Storm was not quite that co-operative. His eyes flared with wild resentment, suspicion, when the attendants ushered Kingston into the cell.

"You see, doctor," one of the attendants said with soothing irony, and not too concealed humor, "we provide you with a patient and everything. We'll move in another couch, and you two can just lie back, relax, and just tell each other all about what's in your subconscious."

"Oh, no you don't," Storm said instantly, and backed into a corner of the cell with an attitude of exaggerated rejection. "That's an old trick. Pretending to be a cell mate so you can learn my secret. That's an old trick, an old, old, old, old, o-l-d—" His lips kept moving, but the sound of his voice trailed away.

"You needn't think you're going to make me listen to your troubles," Kingston snapped at him. "I've got troubles of my own."

Storm's lips ceased moving, and he stared at Kingston without blinking.

"You big-shot scientists try to get along with one another," one of the attendants said as they went out the door.

"Scientists just argue," the other attendant commented. "They never *do* anything."

But Kingston hardly heard them, and hardly noticed them when, a few minutes later, they brought in a cot for him and placed it on the opposite side of the cell from Storm's cot. He was busy analyzing Storm's first reactions. Yes, the pattern was disturbed, possibly demented, certainly regressive—and yet, it was not so much irrational as adolescent, the bitterness of the adolescent when he first begins to really realize that the merchandise of humanity is not living up to the advertising under which it has been sold to him.

Under the attendants' watchful eyes, Kingston changed into the shapeless garments of the inmates. He flared up at them once again, carrying out his pattern of indignation that they should do this to him, but he didn't put much heart into it. No point in overdoing the act.

"Looks like he might have passed his peak," one of the attendants muttered. "He's calming down again. Maybe he won't be too hard to handle." They went out the door again with the admonishment: "Now you fellows be quiet, and you'll get breakfast pretty soon. But if you get naughty—" With his fist and thumb he made an exaggerated motion of working a hypodermic syringe. Storm cowered back into his corner of the cell.

"I've given up trying to convince you numskulls," Kingston said with contempt. "I'll just wait now until my office hears about this."

"Yeah," the attendant said. "Yeah, you just sit tight and wait. Just keep waiting—and quiet!"

The sound of their steps receded down the hallway. Kingston lay back on his couch and said nothing. He knew Storm's eyes were on him, watching him, as nervous, excited, and wary as an animal. The cell was barren, containing only the cots covered with a tough plastic which defied tearing with the bare fingers, and a water closet. There wasn't a seat on the latter because that can be torn off and used as a weapon either against one's self or others. In the wards there would be books, magazines, games, implements of various skills and physical therapies, all under the eyes of watchful attendants; but in these cells there was nothing, because there weren't enough attendants to watch the occupants of each cell.

Kingston lay on his couch and waited. In a little while Storm came out of his corner and sat down on the edge of his own couch. His attitude was half wary, half belligerent.

"You needn't be afraid of me," Kingston said softly, and kept looking upward at the ceiling. "I really am Dr. Heidrich Kingston. I'm a psychiatrist. And I already know all about you and your secrets."

He heard a faint whimper, the rustling of garments on the plastic couch cover, as if Storm were shrinking back against the wall, as if *he* expected this to be the prelude to more punishment for having such secret thoughts. Then a form of reasoning seemed to prevail, and Kingston could feel the tension relaxing in the room.

"You're as crazy as I am," Storm said loudly. There was relief in his voice, and yet regret.

Kingston said nothing. There was no point in pushing it. If his luck held, he would have several days. Miss Verity could be counted on to cut her vacation short and come back ahead of time, but even with that, he should have at least three days. And while Storm was badly disoriented, he could be reached.

"And that's an old, old trick, too," Storm said in a bitter singsong. "Pretending you already know, so I'll talk. Well I'm not a commie! I'm not a traitor! I'm not any of those things. I just think—" He broke off abruptly. "Oh, no you don't!" he exclaimed. "You can't trick me into telling you what I think. That's an old, old, old, old—"

It was quite clear why the therapies used by Moss hadn't worked. Storm was obsessed with guilt. He had been working in the highest echelons of Loyalty and at the same time had been harboring secret doubts that the framework was right. The Moss therapies then were simply punishments for his guilt, punishments which he felt he deserved, punishments which confirmed his wrongdoing. And Moss would be so convinced that Storm's thoughts were entirely wrong, that he couldn't possibly use the technique of agreement to lead Storm out of his syndrome. That was why Moss' past was stainless, why the Security Board trusted him with a Q. S., he was as narrow in his estimate of right and wrong as they.

"Old, old, old, old—" Storm kept repeating. He was stuck in the adolescent groove of bitter cynicism, not yet progressed to the point of realizing that in spite of its faults and hypocrisies, there were some elements in humanity worth a man's respect and faith. Even a thinking man.

It was a full day later before Kingston attempted the first significant move in reaching through to Storm. The previous day had confirmed the pattern of the attendants: A breakfast of adequate but plain food. Moss would never get caught on the technicality so prevalent in many institutions where the inmates can't help themselves—chiseling on food and pocketing the difference. After breakfast a clean-up of the cells and their persons. Four hours alone. Lunch. Carefully supervised and highly limited exercise period. Back to the cell again for another four hours. Supper. And soon, lights out.

It varied, somewhat, from most mental hospital routine; but these were all Q. S. men, each bearing terrible secrets which had snapped their minds. They musn't be allowed to talk to one another. It varied, too, from patient to patient. It varied mainly in that the cells were largely soundproof; they had little of the screaming, raging, cursing, strangling, choking bedlam common in many such institutions.

Moss was a good administrator. He had his wing under thorough control. It was as humane as his limited point of view could make it. There were too few attendants, but then that was always the case in mental hospitals. In this instance it worked in Kingston's favor. There would be little chance of interruption, except at the planned times. In going into another person's mind that was a hazard to be guarded against, as potentially disastrous as a disruption of a major operation.

No reverberation of alarm at his absence from his office reached this far, and Kingston doubted there would be much. Miss Verity was more efficient than Moss and the organization she had set up would run indefinitely during his absence and hers. Decisions, which only he could make, would pile up in the staff offices, but that was nothing unusual in government.

He didn't try to rush Storm. With a combination of the facts he had gleaned from the file and the empathy he possessed, he lay on his cot and talked quietly to the ceiling about Storm. His childhood, his days in school, his attitudes toward his parents, teachers, scout masters, all the carefully tailored and planned sociology surrounding growing youth in respectable circumstances of today. It was called planned youth development, but it could better be called youth suppression, for its object was to quell any divergent tendencies, make the youth docile and complaisant—a good boy, which meant no trouble to anybody.

He translated the standard pattern into specifics about Storm, for obviously, until his breakup, David had been the epitome of a mdoel boy. There are several standard patterns of reaction to this procedure. Eager credulity, where the individual is looking for a concrete father image to carry his burdens; rejective skepticism, where the individual seizes upon the slightest discrepancy to prove the speaker cannot know; occasionally superstitious fear and awe; and even less occasionally a comprehension of how gestalt empathy works. But whatever the pattern of reaction, it is the rare person, indeed, who can keep from listening to an analysis of himself.

Storm lay on his side on his cot, facing Kingston—a good sign because the previous day he had faced the wall—and watched the older man talk quietly and easily at the ceiling. Kingston knew when he came close to dangerous areas from the catch in Storm's breathing, but there was no other sign. Deliberately he broke off in the middle of telling Storm what his reactions had been at the bull session where the radical had been talking.

There was about ten minutes of silence. Several times there was an indrawn breath, as if Storm were starting to say something. But he kept quiet. Kingston picked up the thread and continued on, as if no time had elapsed.

He got his reward during the exercise period. Storm kept close to him, manifestly preferred his company to that of the attendants. They were among the less self-destructive few who were allowed a little time at handball. The previous day Storm had swung on the ball, wildly, angrily, as it to work off some terrible rage by hitting the ball. There hadn't been even the excuse of a game. Storm, younger and quicker, much more intense, had kept the ball to himself. Today Storm seemed the opposite. The few times he did hit the ball he deliberately placed it where Kingston could get it easily. Then he lost interest and sat down in a corner of the court. The attendants hustled them out quickly, to make room for others.

Back in the cell, Kingston picked up the thread again. Genuine accomplishment in gestalt empathy allows one to enter directly into another man's mind; his whole life is laid open for reading. Specific events are often obscure, but the man's pattern of reactions to events, the psychological reality of it, is open to view. Kingston narrated, with neither implied criticism nor praise, until, midafternoon, he sprang a bombshell.

"But you were wrong about one thing, Storm," he said abruptly. He felt Storm's instant withdrawal, the return of hostility. "You thought you were alone. You thought you were the only one with this terrible flaw in your nature. But you were not alone, son. And you aren't alone now.

"You put your finger on the major dilemma facing science today."

Now, for the first time, he glanced over at Storm. The young man was up on his elbow, staring at Kingston with an expression of horror. As easily as that, his secret had come out. And he did not doubt that Kingston knew his thoughts. The rest of it had fitted, and this fitted, too. He began to weep, at first quietly, then with great, wracking sobs.

"Disgrace," he muttered. "Disgrace, disgrace, disgrace. My mother, my father—" He buried his face in his arms. His whole body shook. He turned his face to the wall.

"All over the world, the genuine men of science are fighting out these same problems, David," Kingston said. "You are not alone."

Storm started to put his hands over his ears—then took them away. Kingston appeared not to notice.

"Politicians, not only ours, but all over the world, have discovered that science is a tremendous weapon. As with any other weapon they have seized it and turned it to their use. But it would be a great mistake to cast the politician in the role of villain. He is not a villain.

He simply operates in an entirely different framework from that of science.

"Science does not understand his framework. A man of science grows extremely cautious with his words. He makes no claims he cannot substantiate. He freely admits it when he does not know something. He would be horrified to recommend the imposition of a mere theory of conduct upon a culture. The politician is not bothered by any of this. He has no hesitancy in recommending what he believes be imposed upon a culture; whatever is necessary for him to get the votes he will say.

"The scientist states again and again that saying a thing is true will not make it true. In classical physics this may have been accurate, although there is doubt of its truth in relative physics, and it is manifestly untrue in the living sciences. For often the politician says a thing with such a positive strength of confidence that the people begin operating in a framework of its truth and so implement it that it does become true.

"The public follows the politician by preference. Most of us have never outgrown our emotional childhood, and when the silver cord, the apron strings are broken from our real parents, we set about trying to find parent substitutes to bear the responsibility for our lives. The scientist stands in uncertainty, without panaceas, without sure-fire solutions of how to have all we want and think we want. The politician admits to no such uncertainties. He becomes an excellent father substitute. He will take care of us, bear the brunt of responsibility for us.

"But this clash of frameworks goes much deeper than that. Just as the scientist cannot understand the politician, so the politician does not understand science. Like most people, to him the scientist is just a super trained mechanic. He's learned how to manipulate some laboratory equipment. He has memorized some vague and mysterious higher math formulae. But he's just a highly skilled mechanic, and, as such, is employed by the politician to do a given job. He is not expected to meddle in things which are none of his concern.

"But in science we know this is a false estimation. For science is far more than the development of a skill. It is a frame of thought, a philosophy, a way of life. That was the source of your conflict, son. You were trying to operate in the field of science under the politician's estimation of what it is.

"The scientist is human. He loves his home, his flag, his country. Like any other man he wishes to protect and preserve them. But the political rules under which he is expected to do this come in direct conflict with his basic philosophy and approach to enlightenment. We have one framework, then, forced to make itself subservient to another framework, and the points of difference between the two are so great, that tremendous inner conflicts are aroused.

"The problem is not insuperable. Science has dealt with such problems before. Without risk to home, flag and country, science will find a way to deal with this dilemma, also. You are not alone."

There was a long silence, and then Storm spoke, quite rationally, from his cot.

"That's all very nice," he said, "but there's one thing wrong with it. You're just as crazy as I am, or you wouldn't be here."

Kingston looked over at him and laughed.

"Now you're thinking like the politician, Storm," he said. "You're taking the evidence and saying it can have only one possible interpretation." He was tempted to tell Storm the truth of why he was here, and to show him that science could find a way, without harm, to circumvent the too narrow restrictions placed upon it by the political mind. But that would be unwise. Better never to let anyone know how he had manipulated it so that a simple clerical error could account for the whole chain of events.

"I really am Dr. Heidrich Kingston," he said.

"Yeah," Storm agreed, too quickly. There was derision in his eyes, but there was also pity. That was a good sign, too. Storm was showing evidence that he could think of the plight of someone else, other than himself. "Yeah, sure you are," he added.

"You don't think so, now," Kingston laughed. "But tomorrow, or the next day, my secretary will come to the door, there, and get me out of here."

"Yeah, sure. Tomorrow—or the next day," Storm agreed. "You just go on thinking that, fellow. It helps, believe me, it helps."

"And shortly afterwards you'll be released, too. Because there's no point now in keeping you locked up, incommunicado. I know all about your secrets, you see."

"Yeah," Storm breathed softly. "Tomorrow or the next day, or the day after that, or the day after— Yeah, I think I'll believe it, too, fellow. Yeah, got to believe in something."

In a limited fashion the patterns of human conduct can be accurately predicted. Cause leads to effect in the lives of human beings, just as it does in the physical sciences. The old fellow who had once told Storm that the universe does not hand out printed instructions on how it is put together was only literally correct. Figuratively, he was in error, for the universe does bear the imprints of precisely how it is put together and operates. It is the business of science to learn to read those imprints and know their meanings. Life is a part of the universe, bearing imprints of how it operates, too. And we already read them, after a limited fashion. We couldn't have an organized society, at all, if this were not true.

Kingston had made some movement beyond generalized quantum theory, and could predict the given movements of certain individuals in the total motion of human affairs.

Faithful to the last drawn line on the charted pattern, it was the next morning that Miss Verity, with clenched jaws and pale face, stepped through the cell door, followed by a very worried and incredulous guard.

"Dr. Kingston," she said firmly, then faltered. She stood silent for an instant, fighting to subdue her relief, anger, exasperation, tears. She won. She did not break through the reserve she treasured. She spoke then, quite in the secretarial manner, but she could not subdue a certain triumph in her eyes.

"Dr. Kingston," she repeated, "it seems that while I was on my vacation, you made a . . . ah . . . clerical error."

Further Reading   Mark Clifton

Books

Eight Keys to Eden. Garden City, N.Y.: Doubleday, 1960.
They'd Rather Be Right (with Frank Riley). New York: Gnome Press, 1957.
When They Come from Space. Garden City, N.Y.: Doubleday, 1962.

Stories

"The Conqueror." *Astounding Science Fiction*, August 1952. (*Mutants*, ed. Robert Silverberg.)
"Hang Head, Vandal!" *Amazing Stories*, April 1962. (*The 8th Annual of the Year's Best S-F*, ed. Judith Merril.)
"How Allied." *Astounding Science Fiction*, March 1957. (*Elsewhere and Elsewhen*, ed. Groff Conklin.)
"Sense from Thought Divide." *Astounding Science Fiction*, March 1955. (*SF: The Best of the Best*, ed. Judith Merril.)
"Star, Bright." *Galaxy Science Fiction*, July 1952. (*Second Galaxy Reader of Science Fiction*, ed. H. L. Gold.)
"What Have I Done?" *Astounding Science Fiction*, May 1952. (*The Astounding-Analog Reader, Vol. II,* ed. Harry Harrison and Brian W. Aldiss.)
"What Thin Partitions" (with Alex Apostolides). *Astounding Science Fiction*, September 1953. (*The Best Science Fiction Stories: 1954,* ed. Bleiler and Dikty.)

"Christopher Anvil" (Harry C. Crosby) has only himself to blame for his relative anonymity, for he is a maddeningly uneven writer. At his best, in stories like "A Rose by Other Name" (1960), the widely reprinted "Not in the Literature" (1962), and "Positive Feedback" (1965)—all three from *Astounding/Analog*—he is an inventive and expert manipulator of social trends and processes. Indeed, he has been one of the very best observers (along with Mack Reynolds at *his* best) in all of science fiction of the foibles and presumptuousness of social thinkers and social managers. He was perhaps too successful—he found a formula and worked it to death, and this was one of the main reasons why the 1960s *Analog* always left you with the feeling that you had just read last month's issue again. He was a John Campbell writer who could be relied upon to hew to the formulas of that editor, and, like Randall Garrett, became lost to public view through constant, unchanging exposure. Perhaps he might have flourished artistically in another market—"Mind Partner" would make one think so—but it is also possible that John Campbell brought out the *best* in him, at least kept him working.

Anvil has published more than two hundred stories (and two forgettable novels), and "Mind Partner" may be the best of them. It was "New Wave" before anyone was arguing about the term or anyone in science fiction had even heard of it. Like the best psychological sf, it has a nightmare quality about it that lingers long after the reading.

M.H.G. & J.D.O.

Mind Partner

by CHRISTOPHER ANVIL

Jim Calder studied the miniature mansion and grounds that sat, carefully detailed, on the table.

"If you slip," said Walters, standing at Jim's elbow, "the whole gang will disappear like startled fish. There'll be another thousand addicts, and we'll have the whole thing to do over again."

Jim ran his hand up the shuttered, four-story replica tower that stood at one corner of the mansion. "I'm to knock at the front door and say, 'May I speak to Miss Cynthia?'"

Walters nodded. "You'll be taken inside, you'll stay overnight, and the next morning you will come out a door at the rear and drive away. You will come directly here, be hospitalized and examined, and tell us everything you can remember. A certified check in five figures will be deposited in your account. How high the five figures will be depends on how much your information is worth to us."

"Five figures," said Jim.

Walters took out a cigar and sat down on the edge of his desk. "That's right—10,000 to 99,999."

Jim said, "It's the size of the check that makes me hesitate. Am I likely to come out of there in a box?"

"No." Walters stripped the cellophane wrapper off his cigar, lit it, and sat frowning. At last he let out a long puff of smoke and looked up. "We've hit this setup twice before in the last three years. A city of moderate size, a quietly retired elderly person in a well-to-do part of town, a house so situated that people can come and go without causing comment." Walters glanced at the model of mansion and grounds on the table. "Each time, when we were sure where the trouble was coming from, we've raided the place. We caught addicts, but otherwise the house was empty."

"Fingerprints?"

"The first time, yes, but we couldn't trace them anywhere. The second time, the house burned down before we could find out."

"What about the addicts, then?"

"They don't talk. They—" Walters started to say something, then shook his head. "We're offering you a bonus because we don't know what the drug is. These people are addicted to something, but *what?* They don't accept reality. There are none of the usual withdrawal symptoms. A number of them have been hospitalized for three years and have shown no improvement. We don't *think* this will happen to you—one exposure to it shouldn't make you an addict—but we don't *know*. We have a lot of angry relatives of these people backing us. That's why we can afford to pay you what we think the risk is worth."

Jim scowled. "Before I make up my mind, I'd better see one of these addicts."

Walters drew thoughtfully on his cigar, then nodded and picked up the phone.

Behind the doctor and Walters and two white-coated attendants, Jim went into the room at the hospital. The attendants stood against the wall. Jim and Walters stood near the door and watched.

A blonde girl sat on the cot, her head in her hands.

"Janice," said the doctor softly. "Will you talk to us for just a moment?"

The girl sat unmoving, her head in her hands, and stared at the floor.

The doctor dropped to a half-kneeling position beside the cot. "We want to talk to you, Janice. We need your help. Now, I am going to talk to you until you show me you hear me. You do hear me, don't you, Janice?"

The girl didn't move.

The doctor repeated her name again and again.

Finally she raised her head and looked through him. In a flat, ugly voice, she said, "Leave me alone. I know what you're trying to do."

"We want to ask you just a few questions, Janice."

The girl didn't answer. The doctor started to say something else, but she cut him off.

"Go away," she said bitterly. "You don't fool me. You don't even exist. You're nothing." She had a pretty face, but as her eyes narrowed and her lips drew slightly away from her teeth and she leaned forward on the cot, bringing her hands up, she had a look that tingled the hair on the back of Jim's neck.

The two attendants moved warily from the wall.

The doctor stayed where he was and talked in a low, soothing monotone.

The girl's eyes gradually unfocused, and she was looking through the doctor as if he weren't there. She put her head hard back into her hands and stared at the floor.

The doctor slowly came to his feet and stepped back.

"That's it," he told Jim and Walters.

On the way back, Walters drove, and Jim sat beside him on the front seat. It was just starting to get dark outside. Abruptly Walters asked, "What did you think of it?"

Jim moved uneasily. "Are they all like that?"

"No. That's just one pattern. An example of another pattern is the man who bought a revolver, shot the storekeeper who sold it to him, shot the other customer in the store, put the gun in his belt, went behind the counter and took out a shotgun, shot a policeman who came in the front door, went outside and took a shot at the lights on a theater marquee; he studied the broken lights for a moment, then leaned the shotgun against the storefront, pulled out the revolver, blew out the right rear tires of three cars parked at the curb, stood looking from one of the cars to another and said, 'I just can't be sure, that's all.' "

Walters slowed slightly as they came onto a straight stretch of highway and glanced at Jim. "Another policeman shot the man, and that ended that. We traced that one back to the *second* place we closed up, the place that burned down before we could make a complete search."

"Were these places all run by the same people?"

"Apparently. When we checked the dates, we found that the second place didn't open till after the first was closed, and the third place till the second was closed. They've all operated in the same way. But the few descriptions we've had of the people who work there don't check."

Jim scowled and glanced out the window. "What generally happens when people go there? Do they stay overnight, or what?"

"The first time, they go to the front door, and come out the next morning. After that, they generally rent one of the row of garages on the Jayne Street side of the property, and come back at intervals, driving in after dark and staying till the next night. They lose interest in their usual affairs, and gradually begin to seem remote to the people around them. Finally they use up their savings, or otherwise come to the end of the money they can spend. Then they do like the girl we saw tonight, or like the man in the gun store, or else they follow some other incomprehensible pattern. By the time we find the place and close it up, there are seven hundred to twelve hundred addicts within a fifty-mile radius of the town. They all fall off their rockers inside the same two- to three-week period, and for a month after that, the police and the hospitals get quite a workout."

"Don't they have any of the drug around?"

"That's just it. They must get it all at the place. They use it there. They don't bring any out."

"And when you close the place up—"

"The gang evaporates like a sliver of dry ice. They don't leave any drug or other evidence behind. This time we've got a precise model of their layout. We should be able to plan a perfect capture. But if we just close in on them, I'm afraid the same thing will happen all over again."

"Okay," said Jim. "I'm your man. But if I don't come out the next morning, I want you to come in after me."

"We will," said Walters.

Jim spent a good part of the evening thinking about the girl he'd seen at the hospital, and the gun-store addict Walters had described. He paced the floor, scowling, and several times reached for the phone to call Walters and say, "No." A hybrid combination of duty and the thought of a five-figure check stopped him.

Finally, unable to stay put, he went out into the warm, dark evening, got in his car and drove around town. On impulse, he swung down Jayne Street and passed the dark row of rented garages Walters had mentioned. A car was carefully backing out as he passed. He turned at the next corner and saw the big, old-fashioned house moonlit among the trees on its own grounds. A faint sensation of wrongness bothered him, and he pulled to the curb to study the house.

Seen through the trees, the house was tall and steep-roofed. It reached far back on its land, surrounded by close-trimmed lawn and shadowy shrubs. The windows were tall and narrow, some of them closed by louvered shutters. Pale light shone out through the narrow openings of the shutters.

Unable to place the sensation of wrongness, Jim swung the car away from the curb and drove home. He parked his car, and, feeling tired and ready for sleep, walked up the dark drive, climbed the steps to the porch, and fished in his pocket for his keycase. He felt for the right key in the darkness, and moved back onto the steps to get a little more light. It was almost as dark there as on the porch. Puzzled, he glanced up at the sky.

The stars were out, with a heavy mass of clouds in the distance, and a few small clouds sliding by overhead. The edge of one of the small clouds lit up faintly, and as it passed, a pale crescent moon hung in the sky. Jim looked around. Save for the light in the windows, the houses all bulked dark.

Jim went down the steps to his car and drove swiftly back along Jayne Street. He turned, drove a short distance up the side street, and parked.

This time, the outside of the huge house was dark. Bright light shone out the shutters onto the lawn and shrubbery. But the house was a dark bulk against the sky.

Jim swung the car out from the curb and drove home slowly.

The next morning, he went early to Walters' office and studied the model that sat on the table near the desk. The model, painstakingly constructed from enlarged photographs, showed nothing that looked like a camouflaged arrangement for softly floodlighting the walls of the house and the grounds. Jim studied the location of the trees, looked at the house from a number of angles, noticed the broken slats in different shutters on the fourth floor of the tower, but saw nothing else he hadn't seen before.

He called up Walters, who was home having breakfast, and without mentioning details asked, "Is this model on your table complete?"

Walters' voice said, "It's complete up to three o'clock the day before yesterday. We check it regularly."

Jim thanked him and hung up, unsatisfied. He knelt down and put his eye in the position of a man in the street in front of the house. He noticed that certain parts of the trees were blocked off from view by the mansion. Some of these parts could be photographed from a light plane flying overhead, but other positions would be hidden by foliage. Jim told himself that floodlights *must* be hidden high in the trees, in such a way that they could simulate moonlight.

In that case, the question was—why?

Jim studied the model. He was bothered by much the same sensation as that of a man examining the random parts of a jigsaw puzzle. The first few pieces fitted together, the shapes and colors matched, but they didn't seem to add up to anything he had ever seen before.

As he drove out to the house, the day was cool and clear.

The house itself, by daylight, seemed to combine grace, size, and a sort of starched aloofness. It was painted a pale lavender, with a very dark, steeply slanting roof. Tall arching trees rose above it, shading parts of the roof, the grounds, and the shrubs. The lawn was closely trimmed, and bordered by a low spike-topped black-iron fence.

Jim pulled in to the curb in front of the house, got out, opened a low wrought-iron gate in the fence, and started up the walk. He glanced up at the trees, saw nothing of floodlights, then looked at the house.

The house had a gracious, neat, well-groomed appearance. All the windowpanes shone, all the shades were even, all the curtains neatly hung, all the trim bright and the shutters straight. Jim, close to the house, raised his eyes to the tower. All the shutters there were perfect and even and straight.

The sense of wrongness that had bothered him the day before was back again. He paused in his stride, frowning.

The front door opened and a plump, gray-haired woman in a light-blue maid's uniform stood in the doorway. With her left hand, she smoothed her white apron.

"My," she said, smiling, "isn't it a nice day?" She stepped back and with her left hand opened the door wider. "Come in." Her right hand remained at her side, half-hidden by the ruffles of her apron.

Jim's mouth felt dry. "May I," he said, "speak to Miss Cynthia?"

"Of course you may," said the woman. She shut the door behind him.

They were in a small vestibule opening into a high-ceilinged hallway. Down the hall, Jim could see an open staircase to the second floor, and several wide doorways with heavy dark draperies.

"Go straight ahead and up the stairs," said the woman in a pleasant voice. "Turn left at the head of the stairs. Miss Cynthia is in the second room on the right."

Jim took one step. There was a sudden sharp pressure on his skull, a flash of white light, and a piercing pain and a pressure in his right arm—a sensation like that of an injection. Then there was nothing but blackness.

Gradually he became aware that he was lying on a bed, with a single cover over him. He opened his eyes to see that he was in an airy room with a light drapery blowing in at the window. He started to sit up and his head throbbed. The walls of the room leaned out and came back. For an instant, he saw the room like a photographic negative, the white woodwork black and the dark furniture nearly white. He lay carefully back on the pillow and the room returned to normal.

He heard the quick tap of high heels in the hallway and a door opened beside him. He turned his head. The room seemed to spin in circles around him. He shut his eyes.

When he opened his eyes again, a tall, dark-haired woman was watching him with a faint hint of a smile. "How do you feel?"

"Not good," said Jim.

"It's too bad we have to do it this way, but some people lose their nerve. Others come with the thought that we have a profitable business and they would like to have a part of it. We have to bring these people around to our way of thinking."

"What's your way of thinking?"

She looked at him seriously. "What we have to offer is worth far more than any ordinary pattern of life. We can't let it fall into the wrong hands."

"What is it that you have to offer?"

She smiled again. "I can't tell you as well as you can experience it."

"That may be. But a man going into a strange country likes to have a road map."

"That's very nicely put," she said, "but you won't be going into any strange country. What we offer you is nothing but your reasonable desires in life."

"Is that all?"

"It's enough."

"Is there any danger of addiction?"

"After you taste steak, is there any danger of your wanting more? After you hold perfect beauty in your arms, is there any danger you might want to do so again? The superior is always addicting."

He looked at her for a moment. "And how about my affairs? Will they suffer?"

"That depends on you."

"What if I go from here straight to the police station?"

"You won't. Once we are betrayed, you can never come back. We won't be here. You wouldn't want that."

"Do you give me anything to take out? Can I buy—"

"No," she said. "You can't take anything out but your memories. You'll find they will be enough."

As she said this, Jim had a clear mental picture of the girl sitting on the cot in the hospital, staring at the floor. He felt a sudden intense desire to get out. He started to sit up, and the room darkened and spun around him.

He felt the woman's cool hands ease him back into place.

"Now," she said, "do you have any more questions?"

"No," said Jim.

"Then," she said briskly, "we can get down to business. The charge for your first series of three visits is one thousand dollars per visit."

"What about the next visits?"

"Must we discuss that now?"

"I'd like to know."

"The charge for each succeeding series of three is doubled."

"How often do I come back?"

"We don't allow anyone to return oftener than once every two weeks. That is for your own protection."

Jim did a little mental arithmetic, and estimated that by the middle of the year a man would have to pay sixteen thousand dollars a visit, and by the end of the year it would be costing him a quarter of a million each time he came to the place.

"Why," he asked, "does the cost increase?"

"Because, I've been told to tell those who ask, your body acquires a tolerance and we have to overcome it. If we have to use twice as much of the active ingredient in our treatment, it seems fair for us to charge twice as much."

"I see." Jim cautiously eased himself up a little. "And suppose that I decided right now not to pay anything at all."

She shook her head impatiently. "You're on a one-way street. The only way you can go is forward."

"That remains to be seen."

"Then you'll see."

She stepped to a dresser against the wall, picked up an atomizer, turned the little silver nozzle toward him, squeezed the white rubber bulb, and set the atomizer back on the dresser. She opened the door and went out. Jim felt a mist of fine droplets falling on his face. He tried to inhale very gently to see if it had an odor. His muscles wouldn't respond.

He lay very still for a moment and felt the droplets falling one by one. They seemed to explode and tingle as they touched his skin. He lay still a moment more, braced himself to make one lunge out of the bed, then tried it.

He lay flat on his back on the bed. A droplet tingled and exploded on his cheek.

He was beginning to feel a strong need for breath.

He braced himself once more, simply to move sidewise off the pillow. Once there, he could get further aside in stages, out of the range of the droplets. He kept thinking, "Just a moment now—steady—just a moment—just—Now!"

And nothing happened.

He lay flat on his back on the bed. A droplet tingled and exploded on his cheek.

The need for air was becoming unbearable.

Jim's head was throbbing and the room went dark with many tiny spots of light. He tried to suck in air and he couldn't. He tried to breathe out, but his chest and lungs didn't move. He could hear the pound of his heart growing fast and loud.

He couldn't move.

At the window, the light drapery fluttered and blew in and fell back.

He lay flat on the bed and felt a droplet tingle and explode on his cheek.

His skull was throbbing. His heart writhed and hammered in his chest. The room was going dark.

Then something gave way and his lungs were dragging in painful gasps of fresh air. He sobbed like a runner at the end of a race. After a long time, a feeling of peace and tiredness came over him.

The door opened.

He looked up. The woman was watching him sadly. "I'm sorry," she said. "Do you want to discuss payment?"

Jim nodded.

The woman sat down in a chair by the bed. "As I've explained, the initial series of three visits cost one thousand dollars each. We will accept a personal check or even an I. O. U. for the first payment. After that, you must have cash."

Jim made out a check for one thousand dollars.

The woman nodded, smiled, and folded the check into a small purse. She went out, came back with a glass of colorless liquid, shook a white powder into it, and handed it to him.

"Drink it all," she said. "A little bit can be excruciatingly painful."

Jim hesitated. He sat up a little and began to feel dizzy. He decided he had better do as she said, took the glass and drained it. It tasted exactly like sodium bicarbonate dissolved in water. He handed her the glass and she went to the door.

"The first experiences," she said, "are likely to be a little exuberant. Remember, your time sense will be distorted, as it is in a dream." She went out and shut the door softly.

Jim fervently wished he were somewhere else. He wondered what she had meant by the last comment. The thought came to him that if he could get out of this place, he could give Walters and the doctors a chance to see the drug in action.

He got up, and had the momentary sensation of doing two things at once. He seemed to lie motionless on the bed and to stand up at one and the same time. He wondered if the drug could have taken effect already. He lay down and got up again. This time he felt only a little dizzy. He went to the window and looked out. He was in a second-story window, and the first-floor rooms in this house had high ceilings. Moreover, he now discovered he was wearing a sort of hospital gown. He couldn't go into the street in that without causing a sensation, and he didn't know just when the drug would take effect.

He heard the soft click of the door opening and turned around. The woman who had talked to him came in and closed the door gently behind her. Jim watched in a daze as she turned languorously, and it occurred to him that no woman he had ever seen had moved quite like that, so the chances were that the drug had taken effect and he was imagining all this. He remembered that she had said the first experiences were likely to be a little exuberant, and his time sense distorted as in a dream.

Jim spent the night, if it was the night, uncertain as to what was real and what was due to the drug. But it was all vivid, and realistic events shaded into adventures he *knew* were imaginary, but that were so bright and satisfying that he didn't care if they were real or not. In these adventures, the colors were pure colors, and the sounds were clear sounds, and nothing was muddied or uncertain as in life.

It was so vivid and clear that when he found himself lying on the bed with the morning sun streaming in, he was astonished that he could remember not a single incident save the first, and that one not clearly.

He got up and found his clothes lying on a chair by the bed. He dressed rapidly, glanced around for the little atomizer and saw it was gone. He stepped out into the hall and there was a sudden sharp pressure on his skull, a flash of white light, and a feeling of limpness. He felt strong hands grip and carry him. He felt himself hurried down a flight of steps, along a corridor, then set down with his back against a wall.

The plump, gray-haired woman took a damp cloth and held it to his head. "You'll be all over that in a little while," she said. "I don't see why they have to do that."

"Neither do I," said Jim. He felt reasonably certain that she had done the same thing to him when he came in. He looked around, saw that they were in a small bare entry, and got cautiously to his feet. "Is my car still out front?"

"No," she said. "It's parked in back, in the drive."

"Thank you," he said. "Say good-by to Miss Cynthia for me."

The woman smiled. "You'll be back."

He was very much relieved to get outside the house. He walked back along the wide graveled drive, found his car, got in, and started it. When he reached the front of the house, he slowed the car to glance back. To his surprise, the two shutters on the third floor of the tower had broken slats. He thought this had some significance, but he was unable to remember what it was. He sat for a moment, puzzled, then decided that the important thing was to get to Walters. He swung the car out into the early morning traffic, and settled back with a feeling compounded of nine parts relief and one part puzzlement.

What puzzled him was that anyone should pay one thousand dollars for a second dose of that.

The doctors made a lightning examination, announced that he seemed physically sound, and then Walters questioned him. He described the experience in close detail, and Walters listened, nodding from time to time. At the end, Jim said, "I'll be *damned* if I can see why anyone should go back!"

"That *is* puzzling," said Walters. "It may be that they were all sensation-seekers, though that's a little odd, too. Whatever the reason, it's lucky you weren't affected."

"Maybe I'd better keep my fingers crossed," said Jim.

Walters laughed. "I'll bring your bankbook in to keep you happy." He went out, and a moment later the doctors were in again. It wasn't until the next morning that they were willing to let him go. Just as he was about to leave, one of them remarked to him, "I hope you never need a blood transfusion in a hurry."

"Why so?" Jim asked.

"You have one of the rarest combinations I've ever seen." He held out an envelope. "Walters said to give you this."

Jim opened it. It was a duplicate deposit slip for a sum as high as five figures could go.

Jim went out to a day that wasn't sunny, but looked just as good to him as if it had been.

After careful thought, Jim decided to use the money to open a detective agency of his own. Walters, who caught the dope gang trying to escape through an unused steam tunnel, gave Jim his blessing, and the offer of a job if things went wrong.

Fortunately, things went very well. Jim's agency prospered. In time, he found the right girl, they married, and had two boys and a girl. The older boy became a doctor, and the girl married a likable fast-rising young lawyer. The younger boy had a series of unpleasant scrapes and seemed bound on wrecking his life. Jim, who was by this time very well to do, at last offered the boy a job in his agency, and was astonished to see him take hold.

The years fled past much faster than Jim would have liked. Still, when the end came near, he had the pleasure of knowing that his life's work would be in the capable hands of his own son.

He breathed his last breath in satisfaction.

And woke up lying on a bed in a room where a light drapery blew back at the window and the morning sun shone in, and his clothes were folded on a chair by his bed.

Jim sat up very carefully. He held his hand in front of his face and turned it over slowly. It was not the hand of an old man. He got up and looked in a mirror, then sat down on the edge of the bed. He was young, all right. The question was, was this an old man's nightmare, or was the happy life he had just lived in a dope addict's dream?

He remembered the woman who had doped him saying, "What we offer you is nothing but your reasonable desires in life."

Then it had all been a dream.

But a dream should go away, and this remained clear in his memory.

He dressed, went out in the hall, felt a sudden pressure on his skull, a flash of white light, and a feeling of limpness.

He came to in the small entry, and the plump, gray-haired woman carefully held a damp cool cloth to his head.

"Thanks," he said. "Is my car out back?"

"Yes," she said, and he went out.

As he drove away from the house he glanced back and noticed the two broken shutters on the third floor of the tower. The memory of his dream about this same event—leaving the place—jarred him. It seemed that those broken shutters meant something, but he was unable to remember what. He trod viciously on the gas pedal, throwing a spray of gravel on the carefully tailored lawn as he swung into the street.

He *still* did not see why anyone should go back there with anything less than a shotgun.

He told Walters the whole story, including the details of his "life," that he remembered so clearly.

"You'll get over it," Walters finally said, when Jim was ready to leave the hospital. "It's a devil of a thing to have happen, but there's an achievement in it you can be proud of."

"You name it," said Jim bitterly.

"You've saved a lot of other people from this same thing. The doctors have analyzed the traces of drug still in your blood. They think they can neutralize it. Then we are going to put a few sturdy men inside that house, and while they're assumed to be under the influence, we'll raid the place."

The tactic worked, but Jim watched the trial with a cynical eye. He couldn't convince himself that it was true. He might, for all he knew, be lying in a second-floor room of the house on a bed, while these people, who seemed to be on trial, actually were going freely about their business.

This inability to accept what he saw as real at last forced Jim to resign his job. Using the generous bonus Walters had given him, he took up painting. As he told Walters on one of his rare visits, "It may or may not be that what I'm doing is real, but at least there's the satisfaction of the work itself."

"You're not losing any money on it," said Walters shrewdly.

"I know," said Jim, "and that makes me acutely uneasy."

On his 82nd birthday, Jim was widely regarded as the "Grand Old Man" of painting. His hands and feet felt cold that day, and he fell into an uneasy, shallow-breathing doze. He woke with a start and a choking cough. For an instant everything around him had an unnatural clarity; then it all went dark and he felt himself falling.

He awoke in a bed in a room where a light drapery fluttered at the window, and the morning sun shone into the room.

This time, Jim entertained no doubts as to whether or not this was real. He got up angrily and smashed his fist into the wall with all his might.

The shock and pain jolted him to his heels.

He went out the same way as before, but he had to drive one-handed, gritting his teeth all the way.

The worst of it was that the doctors weren't able to make that hand exactly right afterward. Even if the last "life" had been a dream—even if this one was—he wanted to paint. But every time he tried to, he felt so clumsy that he gave up in despair.

Walters, dissatisfied, gave Jim the minimum possible payment. The gang escaped. Jim eventually lost his job, and in the end he eked out his life at poorly paid odd jobs.

The only consolation he felt was that his life was so miserable that it must be true.

He went to bed sick one night and woke up the next morning on a bed in a room where a light drapery fluttered at the window and the early morning sun shone brightly in.

This happened to him twice more.

The next time after that, he lay still on the bed and stared at the ceiling. The incidents and details of five lives danced in his mind like jabbering monkeys. He pressed his palms to his forehead and wished he could forget it all.

The door opened softly and the tall, dark-haired woman was

watching him with a faint smile. "I told you," she said, "that you couldn't take anything away but memories."

He looked up at her sickly. "That seems like a long, long while ago."

She nodded and sat down. "Your time sense is distorted as in a dream."

"I wish," he said drearily, looking at her, "that I could just forget it all. I don't see why anyone would come back for more of that."

She leaned forward to grip the edge of the mattress, shaking with laughter. She sat up again. "Whew!" she said, looking at him and forcing her face to be straight. "Nobody comes back for *more*. That is the unique quality of this drug. People come back to forget they ever had it."

He sat up. "I can forget that?"

"Oh, yes. *Don't* get so excited! That's what you really paid your thousand dollars for. The forgetfulness drug lingers in your blood stream for two to three weeks. Then memory returns and you're due for another visit."

Jim looked at her narrowly. "Does my body become tolerant of this drug? Does it take twice as much after three visits, four times as much after six visits, eight times as much after nine visits?"

"No."

"Then you lied to me."

She looked at him oddly. "What would you have expected of me? But I didn't lie to you. I merely said that that was what I was told to tell those who asked."

"Then what's the point of it?" Jim asked.

"What's the point of bank robbery?" She frowned at him. "You ask a lot of questions. Aren't you lucky I know the answers? Ordinarily you wouldn't get around to this till you'd stewed for a few weeks. But you seem precocious, so I'll tell you."

"That's nice," he said.

"The main reason for the impossible rates is so you can't pay off in money."

"How does that help you?"

"Because," she said, "every time you bring us a new patron, you get three free visits yourself."

"Ah," he said.

"It needn't be so terribly unpleasant, coming here."

"What happens if, despite everything, some sorehead actually goes and tells the police about this?"

"We move."

"Suppose they catch you?"

"They won't. Or, at least, it isn't likely."

"But you'll leave?"

"Yes."

"What happens to me?"

"Don't you see? We'll *have* to leave. Someone will have betrayed us. We couldn't stay because it might happen again. It isn't right from your viewpoint, but we can't take chances."

For a few moments they didn't talk, and the details of Jim's previous "lives" came pouring in on him. He sat up suddenly. "Where's that forgetfulness drug?"

She went outside and came back with a glass of colorless liquid. She poured in a faintly pink powder and handed it to him. He drank it quickly and it tasted like bicarbonate of soda dissolved in water.

He looked at her. "This isn't the same thing all over again, is it?"

"Don't worry," she said. "You'll forget."

The room began to go dark. He leaned back. The last thing he was conscious of was her cool hand on his forehead, then the faint click as she opened the door to go out.

He sat up. He dressed, drove quickly to Walters and told him all he could remember. Walters immediately organized his raid. Jim saw the place closed up with no one caught.

After two weeks and four days, the memories flooded back. His life turned into a nightmare. At every turn, the loves, hates, and tiny details of six separate lives poured in on him. He tried drugs in an attempt to forget, and sank from misery to hopeless despair. He ended up in a shooting scrap as Public Enemy Number Four.

And then he awoke and found himself in a bed in a room with a light drapery blowing in at the window, and the early morning sun shining brightly in.

"Merciful God!" he said.

The door clicked shut.

Jim sprang to the door and looked out in the carpeted hall. There was the flash of a woman's skirt; then a tall narrow door down the hallway closed to shut off his view.

He drew back into the room and shut the door. The house was quiet. In the distance, on the street, he could hear the faint sound of a passing car.

He swallowed hard. He glanced at the window. It had been, he reasoned, early morning when he had talked to the woman last. It was early morning now. He recalled that before she went out she said, "You'll forget." He had then lived his last miserable "life"— and awakened to hear the click as the door came shut behind her.

That had all taken less than five seconds of actual time.

He found his clothes on a nearby chair and started to dress. As he did so, he realized for the first time that the memories of his "lives" were no longer clear to him. They were fading away, almost as the memories of a dream do after a man wakes and gets up. *Almost* as the memories of a dream, but not quite. Jim found that if he thought of them, they gradually became clear again.

He tried to forget and turned his attention to the tree he could see through the window. He looked at the curve of its boughs, and at a black-and-yellow bird balancing on a branch in the breeze.

The memories faded away, and he began to plan what to do. No sooner did he do this than he remembered with a shock that he had said to Walters, "If I don't come out next morning, I want you to come in after me."

And Walters had said, "We will."

So that must have been just last night.

Jim finished dressing, took a deep breath, and held out his hand. It looked steady. He opened the door, stepped out into the hall, and an instant too late remembered what had happened six times before.

When he opened his eyes, the plump, gray-haired woman was holding a damp cloth to his forehead and clucking sympathetically.

Jim got carefully to his feet, and walked down the drive to his car. He slid into the driver's seat, started the engine, and sat still a moment, thinking. Then he released the parking brake, and pressed lightly on the gas pedal. The car slid smoothly ahead, the gravel of the drive crunching under its tires. He glanced up as the car reached the end of the drive, and looked back at the tower. Every slat in the shutters was perfect. Jim frowned, trying to remember something. Then he glanced up and down the street, and swung out into the light early morning traffic.

He wasted no time getting to Walters.

He was greeted with an all-encompassing inspection that traveled from Jim's head to his feet. Walters looked tense. He took a cigar from a box on his desk and put it in his mouth unlit.

"I've spent half the night telling myself there are some things you can't ask a man to do for money. But we *had* to do it. Are you all right?"

"At the moment."

"There are doctors and medical technicians in the next room. Do you want to see them now or later?"

"Right now."

In the next hour, Jim took off his clothes, stood up, lay down, looked into bright lights, winced as a sharp hollow needle was forced into his arm, gave up samples of bodily excretions, sat back as electrodes were strapped to his skin, and at last was reassured that he would be all right. He dressed, and found himself back in Walters' office.

Walters looked at him sympathetically.

"How do you feel?"

"Starved."

"I'll have breakfast sent in." He snapped on his intercom, gave the order, then leaned back. He picked up his still unlit cigar, lit it, puffed hard, and said, "What happened?"

Jim told him, starting with the evening before, and ending when he swung his car out into traffic this morning.

Walters listened with a gathering frown, drawing occasionally on the cigar.

A breakfast of scrambled eggs and Canadian bacon was brought in. Walters got up, and looked out the window, staring down absently at the traffic moving past in the street below. Jim ate with single-minded concentration, and finally pushed his plate back and looked up.

Walters ground his cigar butt in the ashtray and lit a fresh cigar. "This is a serious business. You say you remembered the details of each of those six lives *clearly?*"

"Worse than that. I remembered the emotions and the attachments. In the first life, for instance, I had my own business." Jim paused and thought back. The memories gradually became clear again. "One of my men, for instance, was named Hart. He stood about five-seven, slender, with black hair, cut short when I first met him. Hart was a born actor. He could play any part. It wasn't his face. His expression hardly seemed to change. But his manner changed. He could stride into a hotel and the bellboys would jump for his bags and the desk clerk spring to attention. He stood out. He was important. Or he could slouch in the front door, hesitate, look around, blink, start to ask one of the bellboys something, lose his nerve, stiffen his shoulders, shamble over to the desk, and get unmercifully snubbed. Obviously, he was less than nobody. Or, again, he could quietly come in the front door, stroll across the lobby, fade out of sight somewhere, and hardly a person would notice or remember him. Whatever part he played, he lived it. That was what made him so valuable."

Walters had taken the cigar out of his mouth, and listened intently. "You mean this Hart—this imaginary man—is real to you? In three dimensions?"

"That's it. Not only that, I like him. There were other, stronger attachments. I had a family."

"Which seems real?"

Jim nodded. "I realize as I say these things that I sound like a lunatic."

"No." Walters shook his head sympathetically. "It all begins to make sense. Now I see why the girl at the hospital said to the doctor, 'You aren't real.' Does it *hurt* to talk about these 'lives'?"

Jim hesitated. "Not as long as we keep away from the personal details. But it hurt like nothing I can describe to have all six of these sets of memories running around in my head at once."

"I can imagine. All right, let's track down some of these memories and see how far the details go."

Jim nodded. "Okay."

Walters got out a bound notebook and pen. "We'll start with your business. What firm name did you use?"

"Calder Associates."

"Why?"

"It sounded dignified, looked good on a business card or letterhead, and wasn't specific."

"What was your address?"

"Four North Street. Earlier, it was 126 Main."

"How many men did you have working with you?"

"To begin with, just Hart, and another man by the name of Dean. At the end, there were twenty-seven."

"What were their names?"

Jim called them off one by one, without hesitation.

Walters blinked. "Say that over again a little more slowly."

Jim repeated the list.

"All right," said Walters. "Describe these men."

Jim described them. He gave more and more details as Walters pressed for them, and by lunch time, Walters had a large section of the notebook filled.

The two men ate, and Walters spent the rest of the afternoon quizzing Jim on his first "life." Then they had steak and French fries sent up to the office. Walters ate in silence for a moment, then said, "Do you realize that you haven't stumbled once?"

Jim looked up in surprise. "What do you mean?"

Walters said, "Quiz me on the names of every man who ever worked for me. I won't remember all of them. Not by a long shot. You remember every last detail of this dream life with a total recall that beats anything I've ever seen."

"That's the trouble. That's why it's pleasant to forget."

Walters asked suddenly, "Did you ever paint? *Actually,* I mean. I ask because you say you were an outstanding painter in one of these 'lives.'"

"When I was a boy, I painted some. I wanted to be an artist."

"Can you come out to my place tonight? I'd like to see whether you can really handle the brushes."

Jim nodded. "Yes, I'd like to try that."

They drove out together, and Walters got out a dusty paint set in a wooden case, set up a folding easel, and put a large canvas on it.

Jim stood still a moment, thinking back. Then he began to paint.

He lost himself in the work, as he always had, all through the years, and what he was painting now he had painted before. Had painted it, and sold it for a good price, too. And it was worth it. He could still see the model in his mind as he painted with swift precise strokes.

He stepped back.

"My Lady in Blue" was a cheerful girl of seventeen. She smiled out from the canvas as if at any moment she might laugh or wave.

Jim glanced around. For an instant the room seemed strange. Then he remembered where he was.

Walters looked at the painting for a long moment, then looked at Jim, and swallowed. He carefully took the painting from the easel and replaced it with another blank canvas. He went across the room and got a large floor-type ashtray, a wrought-iron affair with a galloping horse for the handle.

"Paint this."

Jim looked at it. He stepped up to the canvas, hesitated. He raised the brush—and stopped. He didn't know where to begin. He frowned and carefully thought back to his first lessons. "Let's see." He glanced up. "Do you have any tracing paper?"

"Just a minute," said Walters.

Jim tackled the paper over the canvas and methodically drew the ashtray on the paper. He had a hard time, but at last looked at the paper triumphantly. "Now, do you have any transfer paper?"

Walters frowned. "I've got carbon paper."

"All right."

Walters got it. Jim put a sheet under his tracing paper, tacked it up again, and carefully went over the drawing with a pencil. He un-tacked the paper, then methodically began to paint. At length, weary and perspiring, he stepped back.

Walters looked at it. Jim blinked and looked again. Walters said, "A trifle off-center, isn't it?"

There was no doubt about it, the ashtray stood too far toward the upper right-hand corner of the canvas.

Walters pointed at the other painting. "Over there we have a masterpiece that you dashed off freehand. Here we have, so to speak, a piece of good, sound mechanical drawing that isn't properly placed on the canvas. This took you longer to do than the other. How come?"

"I had done the other before."

"And you remember the motions of your hand? Is that it?" He put another canvas up. "Do it again."

Jim frowned. He stepped forward, thought a moment, and began to paint. He lost himself in a perfection of concentration. In time, he stepped back.

Walters looked at it. He swallowed hard, glanced back and forth from this painting to the one Jim had done at first. He lifted the painting carefully from the easel and placed it beside the other.

They looked identical.

The sun was just lighting the horizon as they drove back to the office. Walters said, "I'm going in there and sleep on the cot. Can you get back around three this afternoon?"

"Sure."

Jim drove home, slept, ate, and was back again by three.

"This is a devil of a puzzle," said Walters, leaning back at his desk and blowing out a cloud of smoke. "I've had half a dozen experts squint at one of those paintings. I've been offered five thousand, even though they don't know the artist's name. Then I showed them the other painting and they almost fell through the floor. It isn't possible, but each stroke appears identical. How do you feel?"

"Better. And I've remembered something. Let's look at your model."

They went to the big model of the mansion, and Jim touched the upper story of the tower. "Have some of the boys sketch this. Then compare the sketches with photographs."

Soon they were looking at sketches and photographs side by side. The sketches showed the tower shutters perfect. The photographs showed several slats of the shutters broken.

Walters questioned the men, who insisted the shutters were perfect. After they left, Jim said, "Everyone who sketched that place wasn't drugged. And the cameras certainly weren't drugged."

Walters said, "Let's take a look." They drove out past the mansion, and the shutters looked perfect. A new photograph showed the same broken slats.

Back at the office, Walters said, "Just what are we up against here?"

Jim said, "I can think of two possibilities."

"Let's hear them."

"Often you can do the same thing several different ways. A man, for instance, can go from one coastal town to another on foot, riding a horse, by car, by plane, or in a speedboat."

"Granted."

"A hundred years ago, the list would have been shorter."

Walters nodded thoughtfully. "I follow you. Go on."

"Whoever sees those shutters as perfect is, for the time being, in an abnormal mental state. How did he get here? We've assumed drugs were used. But just as there are new ways of going from one city to another, so there may be new ways of passing from one mental state to another. Take subliminal advertising, for instance, where the words, 'THIRSTY,' 'THIRSTY,' 'BEER,' may be flashed on the screen too fast to be consciously seen."

"It's illegal."

"Suppose someone found out how to do it undetected, and decided to try it out on a small scale. What about nearly imperceptible *verbal* clues instead of visual ones?"

Walters' eyes narrowed. "We'll analyze every sound coming out of that place and check for any kind of suspicious sensory stimulus whatever. What's your other idea?"

"Well, go back to your travel analogy. Going from one place to another, any number of animals can outrun, outfly, and outswim a man. Let Man work on the problem long enough, and roll up to the starting line in his rocket-plane, and the result will be different. But until Man has time to concentrate enough thought and effort, the nonhuman creature has an excellent chance to beat him. There are better fliers, better swimmers, better fighters, better—"

Walters frowned. "Better *suggestionists?* Like the snake that's said to weave hypnotically?"

"Yes, and the wasp that stings the trapdoor spider, when other wasps are fought off."

"Hmm. Maybe. But I incline to the subliminal advertising theory myself." He looked at the mansion. "Where would they keep the device?"

"Why not the tower?"

Walters nodded. "It's an easy place to guard, and to shut off from visitors."

Jim said, "It might explain those shutters. They might not care to risk painters and repairmen up there."

Walters knocked the ash off his cigar. "But how do we get in there to find out?"

They studied the model. Walters said, "Say we send in a 'building inspector.' They'll knock him out, hallucinate a complete series of incidents in his mind, and send him out totally ignorant. If we try to raid the place in a group, they'll vanish with the help of that machine. But there must be *some* way."

Jim said thoughtfully, "Those trees overhang the room."

"They do, don't they?"

The two men studied the trees and the tower.

Jim touched one of the arching limbs. "What if we lowered a rope from here?"

Walters tied an eraser on a string and fastened the string to a limb. The eraser hung by the uppermost tower window. Walters scowled, snapped on the intercom, and asked for several of his men. Then he turned to Jim. "We'll see what Cullen thinks. He's done some jobs like this."

Cullen had sharp eyes and a mobile face that grew unhappy as he listened to Walters. Finally, he shook his head. "No, thanks. Ask me to go up a wall, or the side of a building. But not down out of a tree branch on the end of a rope."

He gave the eraser a little flip with his finger. It swung in circles, hit the wall, and bounced away.

"Say I'm actually up there. It's night. The rope swings. The limb bobs up and down. The tree sways. All to a different rhythm. I'm spinning around on the end of this rope. One second this shutter is one side of me. The next second it's on the other side and five feet away. A job is a job, but this is one I don't want."

Walters turned to Jim after Cullen went out. "That settles that."

Jim looked at the tree limb. Two or three weeks from today, he told himself, the memories would come flooding back. The people who had done it would get away, and do it again. And he would have those memories.

Jim glanced at Walters stubbornly. "I am going to climb that tree."

The night was still, with a dark overcast sky as Jim felt the rough bark against the insides of his arms. He hitched up the belt that circled the tree, then pulled up one foot, then another as he sank the climbing irons in higher up. He could hear Cullen's advice: "Practice, study the model, do each step over and over in your head. Then, when you're actually doing it and when things get tight, *hold your mind on what to do next*. Do that. *Then* think of the next step."

Jim was doing this as the dark lawn dropped steadily away. He felt the tree trunk grow gradually more slender, then begin to widen. He worked his way carefully above the limb, refastened the belt, and felt a puff of warm air touch his face and neck, like a leftover from the warm day. Somewhere, a radio was playing.

He climbed, aware now of the rustling around him of leaves.

The trunk widened again, and he knew he was at the place where the trunk separated into the limbs that arched out to form the crown of the tree.

He pulled himself up carefully, and took his eyes from the tree for a moment to look toward the mansion. He saw the slanting tile roof of an entirely different house, light shining down from a dormer window. He glanced around, to see the looming steep-roofed tower of the mansion in the opposite direction. He realized he must have partially circled the tree and lost his sense of direction.

He swallowed and crouched in the cleft between the limbs till he was sure he knew which limb arched over the tower. He fastened the belt and started slowly up. As he climbed, the limb arched, to become more and more nearly horizontal. At the same time, the limb became more slender. It began to respond to his movements, swaying slightly as he climbed. Now he was balancing on it, the steep roof of the tower shining faintly ahead of him. He remembered that he had to take off the climbing irons, lest they foul in the rope later on. As he twisted to do this, his hands trembled. He forced his breath to come steadily. He looked ahead to the steep, slanting roof of the tower.

The limb was already almost level. If he crawled further, it would sag under him. He would be climbing head down. He glanced back, and his heart began to pound. To go back, he would have to inch backwards along the narrow limb.

Cullen's words came to him: "When things get tight, *hold your mind on what to do next*. Do that. *Then* think of the next step."

He inched ahead. The limb began to sag.

There was a rustling of leaves.

The limb swayed. It fell, and rose, beneath him.

He clung to it, breathing hard.

He inched further. The leaves rustled. The limb pressed up, then fell away. He shut his eyes, his forehead tight against the bark, and crept ahead. After a time, he seemed to feel himself tip to one side. His eyes opened.

The tower was almost beneath him.

With his left arm, he clung tightly to the limb. With his right, he felt carefully for the rope tied to his belt. He worked one end of the rope forward and carefully looped it around the limb. He tied the knot that he had practiced over and over, then tested it, and felt it hold.

A breeze stirred the leaves. The limb began to sway.

The dark lawn below seemed to reach up and he felt himself already falling. He clung hard to the limb and felt his body tremble all over. Then he knew he had to go through the rest of his plan without hesitation, lest he lose his nerve completely.

He sucked in a deep breath, swung over the limb, let go with one hand, caught the rope, then caught it with the other hand, looped the rope around one ankle, and started to slide down.

The rope swung. The limb dipped, then lifted. The tree seemed to sway slightly.

Jim clung, his left foot clamping the loop of the rope passed over his right ankle. The swaying, dipping, and whirling began to die down. His hands felt weak and tired.

He slid gradually down the rope. Then the shutter was right beside him. He reached out, put his hand through the break in the slats, and lifted the iron catch. The hinges of the shutters screeched as he pulled them open.

A dead black oblong hung before him.

He reached out, and felt no sash in the opening. He climbed higher on the rope, pushed away from the building, and as he swung back, stepped across, caught the frame, and dropped inside.

The shutters screeched as he pulled them shut, but the house remained quiet. He stood still for a long moment, then unsnapped a case on his belt, and took out a little polarizing flashlight. He carefully thumbed the stud that turned the front lens. A dim beam faintly lit the room.

There was a glint of metal, then another. Shiny parallel lines ran from the ceiling to floor in front of him. There was an odd faint odor.

The house was quiet. A shift of the wind brought the distant sound of recorded music.

Carefully, Jim eased the stud of the flashlight further around, so the light grew a trifle brighter.

The vertical lines looked like bars.

He stepped forward and peered into the darkness.

Behind the bars, something stirred.

Jim reached back, unbuttoned the flap of his hip pocket and gripped the cool metal of his gun.

Something moved behind the bars. It reached out, bunched itself, reached out. Something large and dark slid up the bars.

Jim raised the gun.

A hissing voice said quietly, "You are from some sort of law-enforcement agency? Good."

Jim slid his thumb toward the stub of the light, so he could see more clearly. But the faint hissing voice went on, "Don't. It will do no good to see me."

Jim's hand tightened on the gun at the same instant that his mind asked a question.

The voice said, "Who am I? Why am I here? If I tell you, it will strain your mind to believe me. Let me show you."

The room seemed to pivot, then swung around him faster and faster. A voice spoke to him from all sides; then something lifted him up, and at an angle.

He stared at the dial, rapped it with his finger. The needle didn't move from its pin. He glanced at the blue-green planet on the screen. Photon pressure was zero, and there was nothing to do but try to land on chemical rockets. As he strapped himself into the acceleration chair, he began to really appreciate the size of his bad luck.

Any solo space pilot, he told himself, should be a good mechanic. And an individual planetary explorer should be his own pilot, to save funds. Moreover, anyone planning to explore Ludt VI, with its high gravity and pressure, and its terrific psychic stress, should be strong and healthy.

These requirements made Ludt VI almost the exclusive preserve of big organizations with teams of specialists. They sent out heavily equipped expeditions, caught a reasonable quota of spat, trained them on the way home, and sold the hideous creatures at magnificent prices to the proprietors of every dream parlor in the system. From this huge income, they paid their slightly less huge costs, and made a safe moderate profit on their investment. With a small expedition, it was different.

A small expedition faced risk, and a one-man expedition was riskiest of all. But if it succeeded, the trained spat brought the same huge price, and there were no big-ship bills for fuel, specialists, power equipment, and insurance. This, he thought, had almost been a successful trip. There were three nearly trained spat back in his sleeping compartment.

But, though he was a competent trainer, a skilled explorer, a passable pilot, and in good physical condition, he was no mechanic. He didn't know how to fix what had gone wrong.

He sat back and watched the rim of the world below swing up in the deep blue sky.

There was a gray fuzziness. Jim was standing in the dark, seeing the bars shining faintly before him.

The black knot still clung to the bars.

Somewhere in the old mansion, a phone began to ring.

Jim said, in a low voice, "You were the pilot?"

"No. I was the spat. The others died in the crash. Some of your race found me and we made a—an agreement. But it has worked out differently here than I expected. The experiences I stimulate in your minds are enjoyable to you and to me. Yet either the structure of your brains is different from that of the pilot, or you lack training in mind control. You cannot wipe away these experiences afterward, and though I can do it for you easily, it is only temporary."

A door opened and shut downstairs. There was a sound of feet on the staircase.

The hissing began again. "You must go and bring help."

Jim thought of the rope and the trees. His hand tightened on the gun and he made no move toward the window.

The hissing sound said, "I see your difficulty. I will help you."

There was the crack of a rifle, then several shots outside. Jim swung the shutter open, felt a faint dizziness, and looked down on a warm sunlit lawn some thirty feet below.

A hissing voice said, "Take hold the rope. Now carefully step out. Loop the rope with your foot."

Somewhere in Jim's mind, as he did this, there was an uneasiness. He wondered at it as he climbed up the rope to the bar overhead, swung up onto the bar, slipped and nearly lost his grip. He could see the bar was steady and solid, and he wondered as it seemed to move under him. The green lawn was such a short distance down that there clearly was little danger, and he wondered why his breath came fast as he swung around on the bar, slid down to a sort of resting place where he put on climbing irons before starting down again. Always on the way down, the whistling voice told him that it was just a few feet more, just a few feet, as bit by bit he made his way down, and suddenly heard shots, shouts, and a repeated scream.

Jim stepped off onto the soft lawn, stumbled, and knelt to take off the climbing irons. His heart pounded like a trip-hammer. He realized there was a blaze of spotlights around him. He saw lights coming on in the mansion, and memory returned in a rush. He drew in a deep shaky breath, glanced at the tree, then saw a little knot of people near the base of the tower. He walked over, recognized Walters in the glow of the lights and saw a still figure on the ground.

Walters said, "I shouldn't have let him try it. Cover his face, Cullen."

Cullen bent to draw a coat up over the head of the motionless figure, which was twisted sidewise.

Jim looked down.

He saw his own face.

He was aware of darkness and of something hard beneath him. Voices came muffled from somewhere nearby. He heard the sound of a phone set in its cradle, the slam of a door, the scrape of glass on glass. He breathed and recognized a choking smell of cigar smoke.

Jim sat up.

Nearby was the model of the mansion. Jim swung carefully to his feet, made his way across the room, and opened the door to the next office. He blinked in the bright light, then saw Walters look up and grin. "One more night like this and I retire. How do you feel?"

"I ache all over and I'm dizzy. How did I get here?"

"I was afraid your going in there might misfire and touch off their escape, so I had the place surrounded. We saw you go in, there was about a five-minute pause, and the shutters seemed to come open. A figure came out. Then there was the crack of a rifle from the dormer window of a house across the street. I sent some men into that house, and the rest of us closed in on the mansion. We used the spotlights on our cars to light the place. We'd just found what we thought was your body—with a broken neck—when there was a thud behind us. There you were, and the other body was gone.

"Right then, I thought it was going to be the same as usual. But this time we nailed several men and women in quite a state of confusion. Some of them have fingerprints that match those from the first place we raided. We don't have the equipment yet, because that tower staircase was boarded up tight . . . What's wrong?"

Jim told his own version, adding, "Since that shot came *before* I opened the shutters, the 'figure' you saw go up the rope must have been an illusion, to fool whoever had the gun across the street. And since I heard someone running up the stairs a few minutes before you came in, I don't see how the stairs can be boarded up."

Walters sat up straight. *"Another* illusion!"

Jim said, "It would be nice to know if there's any limit to those illusions."

Walters said, "This afternoon, we tried looking at those shutters through field glasses. Beyond about four hundred feet, you could see the broken slats. So there's a limit. But if there's no equipment, this is uncanny, 'spat' or no 'spat.' "

Jim shook his head. "I don't know. You can use the same electromagnetic laws and similar components to make all kinds of devices—radios, television sets, electronic computers. What you make depends mainly on how you put the parts together. It may be that in the different conditions on some other planet, types of nerve components similar to those we use for thought might be used to create dangerous illusions in the minds of other creatures."

"That still leaves us with a problem. What do we do with this thing?"

"I got the impression it was like a merchant who has to sell his wares to live. Let me go back and see if we can make an agreement with it."

"I'll go with you."

Jim shook his head. "One of us has to stay beyond that four-hundred-foot limit."

The stairs were narrow leading up into the tower. Jim found weary men amidst plaster and bits of board at a solid barricade on the staircase. He scowled at it, then shouted up the stairs, "I want to talk to you!"

There was a sort of twist in the fabric of things. Jim found himself staring at the wall beside the stairs, its plaster gone and bits of board torn loose. The staircase itself was open. He started up.

Behind him, a man still staring at the wall said, "Did you see that? He went *around* somehow."

The back of Jim's neck prickled. He reached a tall door, opened it, turned, and he stood where he had been before.

There was a faint hissing. "I am glad you came back. I can't keep this up forever."

"We want to make an agreement with you. Otherwise, we'll have to use force."

"There is no need of that. I ask only food, water, and a chance to use my faculties. And I would be very happy if the atmospheric pressure around me could be increased. Falling pressure tires me so that it is hard for me to keep self-control."

Jim thought of the first night, where there had been the appearance of light on mansion and grounds, but heavy clouds and only a thin moon in the sky.

The hissing voice said, "It had stormed, with a sharp fall in atmospheric pressure. I was exhausted and creating a wrong illusion. Can you provide what I need?"

"The food, water, and pressure chamber, yes. I don't know about the opportunity to 'use your faculties.' "

"There is a painting in the world now that wasn't there before. You and I did that."

"What are you driving at?"

"I can't increase skill where there has been no practice, no earnest thought or desire. I can't help combine facts or memories where none have been stored. But within these limits I can help you and others to a degree of concentration few men of your world know."

"Could you teach us to concentrate this way on our own?"

"I don't know. We would have to try it. Meanwhile, I have been here long enough to have learned that your race has used horses to extend their powers of movement, dogs to increase their ability to trail by scent, cows and goats to convert indigestible grass and leaves into foodstuffs. These all were your partners in the physical world. It seems to me that I am much the same, but in the mental world."

Jim hesitated. "Meanwhile, you can help us to forget these dream lives?"

"Easily. But, as I say, the effect is not permanent."

Jim nodded. "I'll see what we can do."

He went to tell Walters, who listened closely, then picked up the phone.

Early the next morning, Jim climbed the steps to the high narrow door of the tower, put on dark glasses and went in. Right behind him came a corporal with a creepie-peepie TV transmitter. From outside came the windmill roar of helicopters, and, high up, the rumble of jets.

The corporal opened the shutter and spoke quietly into the microphone. A hissing voice spoke in Jim's mind. "I am ready."

Jim said, "This entire place is being watched by television. If there is any important difference between what observers here report and what the cameras show, this place and everything in it will be destroyed a few seconds later."

"I understand," said the hissing voice. Then it told him how to loosen one of the bars, and Jim loosened it and stood back.

There was the sound of footsteps on the staircase. A large heavy box with one end hinged and open was thrust in the doorway.

On the floor, something bunched and unbunched, and moved past into the box. Jim closed the box and snapped shut the padlock. Men lifted it and started down the staircase. Jim and the corporal followed. As they went out the front door, heavy planks were thrown across to a waiting truck. Sweating men in khaki carried the box up the planks into the truck. Then the rear doors swung shut, the engine roared, and the truck moved away.

Jim thought of the truck's destination, a pressure tank in a concrete blockhouse under a big steel shed out in the desert.

He looked around and saw Walters, who smiled at him and held out a slim envelope. "Good work," said Walters. "And I imagine some hundreds of ex-addicts reclaimed from mental hospitals are going to echo those sentiments."

Jim thanked him, and Walters led him to the car, saying, "Now what you need is sleep, and plenty of it."

"And how!"

Once home, Jim fell into an exhausted sleep, and had a nightmare. In the nightmare, he dreamed that he woke up, and found himself in a bed in a room where a light curtain blew in at the window, and the morning sun shone brightly in.

He sat up, and looked around carefully at the furniture, and felt the solid wall of the room as he asked himself a question that he knew would bother him again.

Which was the nightmare?

Then he remembered his fear as he climbed the tree, and Cullen's advice: "When things get tight, *hold your mind on what to do next.* Do that. *Then* think of the next step."

He thought a moment, then lay back and smiled. He might not be absolutely certain this was real. But even if it wasn't, he felt sure he would win in the end.

No nightmare could last forever.

Further Reading   Christopher Anvil

Stories

"Not in the Literature." *Analog Science Fiction,* October 1962. (*Spectrum 4,* ed. Kingsley Amis and Robert Conquest.)

"Positive Feedback." *Analog Science Fiction,* August 1965. (*Sociology Through Science Fiction,* ed. John Milstead, et al.)

"A Rose by Other Name." *Astounding Science Fiction,* January 1960. (*The 6th Annual of the Year's Best S-F,* ed. Judith Merril.)

"Stranglehold." *Analog Science Fiction,* June 1966. (*Analog 6,* ed. John W. Campbell, Jr.)

"Uncalculated Risk." *Analog Science Fiction,* March 1962. (*Nightmare Age,* ed. Frederik Pohl.)

Kris Neville (born 1925) could have been among the ten most honored science fiction writers of his generation; instead, he virtually abandoned the field after conquering it early on and made himself the leading lay authority in the world on epoxy resins, collaborating on a series of specialized texts that have become the basic works in their field. I can hardly blame him for this decision, and it was in any case carefully thought out. Neville, who sold his first story in 1949 and another fifteen by 1952, concluded early on that the perimeters of the field in the 1950s were simply too close to contain the kind of work he would have to do if he wanted to grow as a writer, and accordingly he quit. A scattering of stories has appeared over the last quarter of a century, and a couple of novels, but except for one abortive attempt to write full-time in the mid-1960s (the field simply could not absorb the kind of work he was doing), Neville has been in a state of diminished production for a long time. Nowadays a short-short story shows up once a year or so in a magazine or original anthology; sometimes written in collaboration with his second wife, Lil, and always so astonishingly above the run of material surrounding it as to constitute an embarrassment to the other writers. Neville, whom I do not claim to know well at all but with whom I did correspond prolifically some years ago, may be among the most intelligent of science fiction writers (only A. J. Budrys seems to have his eclecticism and his breadth) and strikes me as among the few contented people I have ever known.

Neville's best-known story, "Bettyann," appeared in Healy and McComa's *New Tales of Space and Time* in 1951, was anthologized often during the decade, and became the basis for a 1968 novel of the same title (Belmont Books), and very good it is too in its handling of an adolescent female point of view. Neville is one of the few contemporary writers around who understands children and can write about them with understanding; he has shown this in work like "From the Government Printing Office" and in the sequel to "Bettyann," "Overture." (Neville understands, for instance, that for the middle class in a technologized culture children are the necessary victims; only by what is perpetrated on them can the system and the adjustment of adults persist.) Neville has also done some extraordinary political satire—"The Price of Simeryl," published way back in 1966, is an early, savage anti-Vietnam piece—and in work like "New Apples in the Garden" manifests an extraordinary range of subject and character.

Nonetheless, I believe that "Ballenger's People," an obscure story published in *Galaxy* a decade ago, unnoticed and never reprinted, is the best thing he has ever written and was the best American short story published in its crazy year. I submit the story in evidence and need not utter a peep more.

                                                              B.N.M.

Ballenger's People

by KRIS NEVILLE

The radios in the wall came on with a click, and a moment later African drum music issued into the bedroom. Bart Ballenger was instantly awake.

He took a vote, and the consensus was it's Thursday.

He arose and stood before the window and breathed deeply. Thursday was the day to settle accounts with a lawyer on Wilshire Blvd.

Air and sunlight said spring. This, too, was verified democratically.

Ballenger completed the early morning routine against the sound of music. He moved about his two-bedroom apartment checking. All was as the previous evening. No one had entered during the night. The smaller bedroom was in order against the arrival of guests who never came.

He sat at the counter-top divider, between living room and kitchen, eating eggs, drinking coffee. The radios around him, all switched on, played the same music as in the bedroom. He bobbed his head to the rhythm, visualized The Star Walkers. He was in love with the middle drummer, a girl named Angelique Roust.

Ballenger had seen Angelique on TV and instantly fallen in love with her. She replaced his previous love, Miss Terri Paul, flutist, a person, in retrospect, with no bust worthy of mention.

Now it seemed, over the eggs and coffee in the natural brightness of morning, fantastic that such a collection as Miss Terri Paul could have attracted even his momentary attention, much less captivated him for a single minute, let alone nearly five whole months. He vowed against eternity that he would never, never, never show Miss

Terri Paul's TV tapes again, and if he heard her on radio, he would refuse to listen. This would be proof of his love for Angelique.

He finished his coffee. The news was coming on, blaring out over the sounds of cool jazz. There were, in the world, the nations of crime and the nations of law and order; he belonged to the latter. All were democracies, whether they knew it or not, but some were insane. This was scarcely surprising when you considered evolution.

Out came the letter: *Final Notice!* The amount, including postage, was $23.47.

"Ballenger" began the letter, omitting the customary salutation— "your actions indicate you have no intention of paying the enclosed bill. If this bill is not paid immediately, I will be forced to institute legal action, which may involve your employer. You will be liable for all costs incurred in collection. To avoid embarrassment and the extra expense, your check in the amount of $23.47 must be received by return mail. I mean business. This is the last notice I will send before forwarding the bill to the California Courts for collection. F. Terrace Watson, Attorney at Law."

The bill was clearly illegal. Watson had been given every chance to prove his case and had failed dismally.

Item one: Jury trial.

Item two: Superior court review.

Item three: Supreme court decision.

All favored Ballenger. Watson did not care enough even to present his case on the appeal, and Ballenger, out of a sense of fairness, had continued the proceedings on his own initiative. Now this man, Watson, was threatening the very nation itself.

Ballenger folded the letter and replaced it in his inner suit-coat pocket. Breakfast finished, he put the dishes in the machine. Seven-twenty in the morning. Normally time to leave for work. Switchboard opens in exactly thirty-five minutes. Time was a rubber band, stretching out.

He removed his credit-card receipts. We will audit the accounts this morning. Prudent financial management is the foundation of the nation. The Secretary of the Treasury was summoned.

Two dollars and fifty-nine cents, plus tax, for a six-pack of half quart cans of beer. Five cans were still in the refrigerator. The supply would last another month. The Secretary of the Treasury waived the right to appeal and agreed the expense was reasonable. Three dollars and eighty-nine cents for dry cleaning: an unavoidable expense. Ten dollars, thirteen cents: a lube and oil job, rotors adjusted, fuel tank filled. No argument there. Forty-seven cents for a large chocolate bar. They called in the Surgeon General on that one. To the bathroom scale. Ballenger had picked up four ounces by the scale. Back to the accounts. Let's watch that candy. Ballenger agreed.

Four dollars and ten cents, including tips, for dinner in the restaurant last night. This Wednesday's expense was sanctioned by tradition, and recent polls showed it was approved by eighty-three per cent of the citizens. Of the $25 he allowed himself for the period, he still had three dollars plus change. Close enough. The Secretary of the Treasury was satisfied.

Snap! went the rubber band. Five minutes before eight.

Ballenger phoned the switchboard.

"Thank you for calling Meritt and Finch," said the recording. "Space research is our specialty."

He said, "Ballenger from Accounting. I have some personal business to take care of this morning. I'll be in after lunch."

"Thank you for your message, Mr. Ballenger," said the machine.

Traffic above Los Angeles would begin breaking in another fifteen minutes. It was a twenty-minute flight to the office of F. Terrace Watson, Attorney at Law. Leave at eight-fifteen, be there at twenty-five before nine.

Ballenger checked the day-shift workers. Everyone seemed at his job. Pulse was good, heartbeat steady, respiration normal. Swing shift would be going to bed in another hour. Most of the night shift probably hadn't gone back to sleep after voting on the day of the week. They should be up stirring. Should try to get all of today's major business out of the way before nine, nine-thirty, so the swing shift could get their rest.

Some sort of a proxy agreement really must be worked out, if it can be done democratically. We've got to send legislation to that effect up to the next Congress. Note: Cabinet meeting on Sunday should discuss this.

Meanwhile, one of the problems was too many important decisions. The executive himself could do something about that. Should definitely cut down on the number of major decisions, keep them to a bare minimum, try to get them all out of the way before nine o'clock. No excuse for decisions in the middle of the day. A well run country shouldn't have emergencies.

Yet the evils of dictatorships are too well known to review: an evolutionary failure of the organism. Strange so few saw this very point with the clarity of Ballenger.

Promptly at eight-twelve, he buzzed the garage of his departure and left the apartment, checking to be sure the door latch was set to lock. Two minutes later, he was on the roof. The morning rush having passed, the mechanical attendant had already assembled the blades. He stepped in, and the radios came on with the ignition. He hummed in time, tapping the control bar.

Airborne, the Security Forces relaxed. Once again he had remembered to lock the door. The day-shift technicians, well rested, began to supervise the complicated motor activity connected with flying. The pilot stood at the bridge, in command, studying meaningful lights as they flashed their careful traffic patterns, responding with the necessary movements.

Ballenger again wished there were some way to introduce more automation. Perhaps he should take it up with his Scientific Advisory Group. But if the SAG could work out a way, what about unemployment, long solved among nations, but an ever-present internal danger?

No! Better to have jobs for all than to have to worry about chronic unemployment. The thing to avoid was overtime. The union was very difficult when it came to overtime. Four hours off for each hour on. Once, after a very difficult week at the office, he had spent all of Friday in bed to catch up.

The blades joined traffic.

At eight-thirty, between commercials, came the newsbreak. It was the one thing he really did not like about the station. Ballenger frowned in annoyance. The nations of crime seemed to have the upper hand: an aggression in Florida, a war on the streets of Los Angeles. Incomprehensible. Pointless.

He checked again with his legal staff. There was no possible question that Watson's demand was completely illegal. There was no legal way Ballenger could be made to pay. Still, this being a foreign affair, rather than a domestic one, you could never be entirely sure of results.

Ballenger had long fought a mental battle with other nations for territorial integrity. To the things of the flesh, flesh; to the things of the spirit, spirit. It was difficult to know whether or not he was being ignored completely, for no other nation ever made a sign of having heard him on this matter. He called in the Secretary of State. We'll rest our case, said the Secretary, on external law. We will negotiate, but we will not arbitrate.

Music came back on. He wished they'd play one of Angelique's records. It would be good to know she was backing him in this matter.

But of course she was. Angelique was a nation like himself: a hater of injustice everywhere. Hadn't she already proved that, time after time? Hadn't she whispered it to him over TV? Of course she supported him. With the total resources of her body.

Ballenger thought of his job at Meritt and Finch. Wisely, the citizens had expressed their will to him: never talk to anyone at Meritt and Finch unless absolutely necessary. If you don't talk to them, we don't have to be always making decisions. You don't have to be bothering the citizens all the time, getting the swing shift out of bed with emergency votes.

So Ballenger kept busy with his punch cards and forms and rows of figures and files. Feeding the computer. Which was composed of an almost infinite number of little things going yes and no. With such uncomplicated fundamentals as that, it was a mystery the thing could even add.

And Ballenger smiled, and he answered questions, and he never went out to lunch with anyone.

Twenty before nine: a commercial. Traffic was unusually heavy. He had hovered almost motionless for nearly five minutes. Now a lane was open. The building was less than a quarter of a mile away, and he entered the descent level, checking visually. He tensed as an idiot pilot dropped too rapidly. Probably an emerging nation. What's the hurry?

Moments later, he was parked safely. He surrendered the blades to an attendant for a claim check. The check looked all right.

He walked quickly to the elevator and checked the directory posted on the wall. It told him the enemy was on the third floor: Suite 315.

Down he went.

F. Terrace Watson was seated behind his desk in the inner office, surrounded by file cabinets, an addressograph machine, a postage meter, a voice typer and a computer with memory storage.

Watson looked up from his desk in the inner office when he heard the corridor door open. It was too early for the mail drop. Who could it be at this hour? His part-time secretary, an expensive extravagance which flattered his ego, would not be in until after lunch for the mailing, so he arose and went through the door to greet the visitor, presumably a salesman.

Ballenger stood nervously beside the vacant receptionist's desk. He was dressed in a conservative suit, a style which had not changed appreciably for the last sixty years, in contrast to the vacillation of women's fashions; he was short, had a receding hairline and weighed no more than 120 pounds.

Watson was a tall man, many pounds Ballenger's superior, with a face that was heavy from rich foods and the eyes of a dictator.

Suppose the unsupposable, Ballenger's Chief of Planning Operations whispered. Consider every possibility, no matter how remote. A nation prepares for all contingencies. Meritt and Finch would demand an explanation for his refusal to pay this illegal bill.

"You are F. Terrace Watson?" he asked. "My name is Bart Ballenger."

And if Ballenger, as Chief Executive, allowed the job at Meritt and Finch to be lost, the citizens would most certainly revolt and throw him out of office. With no one to run the nation, it would become very sick.

"Yes?" asked Watson. "What can I do for you? If it's about employment—"

"You don't know me?" asked Ballenger in amazement. "You are F. Terrace Watson, the attorney?" Ballenger was disturbed by the development. How could the attorney, who had written him so many letters, each signed with a savage flourish, fail to recognize the name Bart Ballenger? There was a mystery, here. What did the Secretary of Defense think?

Watson searched his thoughts. Someone from one of his ex-wives? Someone from Ernie, trying to collect the little bit he still owed from the Santa Anita meeting? A process server?

Ballenger brought out the letter.

Ballenger had been with Meritt and Finch for eleven years; he could never find another job as good. So Watson, at all costs, must be stopped from notifying them. How could Ballenger present a legal brief to Mr. Herreras in defense of his refusal to pay this illegal bill? Mr. Herreras did not even know that he was one nation, under God, with all kinds of people inside him, and it isn't safe to talk to fascists who don't even understand that elementary fact. Evolution decrees their defeat, but natural selection is a slow process.

"It's about this," said Ballenger.

Instantly Watson assumed the stern countenance and demeanor appropriate to the profession. "Let's see, Mr. Ballenger. I believe it's about the overdue account that you wish to see me?" He reached out for the letter and glanced at the amount. "Twenty-three dollars and forty-seven cents."

"I want to talk to you about that."

"Well, let's just step into the office, here, Mr. Ballenger. I'm glad you realize just how serious this matter is. I'm glad to see you've come down in person to straighten it out. Please sit down."

As Watson walked around his desk to his chair, a tiny doubt opened a crevasse in his thoughts and uneasiness leaked out. In the memory of his profession, which was long and honorable, had anyone ever called personally? Not that he was aware of. This was the most mail order of all businesses, composed of fleshless names, first-class postage stamps, white paper, black print, stern taped warnings for the larger delinquents. Human breath sent it into disarray, and Watson felt uncomfortable in his own office. Let us explore the situation, which may be delicate or fraught with annoyance.

"Now," said Watson, after seating himself, "Mr. Ballenger, if you'll just let me have your check for $23.47, we can put an immediate end to this matter, and you will be spared any possible embarrassment and inconvenience. If the amount is a little too much for you right now, I know we can work out a satisfactory payment plan. Many of my accounts pay as little as five dollars a week. I understand how people can get in over their heads on matters like this, and I want to be as reasonable as I can be."

"It's not the money, you know that," said Ballenger, running the words together, still standing.

Watson frowned sternly. He made it a practice of ignoring all letters from accounts which did not contain money. Had Ballenger written protesting the bill? "Do I understand there's been some mistake? From the account number, here, this is for some musical tapes, isn't it? Didn't you receive the merchandise? Was the recording poor? Fuzzy pictures? If that's the case, I'll have to go back to the company with this, and if their records are in order, and if you haven't complained within the required time—" He left unspoken any direct threat.

Ballenger observed that the attorney was introducing irrelevant material. "I received the tapes, they were satisfactory in quality," he said. Diplomatic Corp personnel came forward with advice, prepared with documents. The Secretary of State cleared his throat. "I think you will have to agree, as an attorney and a specialist, that asking us to pay for these Miss Terri Paul tapes is the equivalent of demanding we pay alimony. You have no proof whatever that indicates we have ever been married."

Watson rolled the key to the voice typer between thumbs and forefingers. The accounts, of whom this man was one, were purchases at twenty-five cents on the dollar in blocks of one thousand. A few were always totally uncollectable because of legitimate reasons: merchandise returned and not credited, defective merchandise, incorrect merchandise, unordered merchandise. . . . Out of this group of ten to twenty in each block of accounts, one or two might threaten legal or other action upon receipt of dunning letters. Standard practice ignored them. They had no case; the dunning letters always complied exactly with the applicable laws of the State of California.

Such people, however, were nuisances, and Watson considered for the merest instant whether or not Ballenger might be an unusually aggressive example of that type. But any suspicion that Ballenger was contemplating a law suit evaporated, and Watson saw that he was dealing, instead, with a maniac. New forms of insanity were breaking out all over, as a tragic consequence of universal peace.

The sensible thing, Watson knew, was to stand from his chair, ease the man quietly from the office, lock the door and hope Ballenger would not come back.

"You're perfectly correct, Mr. Ballenger. There is no reason for you to pay this bill. I'll see that you're not bothered by it any more. A tragic misunderstanding for which I apologize."

Watson stood up. He moved to the side of the desk. Would more reassurance be required? It was difficult to know. "I'm sure this alimony matter will work out, too," he added.

Ballenger was outweighed by one hundred pounds and was a good six inches shorter than his enemy. One equalized such contests. He looked up at the attorney. So now he was going to be threatened with alimony. What was behind that threat? He was in trouble enough already.

Better ask the Secretary of the Interior: have we ever to your knowledge been liable for alimony? The answer, in the negative, came back. Still dissatisfied, he said, This is a very serious matter; could we be liable without our knowledge? His Scientific Advisor assured him that it was completely impossible.

"I deny any knowledge of alimony," Ballenger told Watson.

"Just don't worry about anything," said Watson, soothingly.

Ballenger realized this might be even worse than he had anticipated. What would Mr. Herreras say to this? Charges were piling up too rapidly. From his own logic, which was impeccable, sprang a new accusation.

Could this man Watson know Miss Terri Paul and her sorry collection of constituents? Was there a conspiracy, had treaties been made against him, was aggression contemplated?

Watson spoke as though to a child. "You just put it out of your mind. Go home and rest. You don't feel very good this morning."

Ballenger felt panic. The Chief Medical Officer said, I'm afraid we've run into another nut, here. The world is full of such nations, they cause all the trouble.

This one, said the Chief of Security Forces, is a lawyer. Lawyers are the most dangerous of all. They can exhume treaties to the days of King John to cite against us.

Watson, looking down on the man he completely dominated physically, felt a moment of compassion. Ballenger was sick; he needed help. Watson decided to probe the extent of this post-Freudian psychosis, to divine in which direction help for the poor, disturbed man might lie. "You have some relatives here?"

"The question," said Ballenger, "is an insult to national dignity! I am perfectly capable of fighting my own wars!"

A little flicker of fear came to Watson. Against the power of a madman, his physical advantage might be canceled. Ballenger might be capable of hurting him and, beyond that, might constitute a larger menace. The idea, half formed, that it would be possible to reason Ballenger into seeking medical attention, vanished. No other avenue of assistance lay open to the attorney. In the absence of criminal conduct, only a relative could have Ballenger committed.

Watson could prefer a misdemeanor charge: but if the insanity were temporary, or if Ballenger could recover sufficiently to conceal it from the judge, then Watson himself might be in an unfortunate and vulnerable legal position: a suit for false arrest, or worse. The thing to do was definitely to get him out of the office as soon as possible.

"Come along, now," said Watson, reaching out. "Let's walk out here in the corridor." Once in the corridor, Watson could duck back in the office, slam the door and lock it. If Ballenger stayed outside, an anonymous call to the police might then result in his detention for questioning and lead to the court sending him to the sanctuary the state provided for such disturbed people.

Ballenger shrugged off the hand. He checked to see that all his people were awake. A crisis was near. Once the man, Watson, got him into the corridor, he would be attacked. All the other nations in the building would see it, of course, but none would come to his defense. Ballenger had made no alliances here. His alliances were with the entertainment industry, in Hollywood, in New York City, in the TV industry. They were too far away to help him now! Could they even hear his cries?

What wild charges Watson would make! And could the nation, with the best legal minds available, refute them? Watson was one of the extremely mad ones: a prisoner of the past. He had not been able to escape evolution's *cul de sac:* specialization. Watson treated all the organic components within himself with total contempt for their civil rights. Logical thought was impossible with him. Ballenger confronted a primitive organism.

So Watson was threatening to consider it as an international matter, beyond reasonable compromise. Ballenger had come prepared for that. Was all diplomacy, forever, for nothing? Make one more try at private negotiation.

"You'll never get us before the United Nations," Ballenger said. "You know it's stacked against us; you know we wouldn't have a fair chance to defend ourselves; we're outnumbered."

Ballenger sounded the alarm. Everyone was apprised of the situation. Are you behind me, citizens? he cried. A resounding 97 per cent: yes!

Red alert! cried Ballenger's Secretary of Defense. To arms! To arms! Man the barricades! Prepare to repel the invasion!

Watson's hand came out once more. It fixed on Ballenger's shoulder. "Come along now. I think it's time for you to leave!"

The Secretary of Defense told Ballenger: He's getting ready for a sneak attack! Hurry!

Ballenger acted then. He declared a national emergency. The soldiers came forward, waves of them.

Scientists readied the missile launcher site and took control of the panel with flashing lights.

Get out of my way! snarled the Secretary of Defense to the Secretary of State. This is exclusively a military matter, now!

Ballenger removed the missile launcher from its hidden silo and twisted to his left, firing upward, once, bang!

There was silence. The sound of Watson's body as it met the carpet. Silence.

We had to defend ourselves, he told the citizens. It was us or them. Eighty-one per cent approved the action. The pacifists, less than ten per cent of the population, had continued that portion of the work which had not contributed to the war effort. They now returned to full participation in the society.

Ballenger congratulated the Secretary of Defense for always being prepared and put the missile launcher in his pocket.

The Security Forces took over. He had touched nothing in the office. No fingerprint problem.

Two and a half minutes later, he was at the roof garage. He presented the printed claim check for the blades.

Ninety seconds later still, the Security Forces withdrew, and the technicians took over. He was at the control bar. The music of strings and oboes came from the radios. He looked at his watch. Just after nine. The swing shift people could get their sleep. He ended the emergency.

He asked the Secretary of the Treasury: How was that? That's the kind of war you like, isn't it? Seventy-seven cents is all it cost us this time. Seventy-five cents for parking, two cents for the bullet. I run an economical administration.

Some two hours later, when he was preparing to go to work, the Security Force people remembered the letter on Attorney Watson's desk, but by then it was too late to do anything about it but fire the Security Chief.

Further Reading   Kris Neville

Books

Bettyann. New York: Belmont Books, 1968.
Mission: Manstop. New York: Leisure Books, 1971. (Short fiction.)
The Mutants. New York: Belmont Books, 1966.
Special Delivery. New York: Belmont Books, 1967.
The Unearth People. New York: Belmont Books, 1964.

Stories

"Bettyann." *New Tales of Space and Time,* 1951.
"Cold War." *Astounding Science Fiction,* October 1949. (*The Astounding Science Fiction Anthology,* ed. John W. Campbell.)
"Experimental Station." *Super Science Stories,* September 1950. (*Science Fiction Adventures in Mutation,* ed. Groff Conklin.)
"Franchise." *Astounding Science Fiction,* February 1951. (*Stories for Tomorrow,* ed. William Sloane.)
"From the Government Printing Office." *Dangerous Visions,* 1967.
"Gratitude Guaranteed" (with R. Bretnor). *The Magazine of Fantasy and Science Fiction,* August 1953. (*Twenty Years of F & SF,* ed. Ferman and Mills.)
"New Apples in the Garden." *Analog Science Fiction,* July 1963. (*One Hundred Years of Science Fiction,* ed. Damon Knight.)
"Old Man Henderson." *The Magazine of Fantasy and Science Fiction,* June 1951. (*Best from Fantasy and Science Fiction,* ed. Anthony Boucher and J. Francis McComas.)
"Pacem Est" (with K. M. O'Donnell). *Infinity,* 1970.
"Pater Familias" (with Barry N. Malzberg). *The Magazine of Fantasy and Science Fiction,* March 1972. (*The Best of Barry N. Malzberg.*)
"Underground Movement." *The Magazine of Fantasy and Science Fiction,* June 1952. (*Mission: Manstop.*)

It has always been difficult to locate the real Randall Garrett. Here is a man who during the period 1958–64 appeared more frequently in *Astounding/Analog* than any other writer; whose work has never been appreciated—in fact, it has been vilified on more than one occasion; whose best novel-length efforts were done in collaboration, thus rendering evaluation difficult; and whose numerous appearances in the most prestigious and best-paying sf magazine eventually, as Barry Malzberg says, "got him identified, in the field and perhaps in his own mind, as a house creature, a kind of walking, breathing, fiction-writing John Campbell editorial."

Now in his early fifties and writing and selling science fiction again after a decade's hiatus, he may yet fulfill the potential he clearly showed in "The Hunting Lodge" and in other works, such as "Fighting Division" (sf, like other areas of literature, really needs a "Reborn Writer of the Year" Award, to recognize those individuals who have overcome the pain and frustration of trying to write and publish quality material).

His solo novels include *Unwise Child* (1962), *Anything You Can Do . . .* (1963, as "Darrel T. Langart"), and *Too Many Magicians* (1966), perhaps his best-known effort. He also published two novels in collaboration with Robert Silverberg as "Robert Randall," but more important were his efforts with Laurence M. Janifer (another underappreciated writer) under the name "Mark Phillips"—and one wishes that Mark Phillips, Rog Phillips, and Peter Phillips had chosen other names, since they were all talented and are all confused with one another. The three Garrett-Janifer novels, *Brain Twister* (1962) and *The Impossibles* and *Supermind* (both 1963), are interesting, clever works that deserve to be back in print.

"The Hunting Lodge" is simply one of the most exciting and skillfully plotted stories ever produced in this field.

M.H.G. & J.D.O.

The Hunting Lodge

by RANDALL GARRETT

"We'll help all we can," the Director said, "but if you're caught, that's all there is to it."

I nodded. It was the age-old warning: *If you're caught, we disown you.* I wondered, fleetingly, how many men had heard that warning during the long centuries of human history, and I wondered how many of them had asked themselves the same question I was asking:

Why am *I* risking *my* neck?

And I wondered how many of them had had an answer.

"Ready, then?" the Director asked, glancing at his watch. I nodded and looked at my own. The shadow hands pointed to 2250.

"Here's the gun."

I took it and checked its loading. "Untraceable, I suppose?"

He shook his head. "It can be traced, all right, but it won't lead to us. A gun which couldn't be traced almost certainly would be associated with us. But the best thing to do would be to bring the gun back with you; that way, it's in no danger of being traced."

The way he said it gave me a chill. He wanted me back alive, right enough, but only so there would be no evidence.

"O.K." I said. "Let's go."

I put a nice, big, friendly grin on my face. After all, there was no use making him feel worse than necessary. I knew he didn't like sending men out to be killed. I slipped the sleeve gun into its holster and then faced him.

"Blaze away!"

He looked me over, then touched the hypno controls. A light hit my eyes.

I was walking along the street when I came out of it, heading toward a flitter stand. An empty flitter was sitting there waiting, so I climbed in and sat down.

Senator Rowley's number was ORdway 63-911. I dialed it and leaned back, just as though I had every right to go there.

The flitter lifted perfectly and headed northwest, but I knew perfectly well that the scanners were going full blast, sorting through their information banks to find me.

A mile or so out of the city, the flitter veered to the right, locked its controls, and began to go around in a tight circle.

The viewphone lit up, but the screen stayed blank. A voice said: "Routine check. Identify yourself, please."

Routine! I knew better. But I just looked blank and stuck my right forearm into the checker. There was a short hum while the ultrasonic scanners looked at the tantalum identity plate riveted to the bone.

"Thank you, Mr. Gifford," said the voice. The phone cut off, but the flitter was still going in circles.

Then the phone lit again, and Senator Rowley's face—thin, dark, and bright-eyed—came on the screen.

"Gifford! Did you get it?"

"I got it, sir," I answered quietly.

He nodded, pleased. "Good! I'll be waiting for you."

Again the screen went dark, and this time the flitter straightened out and headed northwest once more.

I tried not to feel too jittery, but I had to admit to myself that I was scared. The senator was dangerous. If he could get a finger into the robot central office of the flitters, there was no way of knowing how far his control went.

He wasn't supposed to be able to tap a flitter any more than he was supposed to be able to tap a phone. But neither one was safe now.

Only a few miles ahead of me was the Lodge, probably the most tightly guarded home in the world.

I knew I might not get in, of course, Senator Anthony Rowley was no fool, by a long shot. He placed his faith in robots. A machine might fail, but it would never be treacherous.

I could see the walls of the Lodge ahead as the flitter began to lose altitude. I could almost feel the watching radar eyes that followed the craft down, and it made me nervous to realize that a set of high-cycle guns were following the instructions of those eyes.

And, all alone in that big mansion—or fortress—sat Senator Rowley like a spider in the middle of an intangible web.

The public flitter, with me in it, lit like a fly on the roof of the mansion. I took a deep breath and stepped out. The multiple eyes of the robot defenses watched me closely as I got into the waiting elevator.

The hard plastic of the little sleeve gun was supposed to be transparent to X rays and sonics, but I kept praying anyway. Suddenly I felt a tingle in my arm. I knew what it was; a checker to see if the molecular structure of the tantalum identity plate was according to government specifications in every respect.

Identity plates were furnished only by the Federal government, but they were also supposed to be the only ones with analyzers. Even the senator shouldn't have had an unregistered job.

To play safe, I rubbed at the arm absently. I didn't know whether Gifford had ever felt that tingle before or not. If he had, he might ignore it, but he wouldn't let it startle him. If he hadn't, he might not be startled, but he wouldn't ignore it. Rubbing seemed the safest course.

The thing that kept running through my mind was—*how much did Rowley trust psychoimpressing?*

He had last seen Gifford four days ago, and at that time, Gifford could no more have betrayed the senator than one of the robots could. Because, psychologically speaking, that's exactly what Gifford had been—a robot. Theoretically, it is impossible to remove a competent psychoimpressing job in less than six weeks of steady therapy. It *could* be done in a little less time, but it didn't leave the patient in an ambient condition. And it couldn't, under any circumstances, be done in four days.

If Senator Rowley was thoroughly convinced I was Gifford, and if he trusted psychoimpression, I was in easy.

I looked at my watch again. 2250. Exactly an hour since I had left. The change in time zones had occurred while I was in the flitter, and the shadow hands had shifted back to accommodate.

It seemed to be taking a long time for the elevator to drop; I could just barely feel the movement. The robots were giving me a very thorough going over.

Finally, the door slid open and I stepped out into the lounge. For the first time in my life, I saw the living face of Senator Anthony Rowley.

The filters built into his phone pickup did a lot for him. They softened the fine wrinkles that made his face look like a piece of old leather. They added color to his grayish skin. They removed the yellowishness from his eyes. In short, the senator's pickup filters took two centuries off his age.

Longevity can't do everything for you, I thought. But I could see what it *could* do, too, if you were smart and had plenty of time. And those who had plenty of time were automatically the smart ones.

The senator extended a hand. "Give me the briefcase, Gifford."

"Yes, sir." As I held out the small blue case, I glanced at my watch. 2255. And, as I watched, the last five became a six.

Four minutes to go.

"Sit down, Gifford." The senator waved me to a chair. I sat and watched him while he leafed through the supposedly secret papers.

Oh, they were real enough, all right, but they didn't contain any information that would be of value to him. He would be too dead for that.

He ignored me as he read. There was no need to watch Gifford. Even if Gifford had tried anything, the robotic brain in the basement of the house would have detected it with at least one of its numerous sensory devices and acted to prevent the senator's death long before any mere human could complete any action.

I knew that, and the senator knew it.

We sat.

2257.

The senator frowned. "This is all, Gifford?"

"I can't be sure, of course, sir. But I will say that any further information on the subject is buried pretty deeply. So well hidden, in fact, that even the government couldn't find it in time to use against you."

"Mmmmmm."

2258.

The senator grinned. "This is it," he said through his tight, thin, old lips. "We'll be in complete control within a year, Gifford."

"That's good, sir. Very good."

It doesn't take much to play the part of a man who's been psychoimpressed as thoroughly as Gifford had been.

2259.

The senator smiled softly and said nothing. I waited tensely, hoping that the darkness would be neither too long nor too short. I made no move toward the sleeve gun, but I was ready to grab it as soon as—

2300!

The lights went out—and came on again.

The senator had time to look both startled and frightened before I shot him through the heart.

I didn't waste any time. The power had been cut off from the Great Northwestern Reactor, which supplied all the juice for the whole area, but the senator had provided wisely for that. He had a reactor of his own built in for emergencies; it had cut in as soon as the Great Northwestern had gone out.

But cutting off the power to a robot brain is the equivalent of hitting a man over the head with a blackjack; it takes time to recover. It was that time lapse which had permitted me to kill Rowley and which would, if I moved fast enough, permit me to escape before its deadly defenses could be rallied against me.

I ran toward a door and almost collided with it before I realized that it wasn't going to open for me. I had to push it aside. I kept on running, heading for an outside entrance. There was no way of knowing how long the robot would remain stunned.

Rowley had figured he was being smart when he built a single centralized computer to take over all the defenses of the house instead of having a series of simple brains, one for each function. And, in a way, I guess he was right; the Lodge could act as a single unit that way.

But Rowley had died because he insisted on that complication; the simpler the brain, the quicker the recovery.

The outside door opened easily enough; the electrolocks were dead. I was still surrounded by walls; the nearest exit was nearly half a mile away. That didn't bother me; I wasn't going to have to use it. There was a high-speed flitter waiting for me above the clouds.

I could hear it humming down toward me. Then I could see it, drifting down in a fast spiral.

Whoom!

I was startled for a timeless instant as I saw the flitter dissolve in a blossom of yellow-orange flame. The flare, marking the end of my escape craft, hung in the air for an endless second and then died slowly.

I realized then that the heavy defenses of the Lodge had come to life.

I didn't even stop to think. The glowing red of the fading explosion was still lighting the ground as I turned and sprinted toward the garage. One thing I knew; the robot would not shoot down one of the senator's own machines unless ordered to do so.

The robot was still not fully awake. It had reacted to the approach of a big, fast-moving object, but it still couldn't see a running man. Its scanners wouldn't track yet.

I shoved the garage doors open and looked inside. The bright lights disclosed ground vehicles and nothing more. The flitters were all on the roof.

I hadn't any choice; I had to get out of there, and fast!

The senator had placed a lot of faith in the machines that guarded the Lodge. The keys were in the lock of one big Ford-Studebaker. I shoved the control from auto to manual, turned the key and started the engines.

As soon as they were humming, I started the car moving. And none too soon, either. The doors of the garage slammed after me like the jaws of a man trap. I gunned the car for the nearest gate, hoping that this one last effort would be successful. If I didn't make it through the outer gate, I might as well give up.

As I approached the heavy outer gates, I could see that they were functioning; I'd never get them open by hand. But the robot was still a little confused. It recognized the car and didn't recognize me. The gates dropped, so I didn't even slow the car. Pure luck again.

And close luck, at that. The gates tried to come back up out of the ground even as the heavy vehicle went over them; there was a loud bump as the rear wheels hit the top of the rising gate. But again the robot was too late.

I took a deep breath and aimed the car toward the city. So far, so good. A clean getaway.

Another of the Immortals was dead. Senator Rowley's political machine would never again force through a vote to give him another longevity treatment, because the senator's political force had been cut off at the head, and the target was gone. Pardon the mixed metaphor.

Longevity treatments are like a drug; the more you have, the more you want. I suppose it had been a good idea a few centuries ago to restrict their use to men who were of such use to the race that they deserved to live longer than the average. But the mistake was made in putting it up to the voting public who should get the treatments.

Of course, they'd had a right to have a voice in it; at the beginning, the cost of a single treatment had been too high for any individual to pay for it. And, in addition, it had been a government monopoly, since the government had paid for the research. So, if the taxpayer's money was to be spent, the taxpayer had a right to say who it was to be spent on.

But if a man's life hangs on his ability to control the public, what other out does he have?

And the longer he lives, the greater his control. A man can become an institution if he lives long enough. And Senator Rowley had lived long enough; he—

Something snickered on the instrument panel. I looked, but I couldn't see anything. Then something moved under my foot. It was the accelerator. The car was slowing.

I didn't waste any time guessing; I knew what was happening. I opened the door just as the car stopped. Fortunately, the doors had only manual controls; simple mechanical locks.

I jumped out of the car's way and watched it as it backed up, turned around, and drove off in the direction of the Lodge. The robot was fully awake now; it had recalled the car. I hadn't realized that the senator had set up the controls in his vehicles so that the master robot could take control away from a human being.

I thanked various and sundry deities that I had not climbed into one of the flitters. It's hard to get out of an aircraft when it's a few thousand feet above the earth.

Well, there was nothing to do but walk. So I walked.

It wasn't more than ten minutes before I heard the buzzing behind me. Something was coming over the road at a good clip, but without headlights. In the darkness, I couldn't see a thing, but I knew it wasn't an ordinary car. Not coming from the Lodge.

I ran for the nearest tree, a big monster at least three feet thick and fifty or sixty feet high. The lowest branch was a heavy one about seven feet from the ground. I grabbed it and swung myself up and kept on climbing until I was a good twenty feet off the ground. Then I waited.

The whine stopped down the road about half a mile, about where I'd left the Ford-Studebaker. Whatever it was prowled around for a minute or two, then started coming on down the road.

When it finally came close enough for me to see it in the moonlight, I recognized it for what it was. A patrol robot. It was looking for me.

Then I heard another whine. But this one was different; it was a siren coming from the main highway.

Overhead, I heard a flitter whistling through the sky.

The police.

The patrol robot buzzed around on its six wheels, turning its search-turret this way and that, trying to spot me.

The siren grew louder, and I saw the headlights in the distance. In less than a minute, the lights struck the patrol robot, outlining every detail of the squat, ugly silhouette. It stopped, swiveling its turret toward the police car. The warning light on the turret came on, glowing a bright red.

The cops slowed down and stopped. One of the men in the car called out, "Senator? Are you on the other end of that thing?"

No answer from the robot.

"I guess he's really dead," said another officer in a low, awed voice.

"It don't seem possible," the first voice said. Then he called again to the patrol robot. "We're police officers. Will you permit us to show our identification?"

The patrol robot clicked a little as the information was relayed back to the Lodge and the answer given. The red warning light turned green, indicating that the guns were not going to fire.

About that time, I decided that my only chance was to move around so that the trunk of the tree was between me and the road. I had to move slowly so they wouldn't hear me, but I finally made it.

I could hear the policeman saying, "According to the information we received, Senator Rowley was shot by his secretary, Edgar Gifford. This patrol job must be hunting him."

"Hey!" said another voice. "Here comes another one! He must be in the area somewhere!"

I could hear the whining of a second patrol robot approaching from the Lodge. It was still about a mile away, judging from the sound.

I couldn't see what happened next, but I could hear the first robot moving, and it must have found me, even though I was out of sight. Directional heat detector, probably.

"In the tree, eh?" said a cop.

Another called: "All right, Gifford! Come on down!"

Well, that was it. I was caught. But I wasn't going to be taken alive. I eased out the sleeve gun and sneaked a peek around the tree. *No use killing a cop*, I thought, *he's just doing his job.*

So I fired at the car, which didn't hurt a thing.

"Look out!"

"Duck!"

"Get that blaster going!"

Good. It was going to be a blaster. It would take off the treetop and me with it. I'd die quickly.

There was a sudden flurry of shots, and then silence.

I took another quick peek and got the shock of my life.

The four police officers were crumpled on the ground, shot down by the patrol robot from the Lodge. One of them—the one holding the blaster—wasn't quite dead yet. He gasped something obscene and fired the weapon just as two more slugs from the robot's turret hit him in the chest.

The turret exploded in a gout of fire.

I didn't get it, but I didn't have time to wonder what was going on. I know a chance when I see one. I swung from the branch I was on and dropped to the ground, rolling over in a bed of old leaves to take up the shock. Then I made a beeline for the police car.

On the way, I grabbed one of the helmets from a uniformed corpse, hoping that my own tunic was close enough to the same shade of scarlet to get me by. I climbed in and got the machine turned around just as the second patrol robot came into sight. It fired a couple of shots after me, but those patrol jobs don't have enough armament to shoot down a police car; they're strictly for hunting unarmed and unprotected pedestrians.

Behind me there were a couple of flares in the sky that reminded me of my own exploding flitter, but I didn't worry about what they could be.

I was still puzzled about the robot's shooting down the police. It didn't make sense.

Oh, well, it had saved my neck, and I wasn't going to pinch a gift melon.

The police car I was in had evidently been the only ground vehicle dispatched toward the Lodge—possibly because it happened to be nearby. It was a traffic-control car; the regular homicide squad was probably using flitters.

I turned off the private road and onto the highway, easing into the traffic-control pattern and letting the car drift along with the other vehicles. But I didn't shove it into automatic. I didn't like robots just then. Besides, if I let the main control panels take over the guiding of the car, someone at headquarters might wonder why car such-and-such wasn't at the Lodge as ordered; they might wonder why it was going down the highway so unconcernedly.

There was only one drawback. I wasn't used to handling a car at a hundred and fifty to two hundred miles an hour. If something should happen to the traffic pattern, I'd have to depend on my own reflexes. And they might not be fast enough.

I decided I'd have to ditch the police car as soon as I could. It was too much trouble and too easy to spot.

I had an idea. I turned off the highway again at the next break, a few miles farther on. There wasn't much side traffic at that time of night, so I had to wait several minutes before the pattern broke again and a private car pulled out and headed down the side road.

I hit the siren and pulled him over to the side.

He was an average-sized character with a belligerent attitude and a fat face.

"What's the matter, officer? There was nothing wrong with that break. I didn't cut out of the pattern on manual, you know. I was—" He stopped when he realized that my tunic was not that of a policeman. "Why, you're not—"

By then, I'd already cut him down with a stun gun I'd found in the arms compartment of the police car. I hauled him out and changed tunics with him. His was a little loose, but not so much that it would be noticeable. Then I put the helmet on his head and strapped him into the front seat of the police vehicle with the safety belt.

After being hit with a stun gun, he'd be out for a good hour. That would be plenty of time as far as I was concerned.

I transferred as much of the police armory as I thought I'd need into the fat-faced fellow's machine and then I climbed into the police car with him. I pulled the car around and headed back toward the highway.

Just before we reached the control area, I set the instruments for the Coast and headed him west, back the way I had come.

I jumped out and slammed the door behind me as the automatic controls took over and put him in the traffic pattern.

Then I walked back to Fatty's car, got in, and drove back to the highway. I figured I could trust the controls of a private vehicle, so I set them and headed east, toward the city. Once I was there, I'd have to get a flitter, somehow.

I spent the next twenty minutes changing my face. I couldn't do anything about the basic structure; that would have to wait until I got back. Nor could I do anything about the ID plate that was bolted on my left ulna; that, too, would have to wait.

I changed the color of my hair, darkening it from Gifford's gray to a mousy brown, and I took a patch of hair out above my forehead to give me a balding look. The mustache went, and the sides of the beard, giving me a goatee effect. I trimmed down the brows and the hair, and put a couple of tubes in my nostrils to widen my nose.

I couldn't do much about the eyes; my little pocket kit didn't carry them. But, all in all, I looked a great deal less like Gifford than I had before.

Then I proceeded to stow a few weapons on and about my person. I had taken the sleeve gun out of the scarlet tunic when I'd put it on the fat-faced man, but his own chartreuse tunic didn't have a sleeve holster, so I had to put the gun in a hip pocket. But the tunic was a godsend in another way; it was loose enough to carry a few guns easily.

The car speaker said: "Attention! You are now approaching Groverton, the last suburb before the city limits. Private automobiles may not be taken beyond this point. If you wish to by-pass the city, please indicate. If not, please go to the free storage lot in Groverton."

I decided I'd do neither. I might as well make the car as hard to find as possible. I took it to an all-night repair technician in Groverton.

"Something wrong with the turbos," I told him. "Give her a complete overhaul."

He was very happy to do so. He'd be mighty unhappy when the cops took the car away without paying him for it, but he didn't look as though he'd go broke from the loss. Besides, I thought it would be a good way to repay Fat-Face for borrowing his car.

I had purposely kept the hood of my tunic up while I was talking to the auto technician so he wouldn't remember my new face later, but I dropped the hood as soon as I got to the main street of Groverton. I didn't want to attract too much attention.

I looked at my watch. 0111. I'd passed back through the time-change again, so it had been an hour and ten minutes since I'd left the Lodge. I decided I needed something to eat.

Groverton was one of those old-fashioned suburbs built during the latter half of the twentieth century—sponge-glass streets and sidewalks, aluminum siding on the houses, shiny chrome-and-lucite business buildings. Real quaint.

I found an automat and went in. There were only a few people on the streets, but the automat wasn't empty by a long shot. Most of the crowd seemed to be teen-age kids getting looped up after a dance. One booth was empty, so I sat down in it, dialed for coffee and ham and eggs, and dropped in the indicated change.

Shapeless little blobs of color were bouncing around in the tri-di tank in the wall, giving a surrealistic dance accompaniment to "Anna from Texarkana":

> *You should have seen the way she ate!*
> *Her appetite insatiate*
> *Was quite enough to break your pocketbook!*
> *But with a yeast-digamma steak,*
> *She never made a damn mistake—*
> *What tasty snythefoods that gal could cook!*
> *Oh, my Anna! Her algae Manna*
> *Was tasty as a Manna-cake could be!*
> *Oh, my Anna—from Texarkana!*
> *Oh, Anna, baby, you're the gal for me!*

I sipped coffee while the thing went through the third and fourth verses, trying to figure a way to get into the city without having to show the telltale ID plate in my arm.

"Anna" was cut off in the middle of the fifth verse. The blobs changed color and coalesced into the face of Quinby Lester, news analyst.

"Good morning, free citizens! We are interrupting this program to bring you an announcement of special importance."

He looked very serious, very concerned, and, I thought, just a little bit puzzled. "At approximately midnight last night, there was a disturbance at the Lodge. Four police officers who were summoned to the Lodge were shot and killed by Mr. Edgar Gifford, the creator of the disturbance. This man is now at large in the vicinity. Police are making an extensive search within a five-hundred-mile radius of the Lodge.

"Have you seen this man?"

A tri-di of Gifford appeared in place of Lester's features.

"This man is armed and dangerous. If you see him, report immediately to MONmouth 6-666-666. If your information leads to the capture of Edgar Gifford, you will receive a reward of ten thousand dollars. Look around you! He may be near you now!"

Everybody in the automat looked apprehensively at everybody

else. I joined them. I wasn't much worried about being spotted. When everybody wears beards, it's hard to spot a man under a handful of face foliage. I was willing to bet that within the next half hour the police would be deluged with calls from a thousand people who honestly thought they had seen Edgar Gifford.

The cops knew that. They were simply trying to scare me into doing something foolish.

They needn't have done that; I was perfectly capable of doing something foolish without their help.

I thought carefully about my position. I was about fifteen miles from safety. Question: Could I call for help? Answer: No. Because I didn't know the number. I didn't even know who was waiting for me. All that had been erased from my mind when the Director hypnoed me. I couldn't even remember who I was working for or why!

My only chance was to get to Fourteenth and Riverside Drive. They'd pick me up there.

Oh, well, if I didn't make it, I wasn't fit to be an assassin, anyway.

I polished off the breakfast and took another look at my watch. 0147. I might as well get started; I had fifteen miles to walk.

Outside, the streets were fairly quiet. The old-fashioned streets hadn't been built to clean themselves; a robot sweeper was prowling softly along the curb, sucking up the day's debris, pausing at every cross street to funnel the stuff into the disposal drains to be carried to the processing plant.

A few people were walking the streets. Ahead of me, a drunk was sitting on the curb sucking at a bottle that had collapsed long ago, hoping to get one last drop out of it.

I decided the best way to get to my destination was to take Bradley to Macmillan, follow Macmillan to Fourteenth, then stay on Fourteenth until I got to Riverside Drive.

But no free citizen would walk that far. I'd better not look like one. I walked up to the swiller.

"Hey, Joe, how'd you like to make five?"

He looked up at me, trying to focus. "Sure, Sid, sure. Whatta gotta do?"

"Sell me your tunic."

He blinked. "Zissa gag? Ya get 'em free."

"No gag. I want your tunic."

"Sure. Fine. Gimme that five."

He peeled off the charity brown tunic and I handed him the five note. If I had him doped out right, he'd be too drunk to remember what had happened to his tunic. He'd be even drunker when he started on that five note.

I pulled the brown on over the chartreuse tunic. I might want to get into a first-class installation, and I couldn't do it wearing charity brown.

"LOOK OUT!"

CLIK LIK LIK LIK LIK LIK LIK!

I felt something grab my ankle and I turned fast. It was the street cleaner! It had reached out a retractable picker and was trying to lift me into its hopper!

The drunk, who had done the yelling, tried to back away, but he stumbled and banged his head on the soft sidewalk. He stayed down —not out, but scared.

Another claw came out of the cleaner and grabbed my shoulder. The two of them together lifted me off the ground and pulled me toward the open hopper. I managed to get my gun out. These cleaners weren't armored; if I could only get in a good shot—

I fired three times, blowing the pickup antenna off the control dome. When the claws opened, I dropped to the sidewalk and ran. Behind me, the robot, no longer under the directions of the central office, began to flick its claws in and out and run around in circles. The drunk didn't manage to get out from under the treads in time.

A lot of people had stopped to watch the brief tussle, a few of them pretty scared. It was unheard of for a street cleaner to go berserk like that,

I dodged into an alleyway and headed for the second level. I was galloping up the escalator full tilt when the cop saw me. He was on the other escalator, going down, but he didn't stay there long.

"Halt!" he yelled, as he vaulted over the waist-high partition and landed on the UP escalator. By that time, I was already on the second level and running like mad.

"Halt or I fire!" he yelled.

I ducked into a doorway and pulled out the stun gun. I turned just in time to see one of the most amazing sights I have ever been privileged to witness. The cop was running toward me, his gun out, when he passed in front of a bottled goods vendor. At that instant, the vendor opened up, delivering a veritable avalanche of bottles into the corridor. The policeman's foot hit one of the rubbery, bouncing cylinders and slipped just as he pulled the trigger.

His shot went wild, and I fired with the stun gun before the cop could hit the floor. He lay still, bottles rolling all around him.

I turned and ran again. I hadn't gone far before another cop showed up, running toward me. I made a quick turn toward the escalators and went down again toward street level.

The cop wasn't prepared for what happened to him when he stepped on the escalator. He was about halfway down, running, when the belt suddenly stopped and reversed itself. The policeman pitched forward on his face and tumbled down the stair.

I didn't wait to see what happened next. I turned the corner, slowed down, and walked into a bar. I tried to walk slowly enough so that I wouldn't attract attention and headed for the rest room.

I went in, locked the door behind me, and looked around.

As far as I could tell, there were no sensory devices in the place, so I pulled the last of my make-up kit out and went to work. This time, I went whole hog. Most of the hair went from the top of my head, and what was left became pure white. I didn't take off the goatee; a beardless man would stand out. But the goatee went white, too.

Then a fine layer of plastic sprayed on my face and hands gave me an elderly network of wrinkles.

All the time I was doing this, I was wondering what was going on with the robots. It was obvious to me that the Lodge was connected illegally with every robot service in the city—possibly in the whole sector.

The street sweeper had recognized me and tried to get me; that was clear enough. But what about the vending machine and the escalator? Was the Lodge's master computer still foggy from the power cutoff? It shouldn't be; not after two hours. Then why had the responses been so slow? Why had they tripped the cops instead of me? It didn't make sense.

That's when it hit me. *Was Rowley really dead?*

I couldn't be absolutely sure, could I? And the police hadn't said anything about a murder. Just a "disturbance." No, wait. The first cops, the ones whose car I'd taken. What had they said the robot reported? I couldn't remember the exact words.

It still didn't settle the question.

For a moment, I found myself wishing we had a government like the United States had had back in the third quarter of the Twentieth Century, back in the days of strong central government, before everybody started screaming about Citizen's Rights and the preservation of the status quo. There wouldn't be any of this kind of trouble now—maybe.

But they had other kinds just as bad.

This wasn't the best of all possible worlds, but I was living in it. Of course, I didn't know how long that happy situation would exist just then.

Somebody rapped on the door.

I didn't know who it was, but I wasn't taking any chances. Maybe it was a cop. I climbed out the back window and headed down the alley toward Bradley Avenue.

If only I could get rid of that plate in my arm! The average citizen doesn't know it, but it isn't really necessary to put your arm in an ID slot to be identified. A sonobeam can pick up a reflected recording from your plate at twenty feet if there's a scanner nearby to direct it.

I walked slowly after running the length of the alley, staying in the shadows as much as possible, trying to keep out of the way of anyone and everyone.

For six blocks or so, I didn't see a soul. Then, just as I turned onto West Bradley, I came face to face with a police car. I froze.

I was ready to pull and shoot; I wanted the cop to kill me before he picked me up.

He slowed up, looked at me sharply, looked at his instrument panel, then drove on. I just stood there, flabbergasted. I knew as well as I knew anything that he'd beamed that plate in my arm!

As the car turned at the next corner, I backed into a nearby doorway, trying to figure out what I should do next. Frankly, I was jumpy and scared; I didn't know what they were up to.

I got even more jumpy when the door behind me gave. I turned fast and made a grab for the gun. But I didn't take it out.

The smoothly dressed girl said: "What's the matter, Grandfather?"

It wasn't until then that I realized how rattled I was. I looked like a very old man, but I wasn't acting like one. I paused to force my mind to adjust.

The girl was in green. The one-piece shortsuit, the sandals, the toenails, fingernails, lips, eyes, and hair. All green. The rest of her was a smooth, even shade of pink.

She said: "You needn't be afraid that anyone will see you. We arrange—Oh!"

I knew what she was oh'ing about. The charity brown of my tunic.

"I'm sorry," she said, frowning. "We can't—"

I cut her off this time. "I have money, my dear," I smiled. "And I'm wearing my own tunic." I flashed the chartreuse on her by opening the collar.

"I see, Grandfather. Won't you come in?"

I followed the green girl in to the desk of the Program Planner, a girl who was a deep blue in the same way that the first girl was green. I outlined what I wanted in a reedy, anticipating voice and was taken to a private room.

I locked the door behind me. A plaque on the door was dated and sealed with the City stamp.

GUARANTEE OF PRIVACY

This room has been inspected and sealed against scanners, microphones, and other devices permitting the observation or recording of actions within it, in accordance with the provisions of the Privacy Act.

That was all very fine, but I wouldn't put enough faith in it to trust my life to it. I relaxed in a soft, heavy lounge facing the one-way wall. The show was already going on. I wasn't particularly interested in the fertility rites of the worshipers of Mahrud—not because they weren't intrinsically interesting, but because I had to do some thinking to save my own skin.

Senator Rowley, in order to keep his section under control, had coupled in his own robot's sensory organs with those of the city's Public Services Department and those of various business concerns, most of which were either owned outright or subsidized by the senator.

But something had happened to that computer; for some reason, its actions had become illogical and inefficient. When the patrol car had spotted me on the street, for instance, the sonobeam, which had penetrated the flesh of my arm and bounced off the tantalum plate back to the pickup, had relayed the modified vibrations back to the Central Files for identification. And the Files had obviously given back the wrong information.

What had gone wrong? Was the senator still alive, keeping his mouth shut and his eyes open? If so, what sort of orders was he giving to the robot? I didn't get many answers, and the ones I did get were mutually contradictory.

I was supposed to be back before dawn, but I could see now that I'd never make it. Here in Groverton, there weren't many connections with Public Services; the robot couldn't keep me under observation all the time. But the deeper into the city I penetrated, the more scanners there would be. I couldn't take a private car in, and I didn't dare take a flitter or a ground taxi. I'd be spotted in the subways as soon as I walked in. I was in a fix, and I'd have to think my way out.

I don't know whether it was the music or the soft lights or my lack of sleep or the simple fact that intense concentration is often autohypnotic. At any rate, I dozed off, and the next thing I remember is the girl bringing in the papers.

This gal was silver. I don't know how the cosmeticians had done it, but looking into her eyes was like looking into a mirror; the irises were a glittering silver halo surrounding the dark pupil. Her hair was the same way; not white, but silver.

"Good morning, Grandfather," she said softly. "Here are the newspapers you asked for."

I was thankful for that "Grandfather"; it reminded me that I was an old man before I had a chance to say anything.

"Thank you, my dear, thank you. Just put them here."

"Your coffee will be in in a moment." She moved out as quietly as she had come in.

Something was gnawing at the back of my brain; something like a dream you know you've had but forgotten completely. I concentrated on it a moment, trying to bring it out into the open, but it wouldn't come, so I gave it up and turned to the paper, still warm from the reproducer.

It was splattered all over the front page.

MYSTERIOUS TROUBLE AT THE LODGE

Police Unable to Enter

The Police Department announced this morning that they have been unable, thus far, to pass the defenses of the Lodge after receiving a call last night that Senator Rowley had been shot by his secretary, Mr. Edgar Gifford.

Repeated attempts to contact the senator have resulted in failure, says a Department spokesman.

Thus far, three police flitters under robot control have been shot down in attempting to land at the Lodge, and one ground car has been blown up. Another ground car, the first to respond to the automatic call for help, was stolen by the fleeing Gifford after killing the four officers in the car. The stolen vehicle was recovered early this morning several hundred miles from here, having been reported by a Mr. —

It went on with the usual statement that the police expected to apprehend the murderous Mr. Gifford at any moment.

Another small item in the lower left-hand corner registered the fact that the two men had been accidentally caught by a street cleaner and had proceeded to damage it. One of the men was killed by the damaged machine, but the other managed to escape. The dead man was a charity case, named Brodwick, and his associates were being checked.

So much for that. But the piece that really interested me was the one that said:

SENATOR LUTHER GRENDON OFFERS AID

"Federal Government Should Keep Hands Off," says Grendon.

Eastern Sector Senator Grendon said early this morning that he would do all in his power to aid Northwestern Sector in "apprehending the murderer of my colleague and bring to justice the organization behind him."

"There is," he said, "no need to call in the Federal Government at this time. The citizens of an independent sector are quite capable of dealing with crime within their own boundaries."

Interviewed later, Senator Quintell of Southwestern Sector agreed that there was no need to call in the FBI or "any other Federal Agency."

The other senators were coming in for the kill, even before it was definitely established that the senator was dead.

Well, that was that. I decided I'd better get going. It would be better to travel during the daytime: it's hard for a beam to be focused on an individual citizen in a crowd.

While the other Immortals were foreclosing on Senator Rowley's private property, there might be time for me to get back safely.

The silver girl was waiting for me as I stepped out the door to the private room.

"This way, Grandfather," she said, the ever-present smile on her glittering lips, She started down the corridor.

"This isn't the way out," I said, frowning.

She paused, still smiling. "No, sir, it isn't the way you came in, but, you see, our number has come up. The Medical Board has sent down a checker."

That almost floored me. Somehow, the Lodge had known where I was and had instituted a check against this particular house. That meant that every door was sealed except the one where the robot Medical checker was waiting.

The perfect trap. The checker was armed and armored, naturally; there were often people who did not want to be detained at the hospital—and at their own expense, if they were free citizens.

I walked slowly, as an old man should, stalling for time. The only armament a checker had was a stun gun; that was a point in my favor. But I needed more information.

"My goodness," I said, "you should have called me earlier, my dear, as soon as the checker came."

"It's only been here fifteen minutes, Grandfather," the silver girl answered.

Then there were still plenty of customers in the building!

The girl was just ahead of me in the corridor. I beamed her down with the stun gun and caught her before she hit the floor. I carried her back into the private room I had just left and laid her on the couch.

Then I started pulling down draperies. They were all heavy synthetic stuff that wouldn't burn unless they were really hot. I got a good armful, went back into the corridor, and headed for the opposite end of the building. Nobody bothered me on the way; everybody was still occupied.

At the end of the hall, I piled the stuff on the floor beneath some other hangings. Then I took two of the power cartridges from the stun gun and pried them open. The powder inside ought to burn nicely. It wouldn't explode unless it was sealed inside the gun, where the explosion was channeled through the supersonic whistle in the barrel to form the beam.

I took out my lighter and applied the flame to a sheet of the newspaper I had brought along, then I laid the paper on top of the opened cartridges. I got well back and waited.

I didn't take more than a second or two to ignite the powder. It hissed and went up in a wave of white heat. The plastic curtains started to smolder. Within less than a minute, the hallway was full of thick, acrid smoke.

I knew the building wouldn't burn, but I was hoping none of the other customers was as positive as I.

I yelled "Fire!" at the top of my lungs, then headed for the stairway and ran to the bottom. I waited just inside the street door for action.

Outside, I could hear the soft humming of a guard robot, stationed there by the checker to make sure no one left through that door.

The smoldering of the curtains put out plenty of smoke before they got hot enough to turn in the fire alarm and bring out the firefighter robots stationed in the walls. The little terrier-sized mechanisms scurried all over the place, looking for heat sources to squirt at. Upstairs, a heavy CO_2 blanket began to drift down.

I wasn't worried about the fire robots; they didn't have the sensory apparatus to spot me. All they could find was fire. They would find it and smother it, but the place was already full of smoke, which was all I wanted.

It was the smoke that did the job, really. People don't like to stay in buildings that appear to be burning down, no matter how safe they think they are. Customers came pouring down the stairway and out the door like angry wasps out of a disturbed hive. I went with them.

I knew that a fire signal would change the checker's orders. It couldn't keep people inside a burning building. Unfortunately, I hadn't realized to what extent the Lodge would go to get me, or to what extent it was capable of countermanding normal orders.

The guard robot at the door started beaming down everybody as they came out, firing as fast as it could scan and direct. It couldn't distinguish me from the others, of course; not in that mob. But it was hitting everything that moved with its stun beam. Luckily, it couldn't scan and direct fast enough to get everybody; there were too many. I watched and waited for a second or two until the turret was facing away from the corner, then I ran like the very devil, dodging as I ran.

A stun beam hit the fingers of my left hand, and my arm went dead to the elbow. The guard robot had spotted me! I made it around the corner and ducked into a crowd of people who were idly watching the smoke billowing from the upper windows.

I kept moving through the crowd, trying to put as much distance between myself and the checker's guards as possible. The guard evidently hadn't recognized me, personally, as Gifford, because it realized the futility of trying to cut down everyone in Groverton to find me and gave up on the crowd outside. But it kept hitting the ones who came out the door.

I got away fast. The thing really had me worried. I had no desire whatever to get myself mixed up with a nutty robot, but, seemingly, there was no way to avoid it.

I circled around and went down to Corliss Avenue, parallel to Bradley, for about seven blocks before I finally walked back over to Bradley again. Two or three times, police cars came by, but either they didn't test me with their beams or the answers they got weren't incriminating.

I was less than a block from the city limits when something hard and hot and tingling burned through my nerves like acid and I blacked out.

Maybe you've never been hit by a stun beam, but if you've ever had your leg go to sleep, you know what it feels like. And you know what it feels like when you wake up; that painful tingling all over that hurts even worse if you try to move.

I knew better than to try to move. I just lay still, waiting for the terrible tingling to subside. I had been out, I knew, a little less than an hour. I knew, because I'd been hit by stunners before, and I know how long it takes my body to throw off the paralysis.

Somebody's voice said, "He'll be coming out of it anytime now. Shake him and see."

A hand shook me, and I gasped. I couldn't help it; with my nerves still raw from the stunner, it hurt to be shaken that way.

"Sorry, Gifford," said another voice, different from the first. "Just wanted to see. Wanted to see if you were with us."

"Leave him alone a few minutes," the first voice said. "That hurts. It'll wear off quickly."

It was wearing off already. I opened my eyes and tried to see what was going on. At first, the visual pattern was a blithering swirl of meaningless shapes and crackling colors, but it finally settled down to a normal ceiling with a normal light panel in it. I managed to turn my head, in spite of the nerve-shocks, and saw two men sitting in chairs beside the bed.

One of them was short, round, and blond, with a full set of mutton chops, a heavy mustache, and a clean-shaven, firm chin. The other man was taller, muscular, with a full Imperial and smooth cheeks.

The one with the Imperial said, "Sorry we had to shoot you down that way, Gifford. But we didn't want to attract too much attention that close to the city limits."

They weren't cops, then. Of that much, I could be certain. At least they weren't the police of this sector. So they were working for one of the other Immortals.

"Whose little boys are you?" I asked, trying to grin.

Evidently I did grin, because they grinned back. "Funny," said the one with the mutton chops, "but that's exactly what we were going to ask you."

I turned my head back again and stared at the ceiling. "I'm an orphan," I said.

The guy with the mutton chops chuckled. "Well," he grinned at the other man, "what do you think of that, Colonel?"

The colonel (*Of what?* I wondered) frowned, pulling heavy brows deep over his gray eyes. His voice came from deep in his chest and seemed to be muffled by the heavy beard.

"We'll level with you, Gifford. Mainly because we aren't sure. Mainly because of that. We aren't sure even you know the truth. So we'll level."

"Your blast," I said.

"O.K., here's how it looks from our side of the fence. It looks like this. You killed Rowley. After fifteen years of faithful service, you killed him. Now we know—even if you don't—that Rowley had you psychoimpressed every six months for fifteen years. Or at least he thought he did."

"He *thought* he did?" I asked, just to show I was interested.

"Well, yes. He couldn't have, really, you see. He couldn't have. Or at least not lately. A psychoimpressed person can't do things like that. Also, we know that nobody broke it, because it takes six weeks of steady, hard therapy to pull a man out of it. And a man's no good after that for a couple more weeks. You weren't out of Rowley's sight for more than four days." He shrugged. "You see?"

"I see," I said. The guy was a little irritating in his manner. I didn't like the choppy way he talked.

"For a while," he said, "we thought it might be an impersonation. But we checked your plate"—he gestured at my arm—"and it's O.K. The genuine article. So it's Gifford's plate, all right. And we know it couldn't have been taken out of Gifford's arm and transferred to another arm in four days.

"If there were any way to check fingerprints and eye patterns, we might be able to be absolutely sure, but the Privacy Act forbids that, we have to go on what evidence we have in our possession now.

"Anyway, we're convinced that you are Gifford. So that means somebody has been tampering with your mind. We want to know who it is. Do you know?"

"No," I said, quite honestly.

"You didn't do it yourself, did you?"

"No."

"Somebody's behind you?"

"Yes."

"Do you know who?"

"No. And hold those questions a minute. You said you'd level with me. Who are *you* working for?"

The two of them looked at each other for a second, then the colonel said: "Senator Quintell."

I propped myself up on one elbow and held out the other hand, fingers extended. "All right, figure for yourself. Rowley's out of the picture; that eliminates him." I pulled my thumb in. "You work for Quintell; that eliminates him." I dropped my little finger and held it with my thumb. "That leaves three Immortals. Grendon, Lasser, and Waterford. Lasser has the Western Sector; Waterford, the Southern. Neither borders on Northwestern, so that eliminates them. Not definitely, but probably. They wouldn't be tempted to get rid of Rowley as much as they would Quintell.

"So that leaves Grendon. And if you read the papers, you'll know that he's pushing in already."

They looked at each other again. I knew they weren't necessarily working for Quintell; I was pretty sure it was Grendon. On the other hand, they might have told the truth so that I'd be sure to think it *was* Grendon. I didn't know how deep their subtlety went, and I didn't care. It didn't matter to me who they were working for.

"That sounds logical," said the colonel. "Very logical."

"But we have to know," added Mutton Chops. "We were fairly sure you'd head back toward the city; that's why we set up guards at the various street entrances. Since that part of our prediction worked out, we want to see if the rest of it will."

"The rest of it?"

"Yeah. You're expendable. We know that. The organization that sent you doesn't care what happens to you now, otherwise they wouldn't have let you loose like that. They don't care what happens to Eddie Gifford.

"So they must have known you'd get caught. Therefore, they've got you hypnoed to a fare-thee-well. And we probably won't find anything under the hypno, either. But we've got to look; there may be some little thing you'll remember. Some little thing that will give us the key to the whole organization."

I nodded. That was logical, very logical, as the colonel had said. They were going to break me. They could have done it gently, removed every bit of blocking and covering that the hypnoes had put in without hurting me a bit. But that would take time; I knew better than to think they were going to be gentle. They were going to peel my mind like a banana and then slice it up and look at it.

And if they were working for any of the Immortals, I had no doubt that they could do what they were planning. It took equipment, and it took an expert psychometrician, and a couple of good therapists—but that was no job at all if you had money.

The only trouble was that I had a few little hidden tricks that they'd never get around. If they started fiddling too much with my mind, a nice little psychosomatic heart condition would suddenly manifest itself. I'd be dead before they could do anything about it. Oh, I was expendable, all right.

"Do you want to say anything before we start?" the colonel asked.

"No." I didn't see any reason for giving them information they didn't earn.

"O.K." He stood up, and so did the mutton-chopper. "I'm sorry we have to do this, Gifford. It'll be hard on you, but you'll be in good condition inside of six or eight months. So long."

They walked out and carefully locked the door behind them.

I sat up for the first time and looked around. I didn't know where I was; in an hour, I could have been taken a long ways away from the city.

I hadn't been, though. The engraving on the bed said:

DELLFIELD SANATORIUM

I was on Riverside Drive, less than eight blocks from the rendezvous spot.

I walked over to the window and looked out. I could see the roof of the tenth level about eight floors beneath me. The window itself was a heavy sheet of transite welded into the wall. There was a polarizer control to the left to shut out the light, but there was no way to open the window. The door was sealed, too. When a patient got violent, they could pump gas in through the ventilators without getting it into the corridor.

They'd taken all my armament away, and, incidentally, washed off the thin plastic film on my hands and face. I didn't look so old any more. I walked over to the mirror in the wall, another sheet of transite with a reflecting back, and looked at myself. I was a sad-looking sight. The white hair was all scraggly, the whiskers were ditto, and my face looked worried. Small wonder.

I sat back down on the bed and started to think.

It must have been a good two hours later when the therapist came in. She entered by herself, but I noticed that the colonel was standing outside the door.

She was in her mid-thirties, a calm-faced, determined-looking woman. She started off with the usual questions.

"You have been told you are under some form of hypnotic compulsion. Do you consciously believe this?"

I told her I did. There was no sense in resisting.

"Do you have any conscious memory of the process?"

"No."

"Do you have any conscious knowledge of the identity of the therapist?"

I didn't and told her so. She asked a dozen other questions, all standard build-up. When she was through, I tried to ask her a couple of questions, but she cut me off and walked out of the room before I could more than open my yap.

The whole sanatorium was, and probably had been for a long time, in the pay of Quintell or Grendon—or, possibly, one of the other Immortals. It had been here for years, a neat little spy setup nestled deep in the heart of Rowley's territory.

Leaving the hospital without outside help was strictly out. I'd seen the inside of these places before, and I had a healthy respect for their impregnability. An unarmed man was in to stay.

Still, I decided that since something *had* to be done, something *would* be done.

My major worry was the question of whether or not the room was monitored. There was a single scanner pickup in the ceiling with a fairly narrow angle lens in it. That was interesting. It was enclosed in an unbreakable transite hemisphere and was geared to look around the room for the patient. But it was *not* robot controlled. There was evidently a nurse or therapist at the other end who checked on the patients every so often.

But how often?

From the window I could see the big, old-fashioned twelve-hour clock on the Barton Building. I used that to time the monitoring. The scanner was aimed at the bed. That meant it had looked at me last when I was on the bed. I walked over to the other side of the room and watched the scanner without looking at it directly.

It was nearly three quarters of an hour later that the little eye swiveled around the room and came to a halt on me. I ignored it for about thirty seconds, then walked deliberately across the room. The eye didn't follow.

Fine. This was an old-fashioned hospital; I had known that much. Evidently there hadn't been any new equipment installed in thirty years. Whoever operated the scanner simply looked around to see what the patient was doing and then went on to the next one. Hi ho.

I watched the scanner for the rest of the afternoon, timing it. Every hour at about four minutes after the hour. It was nice to know.

They brought me my dinner at 1830. I watched the scanner, but there was no special activity before they opened the door.

They simply swung the door outward; one man stood with a stun gun, ready for any funny business, while another brought in the food.

At 2130, the lights went out, except for a small lamp over the bed. That was fine; it meant that the scanner probably wasn't equipped for infrared. If I stayed in bed like a good boy, that one small light was all they'd need. If not, they turned on the main lights again.

I didn't assume that the watching would be regular, every hour, as it had been during the day. Plots are usually hatched at night, so it's best to keep a closer watch then. Their only mistake was that they were going to watch *me*. And that was perfectly O.K. as far as I was concerned.

I lay in bed until 2204. Sure enough, the scanner turned around and looked at me. I waited a couple of minutes and then got up as though to get a drink at the wash basin. The scanner didn't follow, so I went to work.

I pulled a light blanket off my bed and stuffed a corner of it into the basin's drain, letting the rest of it trail to the floor. Then I turned the water on and went back to bed.

It didn't take long for the basin to fill and overflow. It climbed over the edge and ran silently down the blanket to the floor.

Filling the room would take hours, but I didn't dare go to sleep. I'd have to wake up before dawn, and I wasn't sure I could do that. It was even harder to lie quietly and pretend I was asleep, but I fought it by counting fifty and then turning over violently to wake myself again. If anyone was watching, they would simply think I was restless.

I needn't have bothered. I dropped off—sound asleep. The next thing I knew, I was gagging. I almost drowned; the water had come up to bed level and had flowed into my mouth. I shot up in bed, coughing and spitting.

Fully awake, I moved fast. I pulled off the other blanket and tied it around the pickup in the ceiling. Then I got off the bed and waded in waist-deep water to the door. I grabbed a good hold on the metal dresser and waited.

It must have been all of half an hour before the lights came on. A voice came from the speaker: "Have you tampered with the TV pickup?"

"Huh? Wuzzat?" I said, trying to sound sleepy. "No. I haven't done anything."

"We are coming in. Stand back from the door or you will be shot."

I had no intention of being that close to the door.

When the attendant opened the door, it slammed him in the face as a good many tons of water cascaded onto him. There were two armed men with him, but they both went down in the flood, coughing and gurgling.

Judging very carefully, I let go the dresser and let the swirling water carry me into the hall. I had been prepared and I knew what I was doing; the guards didn't. By turning a little, I managed to hit one of them who was trying to get up and get his stunner into action. He went over, and I got the stunner.

It only lasted a few seconds. The water had been deep in the confines of the little room, but when allowed to expand into the hall, it merely made the floor wet.

I dispatched the guards with the stunner and ran for the nurse's desk, which, I knew, was just around the corner, near the elevators. I aimed quickly and let the nurse have it; he fell over, and I was at the desk before he had finished collapsing.

I grabbed the phone. There wouldn't be much time now.

I dialed. I said: "This is Gifford. I'm in Dellfield Sanatorium, Room 1808."

That was all I needed. I tossed the stunner into the water that trickled slowly toward the elevators and walked back toward my room with my hands up.

I'll say this for the staff at Dellfield; they don't get sore when a patient tries to escape. When five more guards came down the hall, they saw my raised hands and simply herded me into the room. Then they watched me until the colonel came.

"Well," he said, looking things over.

"Well. Neat. Very neat. Have to remember that one. Didn't do much good, though. Did it? Got out of the room, couldn't get downstairs. Elevators don't come up."

I shrugged. "Can't blame me for trying."

The colonel grinned for the first time. "I don't. Hate a man who'd give up—at any time." He lit a cigarette, his gun still not wavering. "Call didn't do you any good, either. This is a hospital. Patients have reached phones before. Robot identifies patient, refuses to relay call. Tough."

I didn't say anything or look anything; no use letting him think he had touched me.

The colonel shrugged. "All right. Strap him."

The attendants were efficient about it. They changed the wet bedclothes and strapped me in. I couldn't move my head far enough to see my hands.

The colonel looked me over and nodded. "You may get out of this. O.K. by me if you try. Next time, though, we'll give you a spinal freeze."

He left and the door clicked shut.

Well, I'd had my fun; it was out of my hands now. I decided I might as well get some sleep.

I didn't hear any commotion, of course; the room was soundproof. The next thing I knew, there was a Decon robot standing in the open door. It rolled over to the bed.

"Can you get up?"

These Decontamination robots aren't stupid, by any means.

"No," I said. "Cut these straps."

A big pair of nippers came out and began scissoring through the plastic webbing with ease. When the job was through, the Decon opened up the safety chamber in its body.

"Get in."

I didn't argue; the Decon had a stun gun pointed at me.

That was the last I saw of Dellfield Sanatorium, but I had a pretty good idea of what had happened. The Decontamination Squad is called in when something goes wrong with an atomic generator. The Lodge had simply turned in a phony report that there was generator trouble at Dellfield. Nothing to it.

I had seen Decons go to work before; they're smart, efficient, and quick. Each one has a small chamber inside it, radiation shielded to carry humans out of contaminated areas. They're small and crowded, but I didn't mind. It was better than conking out from a psychosomatic heart ailment when the therapists started to fiddle with me.

I smelled something sweetish then, and I realized I was getting a dose of gas. I went by-by.

When I woke up again, I was sick. I'd been hit with a stun beam yesterday and gassed today. I felt as though I was wasting all my life sleeping. I could still smell the gas.

No. It wasn't gas. The odor was definitely different. I turned my head and looked around. I was in the lounge of Senator Anthony Rowley's Lodge. On the floor. And next to me was Senator Anthony Rowley.

I crawled away from him, and then I was *really* sick.

I managed to get to the bathroom. It was a good twenty minutes before I worked up nerve enough to come out again. Rowley had moved, all right. He had pulled himself all of six feet from the spot where I had shot him.

My hunch had been right.

The senator's dead hand was still holding down the programming button on the control panel he had dragged himself to. The robot had gone on protecting the senator because it thought—as it was supposed to—that the senator was still alive as long as he was holding the ORDERS circuit open.

I leaned over and spoke into the microphone. "I will take a flitter from the roof. I want guidance and protection from here to the city. There, I will take over manual control. When I do, you will immediately put all dampers on your generator.

"Recheck."

The robot dutifully repeated the orders.

After that, everything was simple. I took the flitter to the rendezvous spot, was picked up, and, twenty minutes after I left the Lodge, I was in the Director's office.

He kicked in the hypnoes, and when I came out of it, my arm was strapped down while a surgeon took out the Gifford ID plate.

The Director of the FBI looked at me, grinning. "You took your time, son."

"What's the news?"

His grin widened. "You played hob with everything. The Lodge held off all investigation forces for thirty-odd hours after reporting Rowley's death. The Sector Police couldn't come anywhere near it.

"Meanwhile, funny things have happened. Robot in Groverton kills a man. Medic guard shoots down eighteen men coming out of a burning house. Decon Squad invades Dellfield when there's nothing wrong with the generator.

"Now all hell has busted loose. The Lodge went up in a flare of radiation an hour ago, and since then all robot services in the city have gone phooey. It looks to the citizens as though the senator had an illegal hand in too many pies. They're suspicious.

"Good work, boy."

"Thanks," I said, trying to keep from looking at my arm, where the doctor was peeling back flesh.

The Director lifted a white eyebrow. "Something?"

I looked at the wall. "I'm just burned up, that's all. Not at you; at the whole mess. How did a nasty slug like Rowley get elected in the first place? And what right did he have to stay in such an important job?"

"I know," the Director said somberly. "And that's our job. Immortality is something the human race isn't ready for yet. The masses can't handle it, and the individual can't handle it. And, since we can't get rid of them legally, we have to do it this way. Assassination. But it can't be done overnight."

"*You've* handled immortality," I pointed out.

"Have I?" he asked softly. "No. No, son. I haven't; I'm using it the same way they are. For power. The Federal government doesn't have any power any more. I have it.

"I'm using it in a different way, granted. Once there were over a hundred Immortals. Last week there were six. Today there are five. One by one, over the years, we have picked them off, and they are never replaced. The rest simply gobble up the territory and the power and split it between them rather than let a newcomer get into their tight little circle.

"But I'm just as dictatorial in my way as they are in theirs. And when the status quo is broken, and civilization begins to go ahead again, I'll have to die with the rest of them.

"But never mind that. What about you? I got most of the story from you under the hypno. That was a beautiful piece of deduction."

I took the cigarette he offered me and took a deep lungful of smoke. "How else could it be? The robot was trying to capture me. But also it was trying to keep anyone else from killing me. As a matter of fact, it passed up several chances to get me in order to keep others from killing me.

"It had to be the senator's last order. The old boy had lived so long that he still wasn't convinced he was dying. So he gave one last order to the robot:

"'*Get Gifford back here—ALIVE!*'"

"And then there was the queer fact that the robot never reported that the senator was dead, but kept right on defending the Lodge as though he were alive. That could only mean that the ORDERS circuits were still open. As long as they were, the robot thought the senator was still alive.

"So the only way I could get out of the mess was to let the Lodge take me. I knew the phone at Dellfield would connect me with the Lodge—at least indirectly. I called it and waited.

"Then, when I started giving orders, the Lodge accepted me as the senator. That was all there was to it."

The Director nodded. "A good job, son. A good job."

Further Reading   Randall Garrett

Books (all with Laurence M. Janifer as "Mark Phillips")

Brain Twister. New York: Pyramid Books, 1962.
The Impossibles. New York: Pyramid Books, 1963.
Supermind. New York: Pyramid Books, 1963.

Stories

"Fighting Division." *Analog Science Fiction,* August 1965. (*Analog 5,* ed. John W. Campbell, Jr.)
"Sound Decision" (with Robert Silverberg). *Astounding Science Fiction,* October 1956. (*Prologue to Analog,* ed. John W. Campbell, Jr.)

In *Alternate Worlds: An Illustrated History of Science Fiction,* James E. Gunn refers to "the mysterious Peter Phillips" and can offer no more. Gunn (who is, along with no more than ten other people, among the few scholars the field has to date produced) concedes a sense of bewilderment with this writer; I can do no less.

Phillips, who lives in England and would be somewhere between sixty and seventy now, is typical of a certain kind of writer unique to the genres of American fiction: a writer about whom almost nothing is known who comes in, drops one or two or five incredible pieces on the field, and disappears, perhaps never to be heard of again. T. L. Sherred is such a figure,* as are Gary Wright (one story in *Galaxy* in 1967), John T. Lutz (ditto), Alan Arkin (two stories in *Galaxy* in 1955: whatever became of him?). Phillips did somewhere between five and ten in the late forties and early fifties of which three, "Lost Memory," "Dreams Are Sacred," and "Manna," can be characterized as brilliant.

Why does this happen? How can a writer have achieved such evident skill (the outcome of either extraordinary instinct or extraordinary work), make an immediate impression in a sophisticated, specialized field staffed with cynical editors and jaded readers, and then cease to write? Ill health or bad circumstance cannot be the answer; the careers of several of the writers noted above are known to me, and in no case do those explanations apply. A slender gift that yields up its small, precious mysteries and is then emptied? But "Dreams Are Sacred" and "Lost Memory" show amazing imaginative facility; if nothing else, Phillips could have rewritten and expanded the themes into endless semi-sequels if he had desired; many lesser writers have done this. A boredom or disgust with the genre itself? Doubtful; one does not write like this unless one is extremely familiar with the specialized genre as the result of years of reading, and one does not turn so quickly from what one knows so well. Inability to bear the pain that the creation of serious work imposes upon some of us? Here one may be onto something—writing can be for some writers an extraordinarily painful circumstance, and in the long run it is painful for all of us—but dare not pursue it much further.

* Tom Sherred did appear with a novel, *Alien Island,* in 1968 and a couple of short stories a little later than that, but for the twenty years since his remarkable "E for Effort" in *ASF* in 1947 he was known as the author of only that story and two minor, similarly titled others: "Q for Quiet" and "I for Iniquity."

In any case, "Lost Memory" is a remarkable and audacious piece and will not give great comfort to those who take their testaments seriously. "Dreams Are Sacred" is as important and as well written, and the choice in favor of this story was close, even agonizing. . . . "Lost Memory" wins because *everyone,* this writer much among the guilty, seems to have rewritten "Dreams Are Sacred" somewhere along the line but this one is sacred ground.

B.N.M.

Lost Memory

by PETER PHILLIPS

I collapsed joints and hung up to talk with Dak-whirr. He blinked his eyes in some discomfort.

"What do you want, Palil?" he asked complainingly.

"As if you didn't know."

"I can't give you permission to examine it. The thing is being saved for inspection by the board. What guarantee do I have that you won't spoil it for them?"

I thrust confidentially at one of his body-plates. "You owe me a favor," I said. "Remember?"

"That was a long time in the past."

"Only two thousand revolutions and a reassembly ago. If it wasn't for me, you'd be eroding in a pit. All I want is a quick look at its thinking part. I'll vrull the consciousness without laying a single pair of pliers on it."

He went into a feedback twitch, an indication of the conflict between his debt to me and his self-conceived duty.

Finally he said, "Very well, but keep tuned to me. If I warn that a board member is coming, remove yourself quickly. Anyway how do you know it has consciousness? It may be mere primal metal."

"In that form? Don't be foolish. It's obviously a manufacture. And I'm not conceited enough to believe that we are the only form of intelligent manufacture in the Universe."

"Tautologous phrasing, Palil," Dak-whirr said pedantically. "There could not conceivably be 'unintelligent manufacture.' There can be no consciousness without manufacture, and no manufacture without intelligence. Therefore there can be no consciousness without intelligence. Now if you should wish to dispute—"

I turned off his frequency abruptly and hurried away. Dak-whirr is a fool and a bore. Everyone knows there's a fault in his logic circuit, but he refuses to have it traced down and repaired. Very unintelligent of him.

The thing had been taken into one of the museum sheds by the carriers. I gazed at it in admiration for some moments. It was quite beautiful, having suffered only slight exterior damage, and it was obviously no mere conglomeration of sky metal.

In fact, I immediately thought of it as "he" and endowed it with the attributes of self-knowing, although, of course, his consciousness could not be functioning or he would have attempted communication with us.

I fervently hoped that the board, after his careful disassembly and study, could restore his awareness so that he could tell us himself which solar system he came from.

Imagine it! He had achieved our dream of many thousands of revolutions—space flight—only to be fused, or worse, in his moment of triumph.

I felt a surge of sympathy for the lonely traveler as he lay there, still, silent, non-emitting. Anyway, I mused, even if we couldn't restore him to self-knowing, an analysis of his construction might give us the secret of the power he had used to achieve the velocity to escape his planet's gravity.

In shape and size he was not unlike Swen—or Swen Two, as he called himself after his conversion—who failed so disastrously to reach our satellite, using chemical fuels. But where Swen Two had placed his tubes, the stranger had a curious helical construction studded at irregular intervals with small crystals.

He was thirty-five feet tall, a gracefully tapering cylinder. Standing at his head, I could find no sign of exterior vision cells, so I assumed he had some kind of vrulling sense. There seemed to be no exterior markings at all, except the long, shallow grooves dented in his skin by scraping to a stop along the hard surface of our planet.

I am a reporter with warm current in my wires, not a cold-thinking scientist, so I hesitated before using my own vrulling sense. Even though the stranger was non-aware—perhaps permanently—I felt it would be a presumption, an invasion of privacy. There was nothing else I could do, though, of course.

I started to vrull, gently at first, then harder, until I was positively glowing with effort. It was incredible; his skin seemed absolutely impermeable.

The sudden realization that metal could be so alien nearly fused something inside me. I found myself backing away in horror, my self-preservation relay working overtime.

Imagine watching one of the beautiful cone-rod-and-cylinder assemblies performing the Dance of the Seven Spanners, as he's conditioned to do, and then suddenly refusing to do anything except stump around unattractively, or even becoming obstinately motionless, unresponsive. That might give you an idea of how I felt in that dreadful moment.

Then I remembered Dak-whirr's words—there could be no such thing as an "unintelligent manufacture." And a product so beautiful could surely not be evil. I overcame my repugnance and approached again.

I halted as an open transmission came from someone near at hand.

"Who gave that squeaking reporter permission to snoop around here?"

I had forgotten the museum board. Five of them were standing in the doorway of the shed, radiating anger. I recognized Chirik, the chairman, and addressed myself to him. I explained that I'd interfered with nothing and pleaded for permission on behalf of my subscribers to watch their investigation of the stranger. After some argument, they allowed me to stay.

I watched in silence and some amusement as one by one they tried to vrull the silent being from space. Each showed the same reaction as myself when they failed to penetrate the skin.

Chirik, who is wheeled—and inordinately vain about his suspension system—flung himself back on his supports and pretended to be thinking.

"Fetch Fiff-fiff," he said at last. "The creature may still be aware, but unable to communicate on our standard frequencies."

Fiff-fiff can detect anything in any spectrum. Fortunately he was at work in the museum that day and soon arrived in answer to the call. He stood silently near the stranger for some moments, testing and adjusting himself, then slid up the electromagnetic band.

"He's emitting," he said.

"Why can't we get him?" asked Chirik.

"It's a curious signal on an unusual band."

"Well, what does he say?"

"Sounds like utter nonsense to me. Wait, I'll relay and convert it to standard."

I made a direct recording naturally, like any good reporter.

"—after planetfall," the stranger was saying. "Last dribble of power. If you don't pick this up, my name is Entropy. Other instruments knocked to hell, airlock jammed and I'm too weak to open it manually. Becoming delirious, too, I guess. Getting strong undirectional ultra-wave reception in Inglish, craziest stuff you ever heard, like goblins muttering, and I know we were the only ship in this sector. If you pick this up, but can't get a fix in time, give my love to the boys in the mess. Signing off for another couple of hours, but keeping this channel open and hoping . . ."

"The fall must have deranged him," said Chirik, gazing at the stranger. "Can't he see us or hear us?"

"He couldn't hear you properly before, but he can now, through me," Fiff-fiff pointed out. "Say something to him, Chirik."

"Hello," said Chirik doubtfully. "Er—welcome to our planet. We are sorry you were hurt by your fall. We offer you the hospitality of our assembly shops. You will feel better when you are repaired and repowered. If you will indicate how we can assist you—"

"What the hell! What ship is that? Where are you?"

"We're here," said Chirik. "Can't you see us or vrull us? Your vision circuit is impaired, perhaps? Or do you depend entirely on vrulling? We can't find your eyes and assumed either that you protected them in some way during flight, or dispensed with vision cells altogether in your conversion."

Chirik hesitated, continued apologetically: "But we cannot understand how you vrull, either. While we thought that you were unaware, or even completely fused, we tried to vrull you. Your skin is quite impervious to us, however."

The stranger said: "I don't know if you're batty or I am. What distance are you from me?"

Chirik measured quickly. "One meter, two-point-five centimeters from my eyes to your nearest point. Within touching distance, in fact." Chirik tentatively put out his hand. "Can you not feel me, or has your contact sense also been affected?"

It became obvious that the stranger had been pitifully deranged. I reproduce his words phonetically from my record, although some of them make little sense. Emphasis, punctuative pauses and spelling of unknown terms are mere guesswork, of course.

He said: "For godsakemann stop talking nonsense, whoever you are. If you're outside, can't you see the airlock is jammed? Can't shift it myself. I'm badly hurt. Get me out of here, please."

"Get you out of where?" Chirik looked around, puzzled. "We brought you into an open shed near our museum for a preliminary examination. Now that we know you're intelligent, we shall immediately take you to our assembly shops for healing and recuperation. Rest assured that you'll have the best possible attention."

There was a lengthy pause before the stranger spoke again, and his words were slow and deliberate. His bewilderment is understandable, I believe, if we remember that he could not see, vrull or feel.

He asked: "What manner of creature are you? Describe yourself."

Chirik turned to us and made a significant gesture toward his thinking part, indicating gently that the injured stranger had to be humored.

"Certainly," he replied. "I am an unspecialized bipedal manufacture of standard proportions, lately self-converted to wheeled traction, with a hydraulic suspension system of my own devising which I'm sure will interest you when we restore your sense circuits."

There was an even longer silence.

"You are robots," the stranger said at last. "Crise knows how you got here or why you speak Inglish, you must try to understand me. I am mann. I am a friend of your master, your maker. You must fetch him to me at once."

"You are not well," said Chirik firmly. "Your speech is incoherent and without meaning. Your fall has obviously caused several serious feedbacks of a very serious nature. Please lower your voltage. We are taking you to our shops immediately. Reserve your strength to assist our specialists as best you can in diagnosing your troubles."

"Wait. You must understand. You are—ogodno that's no good. Have you no memory of mann? The words you use—what meaning have they for you? *Manufacture*—made by hand hand hand damyou. *Healing*. Metal is not healed. *Skin*. Skin is not metal. *Eyes*. Eyes are not scanning cells. Eyes grow. Eyes are soft. My eyes are soft. Mine eyes have seen the glory—steady on, sun. Get a grip. Take it easy. You out there listen."

"Out where?" asked Prrr-chuk, deputy chairman of the museum board.

I shook my head sorrowfully. This was nonsense, but, like any good reporter, I kept my recorder running.

The mad words flowed on. "You call me he. Why? You have no seks. You are knewter. You are *it it it!* I am he, he who made you, sprung from shee, born of wumman. What is wumman, who is silvya what is shee that all her swains commend her ogod the bluds flowing again. Remember. Think back, you out there. These words were made by mann, for mann. Hurt, healing, hospitality, horror, deth by loss of blud. *Deth. Blud.* Do you understand these words? Do you remember the soft things that made you? Soft little mann who konkurred the Galaxy and made sentient slaves of his machines and saw the wonders of a million worlds, only this miserable representative has to die in lonely desperation on a far planet, hearing goblin voices in the darkness."

Here my recorder reproduces a most curious sound, as though the stranger were using an ancient type of vibratory molecular vocalizer in a gaseous medium to reproduce his words before transmission, and the insulation on his diaphragm had come adrift.

It was a jerky, high-pitched, strangely disturbing sound; but in a moment the fault was corrected and the stranger resumed transmission.

"Does blud mean anything to you?"

"No," Chirik replied simply.

"Or deth?"

"No."

"Or wor?"

"Quite meaningless."

"What is your origin? How did you come into being?"

"There are several theories," Chirik said. "The most popular one —which is no more than a grossly unscientific legend, in my opinion —is that our manufacturer fell from the skies, imbedded in a mass of primal metal on which He drew to erect the first assembly shop. How He came into being is left to conjecture. My own theory, however—"

"Does legend mention the shape of this primal metal?"

"In vague terms, yes. It was cylindrical, of vast dimensions."

"An interstellar vessel," said the stranger.

"That is my view also," said Chirik complacently. "And—"

"What was the supposed appearance of your—manufacturer?"

"He is said to have been of magnificent proportions, based harmoniously on a cubical plan, static in Himself, but equipped with a vast array of senses."

"An automatic computer," said the stranger.

He made more curious noises, less jerky and at a lower pitch than the previous sounds.

He corrected the fault and went on: "God that's funny. A ship falls, menn are no more, and an automatic computer has pupps. Oh, yes, it fits in. A self-setting computer and navigator, operating on verbal orders. It learns to listen for itself and know itself for what it is, and to absorb knowledge. It comes to hate menn—or at least their bad qualities—so it deliberately crashes the ship and pulps their puny bodies with a calculated nicety of shock. Then it propagates and does a dam fine job of selective erasure on whatever it gave its pupps to use for a memory. It passes on only the good it found in menn, and purges the memory of him completely. Even purges all of his vocabulary except scientific terminology. Oil is thicker than blud. So may they live without the burden of knowing that they are—ogod they must know, they must understand. You outside, what happened to this manufacturer?"

Chirik, despite his professed disbelief in the supernormal aspects of the ancient story, automatically made a visual sign of sorrow.

"Legend has it," he said, "that after completing His task, He fused himself beyond possibility of healing."

Abrupt, low-pitched noises came again from the stranger. "Yes. He would. Just in case any of His pupps should give themselves forbidden knowledge and an infeeryorrity komplecks by probing his mnemonic circuits. The perfect self-sacrificing muther. What sort of environment did He give you? Describe your planet."

Chirik looked around at us again in bewilderment, but he replied courteously, giving the stranger a description of our world.

"Of course," said the stranger. "Of course. Sterile rock and metal suitable only for you. But there must be some way. . . ."

He was silent for a while.

"Do you know what growth means?" he asked finally. "Do you have anything that grows?"

"Certainly," Chirik said helpfully. "If we should suspend a crystal of some substance in a saturated solution of the same element or compound—"

"No, no," the stranger interrupted. "Have you nothing that grows of itself, that fruktiffies and gives increase without your intervention?"

"How could such a thing be?"

"Criseallmytee I should have guessed. If you had one blade of gras, just one tiny blade of growing gras, you could extrapolate from that to me. Green things, things that feed on the rich brest of erth, cells that divide and multiply, a cool grove of treez in a hot summer, with tiny warmbludded burds preening their fethers among the leeves; a feeld of spring weet with newbawn mise timidly threading the dangerous jungul of storks; a stream of living water where silver fish dart and pry and feed and procreate; a farm yard where things grunt and cluck and greet the new day with the stirring pulse of life, with a surge of blud. Blud—"

For some inexplicable reason, although the strength of his carrier wave remained almost constant, the stranger's transmission seemed to be growing fainter.

"His circuits are failing," Chirik said. "Call the carriers. We must take him to an assembly shop immediately. I wish he would reserve his power."

My presence with the museum board was accepted without question now. I hurried along with them as the stranger was carried to the nearest shop.

I now noticed a circular marking in that part of his skin on which he had been resting, and guessed that it was some kind of orifice

through which he would have extended his planetary traction mechanism if he had not been injured.

He was gently placed on a disassembly cradle. The doctor in
charge that day was Chur-chur, an old friend of mine. He had been
listening to the two-way transmissions and was already acquainted
with the case.

Chur-chur walked thoughtfully around the stranger.

"We shall have to cut," he said. "It won't pain him, since his intra-
molecular pressure and contact senses have failed. But since we can't
vrull him, it'll be necessary for him to tell us where his main brain is
housed or we might damage it."

Fiff-fiff was still relaying, but no amount of power boost would
make the stranger's voice any clearer. It was quite faint now, and
there are places on my recorder tape from which I cannot make even
the roughest phonetic transliteration.

". . . strength going. Can't get into my zoot . . . done for if they
bust through lock, done for if they don't . . . must tell them I need
oxygen . . ."

"He's in bad shape, desirous of extinction," I remarked to Chur-
chur, who was adjusting his arc-cutter. "He wants to poison himself
with oxidation now."

I shuddered at the thought of that vile, corrosive gas he had mentioned, which causes that almost unmentionable condition we all fear
—rust.

Chirik spoke firmly through Fiff-fiff. "Where is your thinking part,
stranger? Your central brain?"

"In my head," the stranger replied. "In my head ogod my head
. . . eyes blurring everything going dim . . . luv to mairee . . . kids
. . . a carry me home to the lone prayree . . . get this bluddy airlock
open then they'll see me die . . . but they'll see me . . . some kind
of atmosphere with this gravity . . . see me die . . . extrapolate
from body what I was . . . what they are damthem damthem
damthem . . . mann . . . master . . . I AM YOUR MAKER!"

For a few seconds the voice rose strong and clear, then faded
away again and dwindled into a combination of those two curious
noises I mentioned earlier. For some reason that I cannot explain, I
found the combined sound very disturbing despite its faintness. It
may be that it induced some kind of sympathetic oscillation.

Then came words, largely incoherent and punctuated by a kind of
surge like the sonic vibrations produced by variations of pressure in
a leaking gas-filled vessel.

". . . done it . . . crawling into chamber, closing inner . . . must
be mad . . . they'd find me anyway . . . but finished . . . want see

them before I die . . . want see them see me . . . liv few seconds,
watch them . . . get outer one open . . ."

Chur-chur had adjusted his arc to a broad, clean, blue-white glare.
I trembled a little as he brought it near the edge of the circular
marking in the stranger's skin. I could almost feel the disruption of
the intra-molecular sense currents in my own skin.

"Don't be squeamish, Palil," Chur-chur said kindly. "He can't feel
it now that his contact sense has gone. And you heard him say that
his central brain is in his head." He brought the cutter firmly up to
the skin. "I should have guessed that. He's the same shape as Swen
Two, and Swen very logically concentrated his main thinking part as
far away from his explosion chambers as possible."

Rivulets of metal ran down into a tray which a calm assistant had
placed on the ground for that purpose. I averted my eyes quickly. I
could never steel myself enough to be a surgical engineer or assembly technician.

But I had to look again, fascinated. The whole area circumscribed
by the marking was beginning to glow.

Abruptly the stranger's voice returned, quite strongly, each word
clipped, emphasized, high-pitched.

"Ar no no no . . . god my hands . . . they're burning through the
lock and I can't get back I can't get away . . . stop it you feens stop
it can't you hear . . . I'll be burned to deth I'm here in the airlock
. . . the air's getting hot you're burning me alive . . ."

Although the words made little sense, I could guess what had happened and I was horrified.

"Stop, Chur-chur," I pleaded. "The heat has somehow brought
back his skin currents. It's hurting him."

Chur-chur said reassuringly: "Sorry, Palil. It occasionally happens during an operation—probably a local thermo-electric effect.
But even if his contact senses have started working again and he
can't switch them off, he won't have to bear this very long."

Chirik shared my unease, however. He put out his hand and awk-
wardly patted the stranger's skin.

"Easy there," he said. "Cut out your senses if you can. If you
can't, well, the operation is nearly finished. Then we'll repower you,
and you'll soon be fit and happy again, healed and fitted and reas-
sembled."

I decided that I liked Chirik very much just then. He exhibited almost as much self-induced empathy as any reporter; he might even
come to like my favorite blue stars, despite his cold scientific exacti-
tude in most respects.

My recorder tape shows, in its reproduction of certain sounds,
how I was torn away from this strained reverie.

During the one-and-a-half seconds since I had recorded the distinct vocables "burning me alive," the stranger's words had become quite blurred, running together and rising even higher in pitch until they reached a sustained note—around E-flat in the standard sonic scale.

It was not like a voice at all.

This high, whining noise was suddenly modulated by apparent words, but without changing its pitch. Transcribing what seem to be words is almost impossible, as you can see for yourself—this is the closest I can come phonetically:

"Eeee ahahmbeeeeing baked aliiive in an uvennn ahdeeerjeee-sussunmuuutherrr!"

The note swooped higher and higher until it must have neared supersonic range, almost beyond either my direct or recorded hearing.

Then it stopped as quickly as a contact break.

And although the soft hiss of the stranger's carrier wave carried on without perceptible diminution, indicating that some degree of awareness still existed, I experienced at that moment one of those quirks of intuition given only to reporters:

I felt that I would never greet the beautiful stranger from the sky in his full senses.

Chur-chur was muttering to himself about the extreme toughness and thickness of the stranger's skin. He had to make four complete cutting revolutions before the circular mass of nearly white-hot metal could be pulled away by a magnetic grapple.

A billow of smoke puffed out of the orifice. Despite my repugnance, I thought of my duty as a reporter and forced myself to look over Chur-chur's shoulder.

The fumes came from a soft, charred, curiously shaped mass of something which lay just inside the opening.

"Undoubtedly a kind of insulating material," Chur-chur explained.

He drew out the crumpled blackish heap and placed it carefully on a tray. A small portion broke away, showing a red, viscid substance.

"It looks complex," Chur-chur said, "but I expect the stranger will be able to tell us how to reconstitute it or make a substitute."

His assistant gently cleaned the wound of the remainder of the material, which he placed with the rest; and Chur-chur resumed his inspection of the orifice.

You can, if you want, read the technical accounts of Chur-chur's discovery of the stranger's double skin at the point where the cut was made; of the incredible complexity of his driving mechanism, involving principles which are still not understood to this day; of the museum's failure to analyze the exact nature and function of the insulating material found in only that one portion of his body; and of the other scientific mysteries connected with him.

But this is my personal, non-scientific account. I shall never forget hearing about the greatest mystery of all, for which not even the most tentative explanation has been advanced, nor the utter bewilderment with which Chur-chur announced his initial findings that day.

He had hurriedly converted himself to a convenient size to permit actual entry into the stranger's body.

When he emerged, he stood in silence for several minutes. Then, very slowly, he said:

"I have examined the 'central brain' in the forepart of his body. It is no more than a simple auxiliary computer mechanism. It does not possess the slightest trace of consciousness. And there is no other conceivable center of intelligence in the remainder of his body."

There is something I wish I could forget. I can't explain why it should upset me so much. But I always stop the tape before it reaches the point where the voice of the stranger rises in pitch, going higher and higher until it cuts out.

There's a quality about that noise that makes me tremble and think of rust.

Further Reading   Peter Phillips

Stories

"C/O Mr. Makepeace." *The Magazine of Fantasy and Science Fiction,* February 1954. (*The Dark Side,* ed. Damon Knight.)

"Counter Charm." *Slant,* 1951. (*50 Short Science Fiction Tales,* ed. Isaac Asimov and Groff Conklin.)

"Dream Are Sacred." *Astounding Science Fiction,* September 1948. (*Spectrum 3,* ed. Kingsley Amis and Robert Conquest.)

"Manna." *Astounding Science Fiction,* February 1949. (*A Science Fiction Argosy,* ed. Damon Knight.)

"Unknown Quantity." *New Worlds,* May 1949. (*The Best from New Worlds Science Fiction,* ed. John Carnell.)

Robert Abernathy is one of a relatively small number of college professors who write (or have written) science fiction—a group that includes Greg Benford, Stanley Schmidt, Phil Klass, James Gunn, and Jack Williamson. Abernathy teaches Slavic languages at the University of Colorado at Boulder, and over the past thirty-eight years or so has produced a corpus of perhaps thirty sf stories and no novels, this last statistic a deadly liability, since you can count the number of famous short-story-only sf writers on one and one-half hands at the most.

His stories appeared in two bunches, one in the early forties (when he contributed to, but was lost in, the "Golden Age" of *Astounding*), the other in the middle fifties. He has been almost totally quiet since. In addition to the present selection, his best work includes "Single Combat," "Pyramid," "Heirs Apparent" (one of the better Cold War stories), and the fantasy "Grandma's Lie Soap," one of his last appearances in the sf magazines.

"Junior" shows him at the top of his creative form, in a story that was chosen by Judith Merril twice, once in her "Best of the Year" series of beloved memory, and again when she selected the "Best of the Best"—the latter, sadly, eleven years ago.

M.H.G. & J.D.O.

Junior

by ROBERT ABERNATHY

"Junior!" bellowed Pater.

"Junior!" squeaked Mater, a quavering echo.

"Strayed off again—the young idiot! If he's playing in the shallows, with this tide going out . . ." Pater let the sentence hang blackly. He leaned upslope as far as he could stretch, angrily scanning the shoreward reaches where light filtered more brightly down through the murky water, where the sea-surface glinted like bits of broken mirror.

No sign of Junior.

Mater was peering fearfully in the other direction, toward where, as daylight faded, the slope of the coastal shelf was fast losing itself in green profundity. Out there, beyond sight at this hour, the reef that loomed sheltering above them fell away in an abrupt cliffhead, and the abyss began.

"Oh, oh," sobbed Mater. "He's lost. He's swum into the abyss and been eaten by a sea monster." Her slender stem rippled and swayed on its base, and her delicate crown of pinkish tentacles trailed disheveled in the pull of the ebbtide.

"Pish, my dear!" said Pater. "There are no sea monsters. At worst," he consoled her stoutly, "Junior may have been trapped in a tidepool."

"Oh, oh," gulped Mater. "He'll be eaten by a land monster."

"There ARE no land monsters!" snorted Pater. He straightened his stalk so abruptly that the stone to which he and Mater were conjugally attached creaked under them. "How often must I assure you, my dear, that WE are the highest form of life?" (And, for his world and geologic epoch, he was quite right.)

"Oh, oh," gasped Mater.

Her spouse gave her up. "JUNIOR!" he roared in a voice that loosened the coral along the reef.

Round about, the couple's bereavement had begun attracting attention. In the thickening dusk tentacles paused from winnowing the sea for their owners' suppers, stalked heads turned curiously here and there in the colony. Not far away a threesome of maiden aunts, rooted en brosse to a single substantial boulder, twittered condolences and watched Mater avidly.

"Discipline!" growled Pater. "That's what he needs! Just wait till I—"

"Now, dear—" began Mater shakily.

"Hi, folks!" piped Junior from overhead.

His parents swiveled as if on a single stalk. Their offspring was floating a few fathoms above them, paddling lazily against the ebb; plainly he had just swum from some crevice in the reef nearby. In one pair of dangling tentacles he absently hugged a roundish stone, worn sensuously smooth by pounding surf.

"WHERE HAVE YOU BEEN?"

"Nowhere," said Junior innocently. "Just playing hide-and-go-sink with the squids."

"With the other *polyps*," Mater corrected him primly. She detested slang.

Pater was eyeing Junoir with ominous calm. "And where," he asked, "did you get that stone?"

Junior contracted guiltily. The surfstone slipped from his tentacles and plumped to the sea-floor in a flurry of sand. He edged away, stammering, "Well, I guess maybe . . . I might have gone a little ways toward the beach . . ."

"You guess! When I was a polyp," said Pater, "the small fry obeyed their elders, and no guess about it!"

"Now, dear—" said Mater.

"And no spawn of mine," Pater warmed to his lecture, "is going to flout my words! Junior . . . COME HERE."

Junior paddled cautiously round the homesite just out of tentacle-reach. He said in a small voice, "I won't."

"DID YOU HEAR ME?"

"Yes," admitted Junior.

The neighbors stared. The three maiden aunts clutched one another with muted shrieks, savoring beforehand the language Pater would now use.

But Pater said "Ulp!"—no more.

"Now, dear," put in Mater quickly. "We must be patient. You know all children go through larval stages."

"When I was a polyp . . ." Pater began rustily. He coughed out an accidentally inhaled crustacean, and started over: "No spawn of mine . . ." Trailing off, he only glared, then roared abruptly, "SPRAT!"

"I won't!" said Junior reflexively, and backpaddled into the coral shadows of the reef.

"That wallop," seethed Pater, "wants a good polyping. I mean—" He glowered suspiciously at Mater and the neighbors.

"Dear," soothed Mater, "didn't you *notice* . . . ?"

"OF COURSE I— Notice what?"

"What Junior was doing. Carrying a stone. I don't suppose he understands why, just yet, but . . ."

"A stone? Ah, uh, to be sure, a stone. Why . . . Why, my dear, do you realize what this MEANS?"

Pater was once more occupied with improving Mater's mind. It was a long job, without foreseeable end—especially since he and his helpmeet were both firmly rooted for life to the same tastefully decorated homesite (garnished by Pater himself with colored pebbles, shells, urchins, and bits of coral in the rather rococo style which had prevailed during Pater's courting days as a free-swimming polyp).

"Intelligence, my dear," pronounced Pater, "is quite incompatible with motility. Just think—how could ideas congeal in a brain shuttled hither and yon, bombarded with ever-changing sense-impressions? Look at the lower species, which swim about all their lives, incapable of taking root or thought! True Intelligence, my dear—as distinguished from Instinct, of course—presupposes the fixed viewpoint."

He paused. Mater murmured, "Yes, dear," as she always did at this point.

Junior undulated past, swimming toward the abyss. He moved a bit heavily now; it was growing hard for him to keep his maturely thickening afterbody in a horizontal posture.

"Just look at the young of our own kind," said Pater. "Scatter-brained larvae, wandering greedily about in search of new stimuli. But, praise be, they mature at last into sensible, sessile adults. While yet the unformed intellect rebels against the ending of carefree polyphood, instinct, the wisdom of Nature, instructs them to prepare for the great change!"

He nodded wisely as Junior came gliding back out of the gloom of deep water. Junior's tentacles clutched an irregular basalt fragment which he must have picked up down the rubble-strewn slope. As he paddled slowly along the rim of the reef, the adult anthozoans located directly below looked up and hissed irritable warnings. He was swimming a bit more easily now, and, if Pater had not been a firm believer in Instinct, he might have been reminded of the grossly materialistic theory, propounded by some iconoclast, according to which a maturing polyp's tendency to grapple objects was merely a matter of taking on ballast.

"See!" declared Pater triumphantly. "I don't suppose he understands *why,* just yet . . . but Instinct urges him infallibly to assemble the materials for his future homesite."

Junior let the rock fragment fall, and began plucking restlessly at a coral outcropping.

"Dear," said Mater, "don't you think you ought to tell him . . . ?"

"Ahem!" said Pater. "The wisdom of Instinct—"

"As you've always said, a polyp needs a parent's guidance," remarked Mater.

"Ahem!" repeated Pater. He straightened his stalk and bellowed authoritatively, "JUNIOR! Come here!"

The prodigal polyp swam warily close. "Yes, Pater?"

"Junior," said his parent solemnly, "now that you are growing up, it behooves you to know certain facts."

Mater blushed a delicate lavender and turned away on her side of the rock.

"Very soon now," said Pater, "you will begin feeling an irresistible urge . . . to sink to the bottom, to take root there in some sheltered location which will be your lifetime site. Perhaps you even have an understanding already with some—ah—charming young polyp of the opposite gender, whom you would invite to share your homesite. Or, if not, you should take all the more pains to make that site as attractive as possible, in order that such a one may decide to grace it with—"

"Uh-huh," said Junior understandingly. "That's what the fellows mean when they say any of 'em'll fall for a few high-class rocks."

Pater marshaled his thoughts again. "Well, quite apart from such material considerations as selecting the right rocks, there are certain —ah—matters we do not ordinarily discuss."

Mater blushed a more pronounced lavender. The three maiden aunts, rooted to their boulder within easy earshot of Pater's carrying voice, put up a respectable pretense of searching one another for water-fleas.

"No doubt," said Pater, "in the course of your harum-scarum adventurings as a normal polyp among polyps, you've noticed the ways in which the lower orders reproduce themselves—the activities of the fishes, the crustacea, the marine worms, will not have escaped your attention."

"Uh-huh," said Junior, treading water.

"You will have observed that among these there takes place a good deal of—ah—maneuvering for position. But among intelligent, firmly rooted beings like ourselves, matters are of course on a less crude and direct plane. What among lesser creatures is a question of tactics belongs, for us, to the realm of strategy." Pater's tone grew confiding. "Now, Junior, once you're settled, you'll realize the importance of being easy in your mind about your offspring's parentage. Remember, a niche in brine saves trying. Nothing like choosing your location well in the first place. Study the currents around your prospective site—particularly their direction and force at such crucial times as flood-tide. Try to make sure you and your future mate won't be too close down-current from anybody else's site, since in a case like that accidents can happen. You understand, Junior?"

"Uh-huh," acknowledged Junior. "That's what the fellows mean when they say don't let anybody get the drop on you."

"Well," said Pater flatly.

"But it all seems sort of silly," said Junior stubbornly. "*I'd* rather just keep moving around and not have to do all that figuring. And the ocean's full of things I haven't seen yet. I don't *want* to grow down!"

Mater paled with shock. Pater gave his spawn a scalding, scandalized look. "You'll learn! You can't beat Biology," he said thickly, creditably keeping his voice down. "Junior, you may go!"

Junior bobbled off, and Pater admonished Mater sternly: "We

must have patience, my dear! All children pass through these larval stages . . ."

"Yes, dear," sighed Mater.

At long last, Junior seemed to have resigned himself to making the best of it.

With considerable exertions, hampered by his increasing bottom-heaviness, he was fetching loads of stones, seaweed and other debris to a spot downslope, and there laboring over what promised to be a fairly ambitious cairn. Judging by what they could see of it, his homesite might even prove a credit to the colony (thus Mater mused) and attract a mate who would be a good catch (so went Pater's thoughts).

Junior was still to be seen at times along the reef in company with his free-swimming friends among the other polyps, at some of whom his parents had always looked askance, fearing they were by no means well-bred. In fact, there was strong suspicion that some of them—waifs from the disreputable shallows district in the hazardous reaches just below the tide-mark—had never been bred at all, but were products of budding, a practice frowned on in polite society.

However, Junior's appearance and rate of locomotion made it clear he would soon be done with juvenile follies. As Pater repeated with satisfaction, you can't beat Biology; as one becomes more and more bottle-shaped the romantic illusions of youth must inevitably perish.

"I always knew there was sound stuff in the youngster," declared Pater expansively.

"At least he won't be able to go around with those ragamuffins much longer," breathed Mater thankfully.

"What does the young fool think he's doing, fiddling round with soapstone?" grumbled Pater, peering critically through the green to try to make out the details of Junior's building. "Doesn't he know it's apt to slip its place in a year or two?"

"Look, dear," hissed Mater acidly, "isn't that the little polyp who was so rude once? . . . I wish she wouldn't keep watching Junior like that. Our northwest neighbor heard *positively* that she's the child of an only parent!"

"Never mind," Pater turned to reassure her. "Once Junior is properly rooted, his self-respect will cause him to keep riffraff at a distance. It's a matter of psychology, my dear; the vertical position makes all the difference in one's thinking."

The great day arrived.

Laboriously Junior put a few finishing touches to his construction

—which, so far as could be seen from a distance, had turned out decent-looking enough, though it was rather questionably original in design, lower and flatter than was customary.

With one more look at his handiwork, Junior turned bottom-end-down and sank wearily onto the finished site. After a minute, he paddled experimentally, but flailing tentacles failed to lift him—he was already rooted, and growing more solidly so by the moment.

The younger polyps peered from the hollows of the reef in round-eyed awe touched with fear.

"Congratulations!" cried the neighbors. Pater and Mater bowed this way and that in acknowledgment. Mater waved a condescending tentacle to the three maiden aunts.

"I told you so!" said Pater triumphantly.

"Yes, dear," said Mater meekly.

Suddenly there were outcries of alarm from the dwellers down-reef. A wave of dismay swept audibly through all the nearer part of the colony. Pater and Mater looked around and froze.

Junior had begun paddling again, but this time in a most peculiar manner—with a rotary twist and a sidewise scoop which looked awkward, but which he performed so deftly that he must have practiced it. Fixed upright as he was now on the platform he had built, he looked for all the world as if he were trying to swim sidewise.

"He's gone mad!" squeaked Mater, grasping at the obvious straw.

"I—" gulped Pater, "I'm afraid not."

At least, they saw, there was method in Junior's actions. He went on paddling in the same fashion—and now he, and his platform with him, were farther away than they had been, and growing more remote all the time.

Parts of the homesite that was not a homesite revolved in some way incomprehensible to eyes that had never seen the like. And the whole affair trundled along, rocking at bumps in the sandy bottom, and squeaking painfully; nevertheless, it moved.

The polyps watching from the reef swam out and frolicked after Junior, watching his contrivance go and chattering questions, while their parents bawled at them to keep away from that.

The three maiden aunts shrieked faintly and swooned in one another's tentacles. The colony was shaken as it had not been since the tidal wave.

"COME BACK!" thundered Pater. "You CAN'T do that!"

"*Come back!*" shrilled Mater. "You can't do *that!*"

"Come back!" gabbled the neighbors. "You can't *do* that!"

But Junior was past listening to reason. Junior was on wheels.

Further Reading   Robert Abernathy

Stories

"The Canal Builders." *Astounding Science Fiction*, January 1945.
"Grandma's Lie Soap." *Fantastic Universe*, February 1956. (*SF: 1957, The Year's Greatest Science Fiction and Fantasy*, ed. Judith Merril.)
"Heirs Apparent." *The Magazine of Fantasy and Science Fiction*, June 1954. (*Best from Fantasy and Science Fiction: 4*, ed. Anthony Boucher and J. Francis McComas.)
"Peril of the Blue World." *Planet Stories*, 1942. (*Flight into Space*, ed. Donald Wollheim.)
"Pyramid." *Astounding Science Fiction*, July 1954. (*The Astounding-Analog Reader, Vol. II*, ed. Harry Harrison and Brian W. Aldiss.)
"Single Combat." *The Magazine of Fantasy and Science Fiction*, January 1955. (*Cities of Wonder*, ed. Damon Knight.)

"Laugh Along with Franz," which appeared in the December 1965 *Galaxy* when Kagan was in his early twenties and just out of Columbia University, is an amazingly prognosticative piece for the time and, in my opinion, foreshadowed not only the mood but the causes of the great student outbreaks (at Columbia and elsewhere) toward the end of the decade. (Of course, the story was written after the 1964 Berkeley Free Speech convulsions and about the time the Vietnam teach-in movement was beginning on the campuses; part of the story is indeed amazingly visionary but another part is simply good documentary, which is as much of a definition of socially oriented science fiction as anything else.) For reasons never clear to me, the story—which was a lead novelette, Kagan's first contribution to *Galaxy,* and prominently billed by the then editor of the magazine, Fred Pohl—was never reprinted. For reasons slightly more clear to me, it was Kagan's last short story for ten years and, as of this writing, his next-to-last story altogether. (He had a piece in a 1975 anthology of originals edited by George Zebrowski.)

Kagan's *first* story, "The Mathenauts," published in *Worlds of If* in 1964, appeared in Judith Merril's best-of-the-year anthology, and he was recognized by a small coterie as being perhaps the most promising writer to come into science fiction in the small lacuna between the class of 1962 (Spinrad, Disch, Zelazny) and the class of 1966 (Dozois, Wolfe, Tiptree, myself). He did not persist, however, and for that reason is almost unknown in the field today; if "Laugh Along with Franz" had been followed by a career like Roger Zelazny's it might have been as well known as, say, "A Rose for Ecclesiastes." Still, as tales of injustice in science fiction go, this is not one of the greats and the point is that genre science fiction received this story as the literary markets of the time probably would not. (Kagan wrote a literary novel that was an essential expansion of the story; it was shown to many literary publishers in the late sixties and never sold.)

Kagan pointed out to me when we spoke after a twelve-year hiatus recently that he is only in his mid-thirties and not finished by a long shot; I vehemently agree and suspect that he will be heard from again. That he chose to stay on the edges of science fiction and kept his ambitions deliberately in check might have been to spare himself much in a present that he could expend in the future.

Kagan, writing in the authorly third person, enclosed the following afterword:

"Since writing this story, Mr. Kagan has gone on to take an M.F.A. and teach courses in film at several colleges. After a series of production jobs, he is writer-producer of "The Science Report," a monthly half-hour TV show seen by about 50 million people over 600 TV stations in 100 foreign countries. He has also written two books of film criticism (*The War Film, Cinema of Stanley Kubrick*) and is completing his Ph.D. at Columbia University. Mr. Kagan still follows the sf field, and hopes to do more fiction in the future."

B.N.M.

Laugh Along with Franz

by NORMAN KAGAN

Alienated Vote: "I cannot vote for any candidate or issue. None of them seem to have anything to do with the real problems of our nation and my life. I think there is something wrong with our society which requires a more fundamental change."—the so-called "Kafka Ballot"
from the voting machines
U. S. of A.
circa 1976 and after.

I

His Tuesday had worked out free, so Zirkle chose to serve the machines. The mechanisms that had made most men superfluous and egged the rest on towards madness still required a few masters. The operator's saddle of N.Y.M.'s device paid ten dollars an hour, he'd have been a fool to turn it down. Though it was a pittance beside the machine's wage: twenty dollars a moment. Phantom money; the pay for a thousand unemployed, unemployable souls in the nation's Emotionally Disturbed Areas.

Barbara stirred and mumbled beside him; he kissed her small happy face and pushed back the long brown hair. She was wonderful in his bed; he looked at her long pale legs for a moment and sighed, then covered them and began to dress. He tried to think about the machine because to think about her would make him want to look at her and then touch her and hold her and then he'd never get out of here. What a wonderful body! Bodies, bodies, ripe young flesh, ah! . . .

Better bodies than minds and words; she was so quiet to strangers, silent but provocative in pullover and jeans with her long brown hair down behind her. But what she thought. How to get along with her? She was hypersensitive, and she *knew* she was hypersensitive and adequate; they'd gone to bed on their *second date* to show he cared for her and why are you such a cold son-of-a-bitch, cold, cold, I know but aren't our bodies fun, our bodies, don't think just bodies . . .

"Michael?" she smiled up at him.

"I've got to go or I'll be late, Barbara. You know."

"Can't you stay. I'll go out and get us breakfast."

"It's forty bucks, kid—listen, I'll call you at twelve."

"It was my fault about last night, Michael," she said faintly, then huskily, "I mean it. I—"

"Okay, fine, but I really gotta go."

"All right, Michael." She smiled lazily and pulled the covers up to her chin again half pout, half invitation. Oh, boy, down those stairs marry her next week but let's get going.

Downstairs it was a cold-bright November morning. Zirkle put his fists in his windbreaker against the brisk wind. The Village at this hour was shabby but sane; brick and stone and concrete buildings that were human sized, but the behemoths that hung their dead tons above everyone's heads uptown. Zirkle hardly saw them; self-obsessed, or Barbara-obsessed. He never noticed the dead handbills in the street, or sign that read "Election Day hours; 8:00–1:00" beside the large brass plate: "Computer Facility: Courant Institute of Mathematical Sciences; New York Multiversity." With some Chock full o' Nuts coffee warming his middle he took the elevator up to the machine room.

The brightly lit room was nearly silent. In the middle, of course, was the big I.C.M. aleph-sub-ninety; a dozen different units connected beneath the floor. At one side a printer stuttered, tape drives raced and paused, shivering in their vacuum columns. Here was the control board, studs and buttons and little GO-boards of lights that blinked and twinkled patterns. Seated at it was the operator; an expressionless man named Kernan. A few other technicians, shirt sleeved, unshaven, moved silently about. The machine ran around the clock except for maintenance time; while Boeing or G.M. didn't have a problem, Los Alamos could always pay for some time. On the lintel of the console was the brief legend; I.C.M. is here to stay.

Zirkle asked the young man what was running, to which Kernan said briskly: "Randall's replacing me—you're programming for some kind of social thing."

Zirkle shrugged; five dollars an hour was five dollars an hour. He walked out of the Machine Room past the Negress receptionist and down the corridor to the Programmer's Library.

The pine-paneled, linoleum-floored, air-conditioned halls of an I.C.M. installation always made him think of a submarine, or a missile-launching site or shelter. Always the funny tension, as if the ghosts of the millions that automation had replaced inhabited the machines, as if the mechanisms had somehow taken the spirit along with the function of those useless people. The Emotionally Disturbed Areas were where zombies dwelt. *I.C.M. is here to stay.*

Zirkle thought about Barbara. There she was in front of him; beautiful and why shouldn't she be? And the old logic—you think you can keep from getting involved. It's just more words and mucous membranes, but all of a sudden she only talks to you and you ask why not, why not? She's so much fun and you never felt so good before, to be *involved* in something . . .

Half a dozen men working in the bright room. Zirkle spotted Randall and Dr. Progoff, the Center's boss, a big, bald man who'd taken his Ph.D. in pure number theory then switched into computers and applied math. He was talking with a thin, well-dressed faculty member. "—sampling is all finished, but how about the machine time? It won't make much sense to finish the run after the real results are in?"

And then Zirkle remembered. But it was too late to register, of course, and anyway it didn't matter, they were all the same, if he voted he'd—

"Vote for Franz!" the faculty man said angrily. "What do you expect, you've alienated them from everything, even themselves? That's why I don't want you to—"

"What difference does it make?" grumbled the mathematician. "The other results have been out for days, and there'll be machines running right along with the balloting."

"I'm talking about self-fulfilling prophecy—the people silly enough to want to have voted for the winner, or uncaring enough to want to have voted for the winner, or uncaring enough to let a machine do their—oh, never mind, never mind, I'll get the decks and the University authorization."

"Fine," said Progoff. "Oh, Zirkle, please go along with Professor Lerner here. When you come back I want you to debug his program and we'll start it at, oh, say eleven, when that neutrino detection study thing is finished."

Zirkle nodded, and followed the thin man, who seemed to be a sociologist, out to the elevators. They got on in silence, but as the car started down the older man said irritably: "Excuse me, but are you planning to vote today? Please don't lie to me."

"Oh, oh, yes sir."

"Well, it looks like you and I will be about the only ones that do."

Outside the day was warming up. Students in bright jackets or coats moved toward the buildings. In the park and the shabby streets around the university, however, the inevitable idlers had begun to cluster. A newsstand caught his eye; AUTOMATION RIOTS, SUBWAY VIOLENCE, HARLEM SIMMERS. But New York headlines had read like that as far back as he could remember.

"Idiots!" grumbled Lerner. "But how can you blame them? I don't know what can be done, that's sure. There's nothing for 'em to do."

Zirkle thought about Barbara, but asked, "I've been wondering about casting a Kafka ballot, sir. It's not that I feel alienated from society, it's just that there doesn't seem to be much choice between—" (And I'd say: will you marry me? And Barbara would say: no, but I admire your taste.)

"No, no, never do that," cried Lerner, as they crossed the street. "That's the danger of the Kafka ballot—it short circuits thinking, people feel rotten so they push the 'Franz' toggle. Originally, the idea was to find out who just didn't care to vote, and who was truly disenchanted. It backfired—it turned out everyone is alienated and unhappy. And our system is now so complex, so limited by the international situation, so geared to accepting technical change, that we can't make fundamental changes in it, so—more alienation, unhappiness, and four years later more Kafka ballots."

The classes changed, and for a few moments they were pushed back along the corridor by a flood of students. The two managed to enter an elevator. As the door closed Zirkle murmured, "I see." (Keep her in my room if I can. Physical contact, dependence important. Story of the guy that sent his girl a love letter every day. So she married the mailman.)

The doors opened, and Lerner swung out and down the corridor. A bearded student in a lab smock got on, whistling: "Girls Are Like Pianos—Upright or Grand!" the newest song of teen favorite Beatle X, the Ghana Wailer.

Lerner unlocked the door to his office. "Less than fifty million voted in the last election. What happens if Franz gets a majority? What then? We'll have a complete collapse of government morale. How could Congress act, how could the President do anything, when everyone knows nobody really wants them at all?"

Zirkle shrugged, it was their tough luck. He never trusted those dirty politicians. Maybe they could have a robot president?

"You know, there's one thing that might apply. It's in the U. S.

Constitution, but it's never been used." The two stood waiting for the elevator, burdened down with tapes and card decks. "If two thirds of the State Legislatures ask for a Constitutional Convention, Congress has to call it. What the C.C. recommends is constitutional if three quarters of the state legislatures approve. If things get bad enough, it might happen. They could abolish the Presidency, cancel the Civil Rights Laws, put controls on I.C.M. and scientists and engineers. My God! They could—"

Lerner was silent until they were back in the Computer Facility. "It's possible, it's possible," he murmured. "The statistics on crime, drug addiction, mental illness. They could—" he gestured out at the park, where the crowd of idlers mixed with the guitar-and-thongs set. "Look at 'em, punch-drunk, slap-happy already, surrendered—they—I might be one of the last sociologists. There won't be any society left to study."

"Ready to get started?" rumbled Progoff behind him. The big mathematician sported a button with the legend: I.C.M. is here to stay. Lerner seemed to take heart when he saw it.

"Surely, Dr. Progoff. I'd like to speak with you for a moment or two first, however." The two of them went into Progoff's office.

"Mike?" said Randall, looking up from his flow charts and systems manuals. "Come on, let's take a break. I could use it."

"All right," said the shaggy young man. He was feeling odd; he wanted his routine, his console and card decks; Barbara kept mixing into his thoughts. Professional life should be an algorithm.

The two young men went to the Programmer's Lounge for coffee. Zirkle liked Randall, a skinny intense young man whose only vice was getting his friends free gifts from the Book-of-the-Month, Record-of-the-Month, Fruit-of-the-Month Clubs, etc., by using his professional knowledge to alter their I.C.M. business reply cards.

Randall was just asking Zirkle to his friend's apartment to watch the election returns when the lounge's ceiling speakers began to rumble.

II

"This is your International Computing Machines science reporter with our special Election Day news summary, Science in the News! Stand by . . . Flash! N.A.S.A. scientists announce the Jove 67, the sixty-seventh attempt to put a robot probe around the planet Jupiter, is completely successful. The machine is circling the giant planet in an almost perfect orbit. Werner and his rocket team are jubilant. Unfortunately, the Jove 67's telemetry system failed at power track, so we are receiving no data at all. But, as Werner has pointed out, the instruments are going round and round perfectly! N.A.S.A. will ask six billion dollars for twenty more probes for Project Jove . . . Congratulations are in order for the two hundred Eastinghouse Science Talent Hunt Winners! The Bronx High School of Science has the most winners, as usual, including the first five: Ephraim Goldstein, Dennis Steinross, David Einsteinmann, Keither Auerstein, and Steiner Steinstein! Steiner Steinstein, the number one man, has won a five-year Accelerated Ph.D. Scholarship to Cal Tech. Steiner's winning entry was a study of the sex life of pigeons.

"Grinning, the pimply, four-eyed adolescent's acknowledgment was, 'To Satan with Playmates! Give me pigeons every time!' . . . Tragedy in an Emotionally Disturbed Area! Tragedy struck this week at the I.C.M.'s 'Cavalcade of Wisdom,' a traveling exhibit touring America's Emotionally Disturbed Areas. According to the official report: The information booklets *Fortran is Fun* and *Your Exciting Future as an I.C.M. Programmer* were distributed to the crowd. The *Sing-a-Song-of-Sets* and *Binary Math Bonanza* exhibitions were also deployed, and an announcer exhorted the crowds to join I.C.M. He was answered with boos, cat-calls and cries of 'Give us real work!' 'Programming what? How to blow us all up?' and 'Build your own Doomsday machines, Dr. Strangelove!' Several rocks were thrown at the exhibit. A fusillade of rotten food and other materials knocked down the announcer, whereupon the security guards opened up on the dirty non-incorporates with tear gas and machine guns. Casualties were heavy—uh, ahem, I.C.M. has decided to discontinue the 'Cavalcades of Wisdom,' at least temporarily. 'I can't understand why young people are reluctant to work toward progress, freedom and happiness by doing what I say as I.C.M. workers—' said corporate executive Allen Rosenberg. 'Programming as the ideal occupation for modern man!' . . .

"Success Story! N.A.S.A. scientists have just finished their Progress Report to Congress on their Project Lucifer. The five hundred billion dollar Moon Station, Project Lucifer, is the outgrowth of the 50 billion dollar Project Cerberus, the temporary moon station, which came out of the five billion dollar Project Apollo moon landing. Jusifying Apollo, Cerberus and Lucifer, which do not seem to have yielded much of practical value, N.A.S.A. chief David Sarlin cried hotly, 'You must believe in pure research—all sorts of wonderful applications come from it in many different areas! Why, we might find a new cheap food supply, or a way to help our emotionally disturbed citizens.' Congressman Steadman asked why the 500 billion should not have been devoted to food research or Disturbed Area Aid, since this might result in great advances for Dr. Sarlin's vaunted space science. Dr. Sarlin did not reply to this, but instead asked for more money for Project Coprophile, an attempt to make the moon habitable. 'I don't care for the direction we're taking,' despaired Congressman Steadman . . . Automated president? A highly placed authority at Michigan Multiversity revealed today that—"

"Automated president? Then I.C.M. will *really* be here to stay," said Randall. "What're you doing after lunch?"

"Huh? Working this afternoon, I suppose." Zirkle was uneasy, then recalled he had to phone Barbara.

Randall explained about the special election hours, and Zirkle rejoiced; he'd spend the afternoon with his girl.

"Voting?"

"No, I didn't even register, I—maybe we'd better get back."

Their timing was good, a few minutes later Zirkle plunged into the debugging of Lerner's prediction program. The actual sequence was fairly short. Zirkle couldn't find any errors, though he lengthened it slightly to save some execution time. This was the work he loved; to seize a field of logical elements and processes; to order and pattern them; then refine that pattern to the limits of logic and the machine. He was a good programmer, but Barbara wasn't home when he called.

Outside, in the pale warmth of a November noon, the streets and park were filled with business people, students, and the inevitable unemployed. Sometimes in the shiny corridors you forgot that New York City was itself one of the largest of the E.D.A.s. Lerner's introduction to the predictor program (to give the debugger some common sense) had noted there was precious little healthy, prosperous ground in the United States; madness or poverty; Manhattan or Appalachia; emotionally disturbed or economically depressed; the statistical chart looked like a warped, engorged and withered chessboard instead of a map; as if the logic of the plenty machine had been sickened and grown cancerous when applied to men.

He stood still, wondering what to do, while the crowds surged around him. Their talk was no comfort.

"I mean, the great thing about it is when you're smoking you have this great feeling, like you're really great, and when you stop smoking it *doesn't go away*. You still feel terrific—"

"So the guidance guy said; 'I kid you not. I.C.M. is here to stay, a college degree is the least, and I'll clue you in, there won't *be* any jobs for less than an M.A., so you'd have to be really crazy to ask for a leave of—"

"Sure, her and her roommate, really emancipated women. If she dares bring a boy in the apartment the other one slams the door, locks it, and gets on the phone to her father. Same thing the other way—"

"Nothing to do so, we drove around in his Cadillac and asked these women for directions, then grabbed their purses. Feigenbaum wanted to beat this little old lady to death with a baseball bat, but I said—"

"Listen, Louise, let's face it, we're both seniors. It's time to stop going out with Negroes and start going out with pre-dentistry majors."

Maybe she went out for something, or to go to the john. Zirkle made his way through the weary crowd across the Park.

"David, I don't care, I want to spend my whole life with you and I know we can work hard enough to have a healthy marriage and bring up some healthy, un-neurotic children."

He tried to stay with the students; they were twitchy but cheerful. Nevertheless he found it hard to avoid the others; business people fearing for their jobs; young men who'd never held any, baffled behind beards and guitars; worst of all those who could not comprehend any other condition; the empty milling smiling ones, many of them from minority groups, some of whom had been on the dole for three generations.

At least here they had something to do; sing and laugh and preen themselves on grass or concrete; jeans and pullovers, flannel shirts and short shorts; a place to go, a system of behavior, people to talk to. Only on Lerner's charts was this place labeled "Failure Pool," but how many people could or cared to compete with steel and spacistors? For this was The Great New Fact of his world: most people were superfluous.

Zirkle shrugged; Barbara was enough concern. And yet the problem held him. Down streets thick with browsers and the bored he sought faces touched with courage or a private cheer, but there was nothing, or perhaps he'd grown unused to gauging other men; the machine mages had little use for such skills.

And Barbara wasn't there. His people success, his all-absorbing triumph outside numbers, only now he was beginning to see how important; skirts, sweaters, jeans, books and prints and Beatle X records and that was all. The room hovered silently around him, suddenly smaller; the big old drafting table they used for studying, the couch that folded out into a double bed, a bunch of snapshots from this summer taped to the wall.

He could go running about now; the Co-Op, bookstore, library, three sorts of friends becoming one. But the relationship was built on trust and self-trust; pride and confidence shored it up. To go racing around would cancel it out, and besides, well, she knew what was doing, if she didn't want any more of—but he didn't carry that

through, just left a note and was down the stairs, out in the street
where people tumbled past, his feet at random this Election Day,
thinking about Kafka.

III

He had read *The Castle* and *The Trial* and remembered them. He
recalled the Land Surveyor, K., in *The Castle* hopelessly trying to
reach the Castle authorities, never even really certain they existed.
The Trial's poor hero was in an even worse state; ignorant of the
reasons for his arrest; his captors refusing to explain or name their
superiors, he spent the rest of his life in court, fighting a charge he
never even knew. Kafka's world was a hideous, desolate, incomprehensible place.

Yet Michael could see how Kafka might mean a great deal to
some people; sometimes he found himself baffled and enraged by organizations like N.Y.M., or occasionally depressed by his work to
the point where it all seemed meaningless. Alienation the feeling was
called. Modern life was too big and complex; people couldn't seem
to feel in touch with anything, they had no place. With automation's
plenty machines, even the goal, duty and purpose of work was gone.
So people felt helpless, small, and afraid. He wished he could think
about these things another way, but the jargon of sociology was all
he knew; Barbara and his courses required nearly all his time. This
was perhaps his first walk outside the campus this year.

On impulse, he stepped from the sunlit street into a bar. After his
eyes had adjusted to the dark narrow crowded room, he began to
casually study the other patrons. In a few minutes he had them
divided up.

The first sort might be nervous, but they had energy and vigor.
They stood up close to the bar and talked or peered at the overhead
screen, or sat at tables in the light. The others stood alone or hung
back in the gloom, like the commoners of some occupied land; sul-
len and sly, waiting for their chance.

He supposed the split was between those with some goal or satisfactory existence, and those on E.D.A. Relief or close to it.

He turned his attention to the screen.

"Let's turn America into a Fairyland!" a smiling young man with
long blond hair and pouting lips cried, "Vote the Gay Ticket!

"Yes indeed, friends, we're not apologizing anymore. No indeed.
In fact, we sincerely believe ours is not just an acceptable way of
life, but rather a desirable, noble, and even preferable sort of existence. For one thing," he chided, "we've got the perfect solution to
the population explosion!"

A dim cheer, interspaced with laughter and a few cat-calls, went up in the bar.

"So remember, vote the Gay Ticket, and life will be one long camping trip. Elect our candidate—he's a homosex-JEWEL!"

Lerner's introduction had mentioned the Homosexual Party. It was to be expected. In a fragmented world where morality had disappeared, where loyalties were hard to come by and harder to hold to, where work was without purpose and impossible to find anyway, people were desperate for any sort of meaning. Even the schizophrenics, desperate to belong, had their own society with its clever "Com'on Behind the Wall of Glass."

He raised his Schiltz and swallowed it slowly. Somebody put some money in the jukebox, and the narrow old room shook to Beatle X's "Girls Are Like Pianos—Upright or Grand." Zirkle finished his drink and set it down. The atmosphere of the bar was thick, depressing. He went out into the afternoon.

Ten blocks further north the monoliths towered all above him; frozen explosions of brass and steel and glass. Empty this afternoon, hanging their dead tons above the street. Here were the Administrations, the Channels, the Records, The Home Offices of automated America. Away and beyond the city were the next step; the plenty machines, the behemoths—steel clean—where people used to be. And what were those people going to do now, those and these too, for paperpushing and cardpunching don't really mean much. Let's face it, friends, I.C.M. is most definitely here to stay.

And here was a pebble in his shoe, and he couldn't fit it into an analogy in his train of thought, it hurt a little so Michael stood on one foot and let it drop out, pygmied by the giants whose sides bore the invisible motto; I.C.M. is here to stay.

He hunkered up his jacket and walked on into the wind. He was suddenly self-conscious about thinking about the Big Problems for so long. Modern man; he philosophizes but doesn't bother to vote.

He knew when he began to think clever that he was running out of brain. Where do you go from here? Most people were now really superfluous, useless really, adrift in some enormous organization. The world was a *Castle,* life was a *Trial,* and why can't you get any further? Why can't you think up something OR-I-GIN-AL, stupid! He walked faster and faster.

So naturally they would get rid of the government. Franz Kafka for President! Why not? The plenty machines satisfied people's material needs, and society was too fragmented, people too worldly wise to accept any ideas or enthusiasms. Consider them now, the "goals" of modern man:

—*space exploration*—but outside his science-fiction friends, he knew few enthusiasts. It was another monolith, too big to like; the heroes too well molded.

—*impoverished nations*—real, true, but their woes seemed too big and too old for single people to enjoy abating. And that problem was finite, and you must ask—is our way any happier?

—*scientific research*—an endless frontier, perhaps, but why bother after the ten thousandth new element, the gigatillionth law?

—*improve our world*—so everyone lives forever, so people have as many children as possible? Everyone can wander around like this, wondering what for?

He snapped back to the world and ran pell-mell across the street to a Rexall to try to call Barbara at the apartment. No answer. Her home out in Staten Island. No answer. Her crazy friend Sandra. No answer, no answer, no answer, and he pounded his fist softly against the wooden wall of the phone booth below the carved exchange:

Nietzschie: God is dead.
God: Nietzschie is dead. You're next!

Zirkle came out of the telephone booth slowly, bought a Milky Way, and started back downtown. He tried to pick up his thoughts once again but it was difficult. He hadn't thought out this way before, and in a few moments realized why: Barbara. Before her he'd gotten most of his satisfaction and self-worth from his skill with the machines. To wonder if making sure I.C.M. is here to stay was enough meaning for a life was dangerous for someone with only that for a purpose. Barbara had set him free, or almost so. Proof: the impulse to call her.

She was so wonderful. He loved to spend his time with her. And sex, yes, sex, sex, sex but also it was to do things; girls were really so nice, to kid around or study across from her or eat lunch and then go up to sport in their room. And she liked him, loved him. Oh, yes, Barbara had set him free.

Oh, yeah, where was he? Destroying the aspirations of his society. All was meaningless, looked at in that funny harsh way, scientific research was, by order from *The Castle,* becoming a programmer to qualify as a Court Clerk in *The Trial.* I.C.M. is here to stay, was a grunt, a belch, as meaningful as their old slogan *Think.* Think about what? Are we better off since I.C.M. is here to stay? So what?

Sometimes, when he was a little kid, he thought the adults were working on some sort of grand project, some wondrous task, which he would take a part in when he grew up. Now he was grown up, but there was no project. So what to do now?

He walked over two blocks and down into the subway. Behind

him, the enormous buildings began to cast the enormous shadows over the avenues. The wind grew colder and fiercer, and raced up and down and around the giants.

IV

Randall's room was a big loft in an old warehouse. Zirkle had already met his roommates: Bennet, the quiet cheerful English major; Oler, the crazy physics major who had to wait till the last term to learn he hated physics, and now taught high-school science to avoid the draft. But Oler was out this evening, as was Barbara when he'd visited their apartment.

The room was typically collegiate, a big raw underheated dim dorm; old wooden desks and chairs, piles of clothing, piles of food, piles of books, piles of lab equipment. Cots. An exotic liquor bottle collection. Chart of the decomposition of a manifold. Swank's "Flip Out Girl of the month." Battered old T.V. that Randall was tuning.

"Get That Degree!" said the device.

"Still too early for the returns," said Randall, his voice muffled from where his slim form was jack-knifed over the set.

"Turn back to that," said Bennet. The English major sat on the arm of one of their big old armchairs, swinging his leg back and forth.

"Fine," said Michael. I.C.M. sponsored that show, and he wanted a check on what he'd been thinking about so much.

The television set roared: "Good evening, ladies and gentlemen, and welcome to *Get That Degree!*—the television show that proves each week that every American without a college degree is a—

"A WORTHLESS, NO GOOD BUM!

"Yes, friends, *Get That Degree!* is brought to you by the International Computing Machines Corporation, which also sponsors those other survey-topping (on our own surveys, that is!), those other survey-topping shows: *This Will Be Your Life!* and *This IS the You That Is!*

"Worried about getting into college, folks? You should be scared stiff! With the population explosion, it is getting tougher and tougher! Not enough teachers, not enough classrooms, especially at those *highly rated prestige schools!!!* Remember that! Why, without a college degree, without those four years and that sheepskin, you won't be able to go to graduate or professional school! And without that, you're *dead!* No high paying job at a giant corporation! No professional status! Roaming the streets like some kind of a bum! Without that college admission, you might even be drafted, and have some Commie blow your brains out! Obviously you've got to be admitted!" he paused, staring at his audience.

"Later on in the show, we'll tell you how to make sure of that thick admissions letter. No guarantees, of course, but a respectable probability. In case you miss it, be sure to write us at Princeton, New Jersey, our *famous* address. Don't forget our famous motto when planning tomorrow. Remember, 'I.C.M. is here to stay!'

"And now, let's Get That Degree! On our show tonight are four famous people you've probably all heard about, or will hear about soon. And here they all are—"

The cameras dropped away from the announcer, focusing on the stage behind him. Two young men and two older ones waited quietly.

"Let's start with our young people," said the excited announcer. "Here, tonight, representing higher education, is the first prize winner in the Eastinghouse Science Talent Hunt—winning an Accelerated Ph.D. Scholarship to Cal Tech, a graduate of the New York City Bronx High School of Science, here he is folks—Steiner Steinstein!"

The wizened, bespectacled young man smiled insolently at the audience. "Nice of you to give me all this money," he said coldly.

"Now let's meet the stupid uneducated bum! Leaving school at twelve, this young man did nothing but bum from town to town, take odd jobs, have as many girl friends and as much fun as he could, and learn to play the guitar. Three months ago, he won nationwide acclaim for his fantastic song hit; 'Girls Are Like Pianos—Upright or Grand!' Here he is, folks—Beatle X!"

The cameras swung to the singer, a rough-looking youngster with his big guitar slung on his back. He smiled.

"Finally, representing authority and tradition, with us are two members of the faculty of New York Multiversity. First, Dr. Progoff of N.Y.M.'s Computing Facility. Dr. Progoff?"

Zirkle's boss stared at the cameras. "I want to wish both boys the best of luck, but I have special feelings for young Steiner Steinstein. America needs people like you, Steiner. The masses of our population need skilled, university-trained leaders like you." Progoff paused. "The more science, the better, of course—I.C.M. is here to stay, ha-ha, so life gets so complicated we've got to have experts, guys like you to boss the bums—uh, ungifted 85% around. My hat's off to you, Steiner Steinstein!"

"Next," cried the announcer, "Lawrence Lerner, Assistant Professor of Sociology at N.Y.M. Dr. Lerner was one member of the committee that proposed the 'alienated vote,' and an expert on our nation's unfortunate Emotionally Disturbed Areas. Dr. Lerner?"

The cameras swung to Lerner's strained features. He spoke slowly.

"I'd rather not speak, if you'll excuse me. It's been a pleasure to be here on your program but I've been involved in the election; in fact I've a prediction program running down at the school, and I'm really exhausted."

"We all understand," said the announcer slowly. Then he paused dramatically.

"Okay, now let's all play *Get That Degree!*"

The cameras panned in on the announcer's sweating, wild-eyed face. "For those of you who've never seen our show, let me explain that *Get That Degree!* is the finest in modern scientific entertainment, utilizing electronic genius and middle-class morality to discover the wonderful personal potentials of our young folks. Yes, it's the enormous capacities of our youth for spontaneity, individuality, creativity and originality that interest us here at I.C.M."

His voice became a monotone. "Therefore, the two contestants have spent the last three weeks filling out ten thousand multiple-choice and short-answer questions, blacking in those little I.C.M. spaces on a dozen tests—personality, aptitude, achievement, creativity, sociability—everything! The results were fed into one of our I.C.M. aleph-sub-nineties, and now, tonight, the game will be resolved. Okay, programmers, let's see the results! Steiner Steinstein first!"

A low hum mounted in pitch and rhythm, lights flashed on a giant mock computer, a siren screamed. Finally the music ceased, and behind the two young men a tremendous crystal panel glowed into life. The cameras closed on it. It read:

I.C.M. Profile:
Steiner Steinstein

This brilliant young man has a brilliant future ahead in Modern Science. You will make many brilliant discoveries, Steiner. Perhaps you will even improve *me*. Because you are brilliant and make brilliant discoveries, you will be happy. You will meet and marry a brilliant girl, and you will have many brilliant children. Love and a brilliant life will be yours. Everyone will love you, you brilliant scientist you. It's been a brilliant pleasure to have you as a card deck, running rough through my insides. I like your brilliant record, son.

"Isn't that terrific folks! Isn't he brilliant!

"Now let's see how our bum made out. Programmers, let's have the profile on our other contestant, Beatle X!"

I.C.M. Profile: Beatle X (?)

I don't understand what this is about. Is this a person? Oh, well, things look black for this youngster. Though he's had a brief, ephemeral success, I see failure and disaster and doom ahead. His I.Q. is less than 140. He can't program a computer or do research. Bad, bad, bad. All he cares about is making money and having fun. He will probably never have any friends. He will always be depressed. Gloom and doom. He can't solve differential equations. I pity him. He will die a long and painful death.

Notice: I.C.M. results only have a respectable probability and are not to be taken as the Word of God. Low scorers might consider a career in the U. S. Army, sometimes called "the stupid man's I.C.M." Or perhaps you are unsuited to an automated culture, and should move to another. Unfortunately, there *are* no others.

"Isn't that terrific, folks," the announcer cried out. "The I.C.M. computer has compared these two very different, unique young men, and discovered the winner and the loser. And the winner is—Mr., but not for long, Steiner Steinstein!"

There was an enormous burst of applause, and the orchestra played two full choruses of "My Son, the Scientist." Steiner bowed modestly in the flame of the spotlight.

"Congratulations, Steiner! And for your prize, I.C.M. is happy to award you a thousand-year post-doctoral fellowship at the Massachusetts Institute of Technology.

"But what about our bum, our loser, Beatle X? Yes, folks, what about the old Beatle?"

A purple spot turned the big shaggy youth's face into a death mask, his guitar into a monster's hump. He stood, shoulders slumped, in the somber cone of light, his baffled face staring at the announcer.

Suddenly, the spot turned blinding white, as if it had become a laser beamed to burn the low-scorer out of existence, like a moth in a torch.

"No folks, I.C.M. hasn't forgotten young X. For young Beatle X still has a chance to Get That Degree, even as you folks in the audience. And he will get it, our mass society needs trained tools and machines. So he'll do it, folks. *He'd damn well better!*" the announcer finished in a scream, his eyes bulging out.

He paused.

"Well, now," the man said cheerily, "before the Beatle tells us his decision, let's have a few words from his friends and relatives. Tell us, old folks, should young Beatle X Get That Degree?"

The lights dimmed down again. On a phosphorescent screen appeared an anonymous city of enormous size. The cameras flung themselves at it, closing in on a great weary apartment tower, filmed a little with smog and filth.

"This is your mother, Beatle," a thin voice quavered. "Please listen to me, dear. Go to their college if you possibly can. Please, do it for me! You made money, but who knows what will happen, who can tell? The only way to be safe is to obey and stay with the big corporations, they're too big to hurt you—I wasn't, I can't, I'm old and weak and tired, help me, do what they say—"

Another voice, gruff and bitter. "This is your old family doctor, Dr. McCaulley. You listen to I.C.M., they have the money and the power. Go to college, you need that degree, you can't get a job and the world doesn't care, you'll drop dead or go crazy like *that,* nothing matters—"

"This is your brother's friend Harold, Beatle. You remember me, don't you. I—I went crazy, there wasn't any work if you weren't a professor, all we could do was hang around and get government money and I wasn't worth anything, it just didn't seem to matter to anybody or me either, nothing to do and sad all the time, might as well—but I.C.M. helped me, Preg, really they did, a hundred thousand on endocrine treatments and I'm all right now, I'm fine and you don't want to go crazy, it's no fun and bad, do what they say, save yourself before—"

"Look at him, folks!" the Master of Ceremonies chortled. "I'll be surprised if he doesn't go for a Ph.D.!" And indeed the young singer was shaking, one shoulder twitching constantly as if to let fall some terrible burden. His guitar had dropped from his limp hand and rested at his feet.

Bennet, shaking with another emotion, strode to the television set and switched channels. More charts, counting boards, and calm-faced men, one of whom murmured; "The slowest election in thirty years, only two per cent of the returns in, but our computer says it looks like—"

Randall had grunted when Bennet had switched stations, but now he refocused his attention on the screen. The English major and Zirkle exchanged a slow look, but said nothing. Zirkle slumped wearily in his chair.

Another part of the same picture, Michael told himself. When things get big they get complicated, so you've got to have an elite of experts (like himself), with high, moral and good motivation. Also, the program crudely tried to counter the violent anti-intellectualism of the alienated, or at least blunt it. But as the pressure gets higher, the sell gets cruder, of course.

He glanced across at Bennet, who was still smiling oddly. "What's so funny?" asked Zirkle lightly.

"Nothing much. That program, in a way. They talk about the 'Kafka Ballot.' Well, *Get That Degree* is a Kafka joke. They ought to call it *Laugh Along with Franz.*"

Zirkle stared across at the other young man, but Bennet returned his gaze evenly and kept on smiling. He'd heard a lot of odd notions, but Kafka as a *comedian?* The writer of *The Castle* and *The Trial* and "Metamorphosis"? Oh, well, the City was an Emotionally Disturbed Area, and college students, English majors especially . . .

"Listen, I want to get some air," said Bennet, getting up. Zirkle nodded and followed him downstairs.

Outside the street was wide and empty, cold and clean and bright under the lamps this November night. The moon lay full halfway up the sky, dull orange. There was no wind, but Zirkle buttoned his jacket and both young men walked quickly, Bennet working harder to keep up with the husky, nerve-taunted math major. Zirkle kept his hand in his knife pocket, for New York City had become quite dangerous after dark. Some of his physics friends had built themselves laser guns in the labs.

"What did you mean about that program being a big Kafka joke?" Michael asked Bennet truculently.

Bennet was silent for a moment. "You haven't taken much lit, have you? It'd take a while to explain—"

"No," said Zirkle, a little tightly. "My major takes 42 points all by itself, and I've got a job and my girl—you met Barbara, didn't you?" He hesitated, ready to plunge off down a street toward home. But five minutes more? What had Bennet meant? "But anyhow I did read the two important books. Bleak, oppressive—how can you call Kafka funny?"

"I see," said Bennet. "You didn't read *Amerika,* did you? Ummm, and in a survey course they try to simplify everything. And after all, Kafka really did have a lot to say about the condition of alienation."

"So?"

"Okay, so now I want you to forget science for a few minutes. Just get away from that point of view and take a look around you!"

"Come on!"

Bennet looked at him sincerely. "To a philosopher, science as a way of looking at things, the I.C.M. approach, is really pretty limited. Consider some of the *basic* questions. Nobody knows why he's here on earth. Nobody knows why people are here, or if they're behaving in the 'right' way. Nobody knows, exept in a very vague way, what'll happen in the future—say a minute from now. You don't know what God is, or what he wants, or why the universe is here."

"That's philosophy—"

"Sure it is. And I think I've seen you with your girl enough to know you care at least a little about such questions—"

"Well . . ." Zirkle's tone was wary and weary in the street. He tried to see what was coming in Bennet's eyes, but that game was useless, as he'd learned a dozen years before.

"Well, what? What about those questions—and everyone knows about them, and thinks about them, don't kid yourself, smart guy.

"Well," Bennet continued sarcastically, then went on in a normal tone of voice, "Well, most people today say—so what. I get along all right, eat, drink, make love—that's enough for me. I'll leave stuff like that alone.

"Scientists, engineers, the guys at I.C.M., have a few small answers to the *important* questions, so naturally they think they have 'em all. And one way or another, they've fitted the modern world around those answers.

"In the last few years, lots of people haven't been satisfied with the first answer. They've tried to take up the second, but for most of 'em, the 'scientific world' is unbearable—students going nuts trying to become physicists, those that automation unemploys feeling worthless, the 'unintellectually gifted' getting frustrated. People who have chosen lives without pleasure or satisfaction—alienated people."

"Okay, take it easy on the lecture," Zirkle told the other young man, although he was becoming excited. Bennet didn't explain everything, but what he said made sense, more sense than—

"Now what Kafka did as a writer was to play games with those terrible fundamental questions I was talking about—what is life? Who is God?, and so on. The terrible guilt we all sometimes feel and can't explain is like the accused's crime in *The Trial*. The Land Surveyor in *The Castle* who can never reach his superiors or find out what they want—well, if you've ever worked in a large organization—"

"Still, I don't think he's so funny—"

"That's because you're thinking as the Land Surveyor, not as the author. Kafka jokes by fantastic exaggeration, like *The Trial* that goes on for a man's whole life."

"Still I don't see—"

"Did you ever read his "Investigations of a Dog"? It's all about this dog philosopher, trying to solve the Greatest Problem of Canine Philosophy: Will the food still come down if dogs don't keep water-

ing the earth? Only whenever he thinks he's beginning to get anywhere on the solution, this other dog from across the street comes to
visit him and gets him so excited he can't think afterwards about the
great problem for hours.

"You see, the dog hasn't a chance of solving the problem, it's an
impossible problem, because the dog hasn't the smallest notion of
what his real relationship to his superiors (man and the Universe)
really is. Kafka's laughing at us, smiling at our notions of what are
the big problems, what God is and what he wants, what are and
aren't distractions. It's the cast of 'Laugh Along with Franz.' Like
that silly show we just watched—as if a million more Steiner Stein-
steins could help each of us with the problems of our lives."

"Okay," said Michael. "Sure, sure, now I see, everyone so grimly
certain they have the answer—" He slackened the pace a little. The
streets were deserted, the moon and stars making them dimly lumi-
nous. Across the dark nation, in a hundred thousand voting booths,
Franz was roaring. "And the Kafka ballot—you think that's another
joke? If no one has faith in the government and everyone's depressed—"

"I really don't know," the English major confessed. "In a way, to
me, it is. But I don't know, I don't want to apply my philosophy that
far. That problem is too big and strange and real."

Michael looked across at him, but the other boy stayed silent.

Presently they came around a corner and were back at the apartment. Neither one cared to speak anymore. They climbed the stairs
wearily. Zirkle stopped just inside the door and said good-by to the
others.

"Hey, Michael, remember Lerner's program, the one you were
debugging this morning?" asked Randall, his lean face peeking out
from behind a massive old armchair. "Well, if I'm right, they got the
results back from the multiversity and put them on about twenty
minutes ago." He gestured at the screen. "With five per cent of the
vote in, the computers said the alienated vote would be a plurality."

"Well, I guess it's still too early to really tell," said Zirkle dully,
knowing he lied. "I guess I'll be seeing you in class tomorrow,
Toby."

"Right-o."

"Nice talking to you, Bennet," Zirkle said.

"Anytime, Zirkle. Be seeing you."

"Sure. G'by."

Michael was out in the street before he realized he should have
called ahead. He shrugged and went on eagerly through streets
somehow wearier than himself. He'd thought too much, he could feel
himself needing Barbara, all the rest seemed foolishness.

And what had came of it, anyhow? Beside the monoliths uptown, and again watching *Get That Degree,* he'd felt a powerful impulse to switch his major, get away from the machines perhaps even quit school. But he'd have to think of some real alternates before he'd do anything.

And all this new swim of ideas. Maybe in stories people made sudden definite decisions, took violent action. Not him. Oddly, in the dynamic modern world, with the greatest freedom of action in history, everyone in every way, became cautious, demurring, passive.

But what would happen when Franz was elected.

Stupid! he told himself . . . Franz Kafka was running. The president would be the real candidate with the greatest number of votes. The alienated voters wouldn't be getting anything, wouldn't be saying anything.

Or, would they? Yes, he could see it, Bennet had been too cautious. The alienated voters were casting the strongest ballot of all. They were *laughing along with Franz.*

The scientists, the government, including both parties, the big corporations and big universities. There was little choice among them, for a vote or for a life. Together, they'd created automation and the Economically Depressed Areas, *Get That Degree!* and the Emotionally Disturbed Areas. Democrat or Republican, I.C.M. or California Multiversity, the differences were only superficial.

Those who'd voted for Kafka had taken a real stand, showed their dissatisfaction with the whole mess. The politicians wouldn't make long speeches about apathy to the electorate; instead, they'd have to defend themselves to the millions who were angry and frustrated and said it.

More than that, they'd asserted that they had personal problems of their own, concerns that were important to them alone and to which the great social structures were irrelevant.

The Kafka Ballot was no solution. But perhaps it was the first step in a new approach. Automation and the Cold War, space flight and over-population—modern problems were too big, they could do little now but terrify and frustrate. The alienated vote could give people a chance to say how they felt; to relax, to "laugh with Franz."

Zirkle thought of Judo. Sometimes you won by relaxing.

That was what the Kafka Ballot was. A request for freedom, to let each person find his own answers in his own way.

Not that he had any, at least not yet.

But at least he had a clearer eye. So he knew how important it was that Barbara should be waiting for him, and she was.

For nearly a minute after he came in he simply watched her in silent pleasure, smiling happily.

In those seconds she tried to tell him about the letter that had come for him at ten, how the machines had made a mistake about him, not recorded his registration, so that he had effectively vanished from the school: they'd cancelled his I.D., bursar receipt, and class admission tickets, taken back his scholarship awards, and sent him a Draft notice. And she'd been excited and been running round for him all day, trying to get someone in authority to admit that he existed.

She was tired and a reaction of annoyance at him had set in, but he didn't let it come out that way. He embraced her powerfully (a lot of that was needed), and teased her anger into ardour, so her fury was exhausted in amorous combat.

Afterwards, staring up at the ceiling with Barbara slumbering warmly beside him, Michael thought of what the machines had done. Perhaps the devices had not really made a mistake at all, but perhaps in some dark aspect were aware . . .

His fatigue explained such foolishness.

"Kizme," mumbled Barbara in the darkness, and he did.

Hovering on the threshold of sleep, his arm around her, Michael wondered, as he would always wonder, what it really was all about, what he really was here for, and finally, what would happen tomorrow and after that.

He awoke before his girl the next day, to silence and grayness.

His eyes touched his library of manuals and texts and tapes, and he hovered on depression. But then he looked at Barbara, and realized with a happy start how nice it was to wake up next to her.

A little while later, he was not too unsettled to learn that Franz Kafka had been elected President.

Further Reading Norman Kagan

Stories

"Four Brands of Impossible." *The Magazine of Fantasy and Science Fiction*, September 1964. (*A Science Fiction Argosy*, ed. Damon Knight.)

"The Mathenauts." *Worlds of If*, July 1964. (*The 10th Annual of the World's Best S-F*, ed. Judith Merril.)

Eight stories and a novel—that is all there is, the total output of Wyman Guin in the science fiction field. And every one of them good to great, some of the most interesting and subtle writing we have seen. Perhaps his only "famous" story is the breathtaking "Beyond Bedlam," too long for inclusion here, but available in *Spectrum II* and *The Galaxy Reader of Science Fiction,* to be found (we hope) at your local library.

Wyman Guin was born in 1915 at Wanette, Oklahoma, and has worked as a marketing and advertising executive in the pharmaceutical field for almost thirty years, mostly in the area of medical and pharmacy education. Outside of sf, he has co-authored a children's book on biological time clocks and an adult cartoon series, *The Gnu Generation* (in press as this is written, Schmidt Publications). He lives in metropolitan New York and is married, with five children.

From his first appearance in the sf magazines in August 1951 to his last in December 1964 (not quite—there is an original short-short in the British collection *Beyond Bedlam* that carries a 1972 copyright), his work was characterized by originality, freshness, and power. His seven American magazine stories were collected in 1967 as *Living Way Out* (Avon), a dumb title in a poorly designed package, which promptly sank like a stone—and which cries to be back in print. Like Philip K. Dick, Guin was a New Wave writer twenty years before the controversy.

His only novel (he reportedly has another in progress), *The Standing Joy* (Avon, 1969, o.p.), is a powerful, hard-to-classify work that combines science fiction, fantasy, the social sciences, and the physical sciences into something wonderful, a fantastic novel in more ways than one. Unlike most of the other writers represented in this book, Guin did not languish in obscurity. His talent *was* recognized by individuals as diverse in personality and literary taste as Isaac Asimov, Robert Silverberg, and Groff Conklin. Unfortunately, he *is* now a forgotten master because of his own small output and the passage of time. This is a shame, for as H. L. Gold noted, "Wyman Guin has the intellect of a Heinlein, the sensitivity of a C. L. Moore, the guts of Philip José Farmer . . . combined with ideas so profoundly original they are decades ahead of the field."

"My Darling Hecate" is one of the eight.

M.H.G. & J.D.O.

My Darling Hecate

by WYMAN GUIN

One time when my wife and I were kids, I packed a hard, icy snow-ball out on the steps of the Clearview grade school and threw it at her. Just as it got to her it bobbed up over her head and went straight through a school window.

The sheriff was there . . . I mean he was a little boy then, and he looked at me in disgust. "If you gotta throw at girls, why don't you hit 'em? Then I can hit you."

I paid no attention to him. I figured I had just made a grand dis-covery . . . my good self *must* have put that miraculous pitch into my arm to keep my bad self from hitting the pretty little girl.

The principal assigned me some after-school jobs to pay for the window and let me go. I went home and got out my baseball. Out in the back yard, I imagined her standing in front of the garage door. Her neat red hair gleamed around the edges of her snowcap and her sweet little face smiled at me. Then I began to throw at her with every grip and windup I could think of.

Not even a spitball thrown underhand would repeat that bobbing zoom. Finally, I was too tired and discouraged to go on, and right then, as innocently as you please, she wandered into our yard.

I let my bad self aim directly at her. That ball performed a sinusoidal hump over her head just as the snowball had and I gave up my dream of pitching for the Yanks. They certainly weren't going to let me use her head for home plate.

I continued to think egocentrically, that the power which had curved the ball was in my arm, and as the years went by, there were a lot more things like that which I misinterpreted. For example, she never kept me waiting for a date. I'd call her any time it occurred to me and she would say, "I'll be ready in ten minutes." Not fifteen minutes or an hour. Ten minutes.

I just took it for granted that she was always able to get ready that fast because a date with me was important to her. I guess her father looked at it like that, too. He would open the massive front door for me and the skin about his pale blue eyes would crinkle. He would reach up and rumple my hair the way he had since I was a kid and he would say, "Son, you must have something I never had. Her mother would fuss all afternoon getting ready for a date and then keep me waiting an hour when I got there. Go on in. She's in the living room."

And there she would be, cool and lovely, gowned like a goddess. Her father would follow me in shaking his lean head. "She was in blue-jeans ten minutes ago."

She would toss her copper hair emphatically. "Father, all you have to do if you're in a hurry is concentrate on what you're doing. Then everything works out for you."

She could say that as if it were more fundamental than Newton's laws of motion.

And that was the way it was after we were married. She just concentrated on what she was doing and it was a marvel to all our friends how easy it was for her to keep an immaculate home and do all the things she did. My wife never could understand why other women needed house help.

Even with the mysterious things that happened, I never caught on. Like the time we had a late afternoon cocktail party that just about wrecked the place, and as the last guest stumbled down the drive to his car and waiting wife, the phone rang. Friends from the city were coming out to con a country dinner from us.

My wife was looking as fresh and lovely as she had before the boys began trying to manhandle her. "Now, darling. It won't be difficult if we just concentrate on what we're doing. You get the cocktail glasses and canape trays from the living room and I'll see about the kitchen."

Well, I went into the living room and wandered around and there weren't any glasses or trays. There were cigarette ashes sleeted across the carpet and wet rings on all the furniture but the biggest part of the mess had disappeared.

I went back to the kitchen. The automatic dishwasher was splashing away, but my wife wasn't there. I went out into the game room and there was my wife casually straightening up a few things and humming happily to herself.

"There *aren't* any glasses in the living room."

She looked at me sort of funny. Then she laughed lightly. "Oh, I must have been gathering them up while everybody was putting on their coats."

"You were helping with their coats."

"Was I? Well, not all the time, I guess."

I got the vacuum sweeper and a waxing cloth and returned to the living room. The carpet wasn't nearly as dirty as I had thought when I first looked at it. In fact, it wasn't dirty at all. The rings on the furniture had all dried up and disappeared, too. I looked around the room and it seemed just fine. Even the smoke was out of the air.

I took the sweeper and the cloth back to the service room and returned to the game room to help her there. The room was immaculate and my wife wasn't around. I finally found her in the kitchen.

"You're difficult to keep up with," I complained.

"Darling, I'm sorry about the glasses in the living room. Sometimes, when I've already done something like that, it seems to me I've only thought about doing it. You know what I mean?"

"No, I've never had that trouble."

"Well, quite often I can't remember whether I've really done a thing or only thought about doing it. I have to go look to find out. Of course," and she laughed with embarrassment, "I'm such a good housekeeper, I almost always find I've really done whatever it was."

All the time she talked, her hands were working busily on the kitchen counter.

"Are you going to give our guests chicken sandwiches?"

"No, these are for us. There's the dinner over there."

She had taken steaks and vegetables out of the freezer and these were stacked neatly on a work-counter in the impeccable kitchen.

"When did you find time to go down to the basement?"

"Oh, I don't remember. When you were in the living room, I think. Here's your sandwich, darling. I thought we ought to have a snack before they arrive. They'll want cocktails before dinner."

You see how it was. She just concentrated and things worked out for her.

But when everyone in Clearview got to talking about that girl and me, you might say that, for the first time in her life, my wife did some *furious* concentrating.

I suppose I *was* taking quite an interest in that girl. She lives in Clearview where my wife and I went to grade school. It's a little village about three miles up the road from where we now live in the country. I drive through Clearview on my way to the city, and the way this thing started, I was to bring this girl home from the city in the evenings. In the mornings, she left for work earlier than I and would take the bus. But in the evenings—and it was my wife's confident idea—I was to bring her *from* her work in the city *to* her home in Clearview.

Which I always did.

Probably I drove slower coming home those evenings. She enjoyed music and the current novels and it was pleasant talking with her.

She had a way of turning sideways in the seat and leaning back against the car door to watch me while I was driving.

"You know, there aren't many people in Clearview I can talk with about things like this," she said. "I think it was wonderful of your wife to arrange for me to ride with you."

"It has been fun."

"Don't you think there are things like this that can change your whole life? I mean you meet someone interesting and adult and, as you talk with them, your point of view is changed for the rest of your life."

I put the car through a curve and then straightened it carefully on the singing pavement. "Yes, I've found it that way."

She sighed and leaned her pretty blonde head back against the window so that, when I glanced at her, her smooth throat curved beautifully up to her tilted chin. She had eyes like Ingrid Bergman's and now they stared dreamily into the dusk that gathered over the highway ahead.

"I want to know many wonderful people and know them intimately so that, when I am old, I will have all those deep moments to remember."

Naturally, we stopped on occasions for a cocktail or two. And of course that New Year's Eve, as we came out of that little bar, I flipped a coin sort of casually and it fell the wrong way. So I had to kiss her a few times.

But there was still no justification for everyone in Clearview to start talking. Especially to my wife.

My wife is an even-tempered girl except when she explodes, and she let things run along that way until spring, which I suppose she considered the dangerous time because she was thinking of goats. She was pleasant to me. But her manner was getting grim except when she spoke directly to me. I didn't stop for any more cocktails with that girl, but I might as well have, because the talk at the big end of the horn in Clearview didn't slow down.

So, one night, my wife had had a few cocktails herself and she slammed the cards onto the table so hard that I got the whole suit of hearts in my eye. She looked like the goddess Hecate storming the wild uplands of Greece on a roundup of faithless lovers. At the time, I was only dismayed to find the goddess talking like a fishwife.

"Well, I've heard it from everyone else. Now I'd like to hear it from you. What goes with you and this girl?"

You know, sometimes I wonder about myself. What do you think I said? I said, "What girl?"

She assumed an enormous calm like an ocean swell coming at me. "You," she said, "are a goat."

You see, I had guessed she was waiting till spring, and this foresight, this grasp of the way she would be thinking, put me on my feet.

"I have done absolutely nothing wrong," I asserted calmly.

The pyrotechnics mounted as we dashed on into "the lovers' quarrel." But she dwelt on certain painful factors and concluded that I was incapable of doing wrong. Finally, too, she excused the other girl for being attracted to me.

"You see, darling, I married you myself. I can't afford to call that little pot black."

What intensified the flush on her cheeks and put that new glitter into her eyes was the insufferable damage to her pride from the tongues of the town.

Our quarrel was over and it hadn't been anything to what came now. I had never seen my wife like this. Fascinated, I watched her grapple the women of Clearview on the cruel hooks of her words. She snapped off their clay feet and jerked the straw out of their heads before hurling them into her sea of venom.

Like a chip, I was swept up and tossed out with a hapless group of gossips.

"If their own marriages weren't such miserable failures, they would have ignored your antics with that little idiot as I did."

I floated forlornly where she had tossed me. Far off, I could see her superb figure, now tensed, now gesticulating, as the surf of words recoiled for more power and came boiling at me. There on the rocking shore she ground the bitter meat she had been after.

They didn't respect her taste. In clothes. In antiques. In homes. I floated near her for a kind word and a tear because they didn't respect her taste in husbands, either. But she had forgotten that small matter.

She didn't let up when we went to bed. I turned out the lights. During a pause in her fury, I dozed. I came bald-eyed awake to find my wife sitting up in her bed concentrating on a mad mutter.

"I'll blot out the town! I'll blot out the whole town!"

There was a rolling boom of thunder that wasn't thunder. There was a brittle shifting in the foundation of the universe. For a stunning moment, everything about us was lighted from within.

I lay there wondering what on earth had happened. After a long time I heard her hushed voice.

"Darling?"

"Yes, honey?"

"What—what do you think that was?"

"It must have been an explosion somewhere. Look, honey, I'm

awfully sorry about this whole thing. We're both exhausted, so let's go to sleep and maybe in the morning you'll feel like making it up."

"I'd like to make it up now."

I flew over there. Her face was still flaming and it made her lips hot and yielding. She whispered wonderful things to me and I whispered things I had never had occasion to think of before.

Next morning, that dark oath and that vast booming were only part of a bad dream that was happily forgotten. We had a fine breakfast and said more wonderful things and I drove off to work marveling that she loved me enough to get that angry.

I drove along Highway 35 whistling the songs I knew. Driving along that way, not paying attention to anything but the hypnotic road, I stopped whistling and broke out in a sweat.

I pulled over to the shoulder and cut the motor.

A meadow lark was singing off to the left. From ahead I could hear another car approaching with a leisurely hum. I knew this spot on Highway 35. I had driven over it a thousand times. Back about a mile, the road went through Clearview. But this morning it hadn't.

The approaching car went by me, a fellow driving alone in a Buick. I started my engine and turned around and followed him back. When he topped the overpass at the North Central tracks, I was about 300 feet behind him. His brake lights went on and he edged to the shoulder as he started down off the bridge.

Instead of making a sharp S-turn through Clearview and south around the village square, Highway 35 stretched ahead, a clean wide sweep to the south through open fields.

Where Highway 17 came in from the northwest to intersect, there was a filling station, a general store and a couple of houses I had never seen. There were two big farms with handsome dairy barns along the near shore of Shadow Lake.

There should have been summer cottages scattered through there. There should have been the streets and buildings of Clearview, half-hidden in trees, running from there nearly to where the Buick was parked on the approach to the overpass.

The driver had got out and was flagging me down. I crawled up behind him with my motor idling and he walked back to me.

There was a truculent air about him. Somebody had just handed him a lead half-dollar. "Say, I don't drive this route very often, but I thought Clearview was right along in here."

I nodded, staring down the slope at the gasoline station. That was the logical place to ask directions, but I wasn't any more anxious than he seemed to be to stop in.

"Weren't you the guy parked on the shoulder about a mile back?"

I nodded again. I was feeling too sick and frightened to talk to him or collect my thoughts.

"Well, why did you come back?"

"Listen," I snapped, "if you've lost your way, that's the man you want to talk to." I indicated the filling station where the attendant had come out and was talking to the driver of a big farm truck.

He turned without another word and got into his car.

After a while, I put my car in gear and rolled slowly behind him down the wide-sweeping curve. Above the strangely empty fields, white-winged gulls turned and flashed toward Shadow Lake.

There was no sharp break between what was familiar and what was new. Mostly things were just missing. There was no sign of violence except that some telephone lines were down. The shabby little depot was gone, too.

I pulled into the filling station behind the Buick and got out. As I did so, the driver of the farm truck was walking up Highway 17. He was not much more than a boy, and, as he walked past me, I could see that his face was pale. Around his mouth and on his cheeks, it made him look yellow.

The filling station attendant called after him, "Hey, come back here and get your truck!"

The boy walked on up Highway 17, the attendant threw his mystification and annoyance at us.

"That guy has been driving me crazy since six o'clock this morning. Says he can't find his dad's farm where he was taking this load of feed. Drives out around Shadow Lake and in fifteen minutes he's back wringing his hands and swearing at me. Now he leaves his truck parked smack in my drive and walks off."

We stood for a moment looking after the crazy boy walking away up Highway 17.

"Well," the attendant broke the silence, "them's my troubles. What can I do for you gentlemen?"

The driver of the Buick came to himself. "Yes," he said in a businesslike hurry. "I'm looking for Clearview."

The attendant stopped in the middle of his smile. His pale blue eyes narrowed to slits that glared at us from his weathered face. "Now," he whispered levelly, "that's enough. What is this? A mass break from the bughouse? You're the ninth one this morning, including a damned fool bus driver."

He walked stiff-legged into the station and came out with a road map. "So you're headed for Clearview? Well, you can see right here it ain't in this state." He almost put his finger through the map.

I studied the section where it should have been, but there was no Clearview indicated. Otherwise his map seemed all right.

The driver of the Buick was frightened now. "It wasn't Clearview I was trying to get to."

The filling station attendant looked at the man for a long time. Then he began to tremble about his chin. Finally he asked quietly, "Where did you want to go, mister?"

"Oaktown."

"I see. Well, you get into your car quietly and drive on down the road about six miles and you'll be in Oaktown."

As the Buick sped away a big "semi" slowed on the highway. The driver leaned from his cab and yelled at us, "Hey, bud, am I still on Highway 35?"

The attendant nodded and waved him along. He was definitely suspicious when he turned to me. "And you?"

"I represent Darrow Chemicals," I lied. "We have a new line we'd like to get distribution on."

"Come on in the station and let's have a smoke while we talk."

I followed him in, saying, "Where do you suppose he got that idea about a town named Clearview?"

"That's his problem, mister. All I know is there ain't such a place." He lit my cigarette for me.

There was something incongruously familiar about him. I fumbled around in my mind, but I didn't hit on it. Perhaps the clothes and the weathered face threw me off.

A little girl with bright red hair came from the living quarters in back of the station and leaned against the door jamb, staring at me. The attendant grinned. "My daughter. Cute, ain't she?"

"Hello. What's your name?"

She wasn't going to answer foolish questions.

"Hecate," the attendant supplied. "Odd name, but common in these parts."

"How long have you lived here?" I asked him.

"Well, now, that's not an easy one to answer." For a moment he hunted frantically in my eyes for something too big for him to grasp. "All my life, I guess."

I stared at him.

He shook his head in embarrassment, but he grinned confidently. "Lots of mysterious things, aren't there? A man could worry if he was a mind to."

"How do you mean, mysterious?"

"Oh, I don't know. Like my wife, for instance. Are you married?"

I nodded. Over his shoulder, I could see, through the window, a man in a business suit wandering aimlessly in a field that stretched toward Shadow Lake. I recognized him. He lived out in the country, but he had owned a store in Clearview.

The attendant questioned me and his voice was very serious. "How old is your wife?"

"Two years younger than I am. About twenty-eight."

He spoke slowly and contemplatively, as if he were enthralled by a problem he couldn't think out. "That's how I thought it ought to be. You see, my wife is eighty-seven."

I could only gape at him. He was no more than thirty-six. Then I thought of the little red-headed girl and glanced at her and back to him.

He sighed deeply. "She's my wife's daughter."

The child turned away slowly, with her eyes lingering on me. Then she darted back into the living quarters.

Both of us became aware of sirens approaching from the city. Two troopers on motorcycles led a squad car down the hill and up to the station. They cut their motors and calmly stood their machines while three plainclothes men and another in uniform got out of the car. The sirens died down a melancholy scale on the quiet spring air.

One of the plainclothes men led the group that got out of the car up to the station.

"What's going on here?" he demanded, as though he intended to put a stop to it in the next ten minutes.

"Nothing's going on here." The attendant displayed a native attitude of uncooperative independence.

"Where's Clearview?"

I saw the attendant collapse. It crashed him in one instant from his isolated confidence.

"I tell you there ain't such a place. There never was. I'm a native here and I never heard of such a place."

He began to cry and sat down on the step, blubbering into a handkerchief.

The troopers had remained by their machines. One of them spoke to the other, and over the weeping of the attendant, I could hear his undisturbed voice. "I never been out this way. Is it really changed?"

"I can't figure it out. Nothing has happened as far as I can see, except the town is gone."

The plainclothes man turned to me. "What are you doing here?"

"I live over there."

"Where's 'over there'?"

"Blue Lake. I live on the lake."

"Have business here this morning?"

"I was on my way to work in the city. I . . . Clearview is gone."

"I can see that for myself. What did you have to do with it?"

"I called my partner east from Tucumcari, New Mexico. We moved the whole thing, men, women and children, to a spot I had picked in western Oregon. We didn't finish till around daylight and I'm dog-tired."

I started for my car, but one of the men grabbed my arm. "Just a moment, mister. You may be an honestly mystified American citizen like the rest of us. On the other hand, this may be a Communist plot and we can't take chances."

"I thought of that, too," I said. "I decided they wouldn't bother planting spies if they could pull off a neat trick like this. Do you reckon there's anyone straightening out a hangover in Washington, D.C., this morning?"

"All we got to deal with is Clearview," he said sullenly.

I was over being angry. That crack about my partner and me not finishing till daylight had rung a little bell that had grown in volume while I talked, until now it was pealing and clanging across my frightened mind. For the first time that morning, I was remembering the awful oath my wife had muttered and that vast booming and that shimmering light in everything.

I began to look as guilty and scared as hell, but my former bravado covered for me. The officers let me go after taking my name, and asking a few questions about how the scene had looked when I first came back to it. Cars were piling up around the intersection and the two troopers were out taking names and directing traffic with an air of "business-as-usual."

As I drove away, I could see, in the rearview mirror, the warning light on top of the squad car. It was still swinging its red, cyclopean glare fruitlessly over the bright new landscape. At the turn-off, I hesitated, and then dismissed the idea of driving on down to Mexico.

My wife was sitting out on the terrace wearing a pretty little sunsuit. From the bowl she held at her breast, she threw crumbs of cornbread to the pigeons. The birds fluttered around her long beautiful legs. The cat lounged in her lap and the spring breeze rippled his black fur against her sunlit flesh. He disdained the pigeons. He was sitting where he belonged and his green eyes followed me intently.

Her smiling blue eyes followed me, too, and the gorgeous copper hair lifted in the breeze, a sacrilegious halo. Her painfully lovely words hung over the quiet terrace unanswered.

"Darling, I was wishing you would come back. I've been thinking delicious things about us all morning. Now we can spend the whole lovely day together, can't we?"

I went into the kitchen and fixed myself a double scotch and water. I came back out onto the terrace and sat down in a deck chair and scorched the cat's green eyes.

"Drinking in the morning?" she asked pleasantly.

"In the morning. All morning."

"Darling, you're so handsome and wonderful, you should drink whenever you wish."

I watched her face. I asked, "What do you think has happened?"

She showed only a little sulkiness at the corners of her mouth. "I'm sure I don't know."

I watched her face closely. "Clearview is gone."

The cat leaped down from her lap and the pigeons exploded in a whirring cloud. Now that that cat had heard the news, he stalked off to commune with Beelzebub.

"I don't understand," my wife said puzzledly.

"Clearview has disappeared. Vanished. There's some other place there with different people."

At first, her expression didn't change. Then, slowly, she looked pleased. I could see she didn't really believe me. It was just that the idea charmed her.

"You think you're not going to have to pay for your sins, don't you?" I said hotly. "Blowing your stack like a hiccuping fury all because a nice little girl with eyes like Ingrid Bergman's gets a crush on me."

I was so mad, I had tears in my eyes. "She *was* a nice girl. Even if she did have designs. That's rather innocent, you know. At least she didn't sit up in *her* bed making *towns* disappear."

My wife raised her chin and stared at me defiantly.

I went on. "You get into that car and drive down to Clearview. Just try to find it. Apologize to some of those poor women you were damning last night."

"I'll do no such thing," she said flatly.

I put down my glass and got up and walked over to her. I took her arm in a firm grip and helped her across the terrace. I gave her just enough of a boot to send her off in a gay mood. She stood beside the car seething and trying to outglare me. Then she flung herself into the seat and spun out of the drive kicking gravel at me.

I went back into the kitchen and whistled a little tune while I fixed another scotch. They were going to have some new problems to think about at the Institute of Higher Learning. Maybe, in the interests of science, they would have to stuff my wife and keep her in a glass jar at Princeton.

She was back almost before she had started. Now that I knew her for what she was, I wasn't a bit surprised that that should be one of her minor powers.

I heard her slide the car half way up the drive and presently she burst in to the kitchen. She stood there with her lower lip trembling.

Do you know what she said? She said, "Oh, darling! Clearview is gone!"

I shrugged. "I saw that for myself. What did you have to do with it?"

"Do you really think what I said last night . . . Is it possible I . . . ?"

"You," I said, "are a witch."

The phone was ringing and I went across the kitchen to answer it. It was the sheriff.

I said, "Oh, hi! I told you I'd get you elected again. You have a pretty soft spot, too. This country is so quiet, it's just melting away."

"Don't be cute. This is a national emergency. The F.B.I. is swarming around us."

"Has the filling station attendant sworn that he is not now and never has been?"

"I'm sorry we have such a smart guy among the witnesses. I'd like the F.B.I. to get a better impression of the folks around here. Have you and your wife patched things up?"

"What do you mean?"

"You know what I mean. Everybody in Oaktown knew she was going to throw the cards at you last night."

"Oaktown, too? They better watch out how they talk over there. My wife . . ."

"You got a good little girl there. I don't know why you have to go fooling around."

I grinned across the kitchen at my wife. "Sheriff says you're a good little girl. I think he means to dance the macabre with."

"You'll have to bring her along," the sheriff said, "to back up your statements at the investigation over here."

"Where Clearview was?"

"No. That's all blocked off. Except we're bringing those strangers in here to Oaktown for the investigation at the courthouse. Everybody else that was there early, including you, is wanted here."

"When?"

"Now."

"I've been drinking."

"You sure are going to hell, aren't you?"

I put the receiver back and turned to my wife. She was standing with her fists clenched at her sides, crying quietly and gritting back the small lonely sound.

I went over and put my arms around her and she just stood that way with her face buried in my shoulder.

"You don't cry much like a witch," I said. "Maybe it isn't true. Neither of us have suspected your powers and the scientists just haven't got around to recording such things."

She raised her head. "Oh, darling, I hope they never do. They mustn't find out."

I stroked her beautiful copper hair reassuringly. "Don't worry about it. We'll go to that investigation and tell them everybody in Clearview was a fellow-traveler and kept documents in pumpkins! That'll put them hot on the wrong scent."

I didn't have to tell them anything like that. They had combed forty or so people, including the filling station attendant and his senile wife and little girl, out of the area formerly occupied by Clearview. Here they all were in the Oaktown courthouse with only one obstinate fact in mind there was no such town as Clearview and there never had been.

After I had been in that room for some time, I began to realize that there were several peculiarities about the group being investigated. The males were of all different ages. The females, however, were of only two ages—very old women, some of whom were married to men in their twenties, and little girls of eight. There were nine little girls of eight and each had a different daddy who held her on his lap or stroked her red hair while she stood beside him.

There were eight little boys who sat solemnly alone.

I began to feel the shade of Sigmund Freud, heavy and oppressive, in that room. Suddenly I understood what had made the filling station attendant seem so familiar.

He was a weathered replica of my wife's father.

All of the men were my wife's father at different ages.

All the little girls were my wife.

The solemn little boys were me.

When I turned to look at my wife, she was very pale. She faced me and blushed. The blush got deeper. It crimsoned her throat and flamed across her cheekbones. She gulped and turned away from me.

"You *ought* to be ashamed," I whispered. "Couldn't you have made at least one of the daddies be me? Couldn't you have given him a pretty young brunette wife for the purpose of spanking your little eight-year-old bottom?"

She shivered and grasped my arm, whispering frantically. "Darling, don't let them find out. Please—please!—don't let them find out."

Some investigation that was! It was short, too. These investigators weren't going to settle for anything less mundane than a Communist plot, and these suspects, who fumbled so earnestly to give any kind of answers at all, became increasingly unworldly.

Finally, when the F.B.I. men had about exhausted their possible attacks and suspicions, a little old lady rose on quaking legs. She pointed a bony finger at a handsome twenty-year-old replica of my wife's father.

She stood that way, pointing the trembling talon. It occurred to me that her faded eyes might once have looked like Ingrid Bergman's and I glanced at my wife in disgust. The whole room was hushed by the terrible sight of the old lady pointing at the young man.

My wife buried her shattered face in her hands.

The chief investigator was disturbed by the old woman's mad silence. "Madam, you have something you wish to say?"

The ancient vocal cords gathered themselves around a knot of anger. "He's one. He's a Communist."

Now that he had this accusation, the investigator knew it wasn't so. "What makes you think so?"

"He's an infidel and he wants free love. He threatened to leave me this morning. He's going to the city to get young girls."

I had to put my arm around my wife and draw her to me. She was sobbing.

The paralyzed silence in the room had become an agony. One of the F.B.I. men burst out plaintively, "I don't think this is a case for our bureau."

With admirable speed, it was decided to hurry the forty or so people who were "from out of this world" back to their strange area and hold them there. The rest of us were dismissed.

Out on the courthouse steps, the spring day was dying in gouts of bloody light. Our friend, the sheriff, came up and tipped his hat to my wife. Of me he asked, "You still drinking?"

"Sure," I answered. "It's the only way to stay sober around here."

"Let's walk over to the Flamingo and I'll buy you folks a martini."

My wife grabbed that martini like it was her mother's hand. The sheriff is a big, sad man and he looked at her sadly. He looked at me sternly.

"I noticed how pale this little girl was during the investigation," he said. "It's a shame a lug like you gives her such a bad time. Why don't you straighten up and keep her name out of the Wednesday bridge gabble?"

"I definitely intend to," I assured him. "I do definitely intend to. There will be no more chits and chats in my young life."

The sheriff turned apologetically to my wife. "I think he means it."

"Oh, she knows I mean it. If I toy with a notion like that, I toy with the fate of hundreds. That isn't what's worrying her. She's trying to be a good little girl and confess she did it."

My wife looked at me as though I had stabbed her.

"Did what?" the sheriff said levelly.

"Blotted out Clearview."

My wife shuddered and gulped the rest of her drink. Then, like a condemned woman forgiving her accuser, she reached over and squeezed my hand. "Darling, is it all right if I have another martini?"

I took a bill out of my pocket and handed it to the sheriff. "I need a word with the prisoner. Be a good fellow and go over to the bar and get three more for us."

He went, with no injury to his dignity, and I took both of her hands in mine. "Darling, you'll see he won't believe it. Nobody will believe it who's going to hear about it. Even if the sheriff was convinced, he probably wouldn't tell any of his colleagues for fear they'd have his head tapped. Of course, if you're going to make a practice of this sort of thing, the sheriff will see his duty and I will have done mine."

"Oh, darling, I won't ever do it again! I won't ever lose my temper and I'll stop concentrating on what I'm doing. Why, darling, if you want to go out with other girls, I'll be happy about it and I'll . . ."

"Hold it! Hold it! Let's not tear out our hair or rend our breasts. Let's just tell the sheriff what happened and then go home and live a quiet life with our love and guilt."

The sheriff came back and put our drinks on the table with domesticated ease. He sat down and looked at me sternly. "Now, what was this you were saying about this little girl?"

"She cast a curse on Clearview. Of course, I suppose every town in the country is being cursed by some woman every night. If there are occasional incantations that make a spot in the universe go 'poof,' then, sooner or later, one of them is going to hit a town. It follows that some women will wake up to find herself a witch."

The sheriff was looking at me with distaste, but I went right ahead. "That's a good theory you can pass along for old time's sake. For your exclusive interest, we have further particulars. Those people you picked up in that area aren't real. They're zombies or something that she created. Those old hags are aged replicas of Clearview women who used to be her friends."

The sheriff had had enough. "Let's have no more of this foolishness. I've known this little girl since she was a little girl, and even if such a thing were possible, she's not the kind."

"She put a stink bomb in the ventilation system at the grade school," I reminded him.

"Let's not forget who's the guilty party at this table. This little girl has had plenty of reason to be angry with those Clearview gossips, but behind all that was you cutting up like a young he-goat."

We both turned in masculine panic, for my wife was sobbing. She did not bow her head or try to hide. The eyes were closed and the full mouth drawn in her pale face, and she was like a tortured saint.

"I did it! I sent all those good people to their doom!" Her remorse streamed down her cheeks and fell into her empty glass. "Oh, darling, how I wish I could bring back all those good people!"

There was a rolling boom of thunder that wasn't thunder. There was a brittle shifting in the foundation of the universe. For a stunning moment, everything about us was lighted from within.

The bartender turned from where he was polishing glasses.

"What on earth happened?"

Sitting there in the Flamingo, my wife and I looked at each other. She pushed her fists into her eyes like a little girl to wipe away her tears. I smiled and she smiled.

The sheriff asked, "Was that it?"

Still looking at me and smiling, my wife nodded and he got up and went out. My wife leaned toward me and kissed my mouth.

Then she said, "You know, I'll have to warn our children about controlling their tempers. Then, too, maybe we can bring them up to have a lack of concentration."

"I suppose so," I said. "Though I *would* like one of them to pitch for the Yanks."

The other day I met that girl from Clearview on the street. After her brief sojourn out-of-this-world she had joined the Salvation Army. She told me she finds it a richly rewarding experience. I wished her luck and got away fast.

She does have eyes like Ingrid Bergman's. Which I don't think I'll mention again to my wife.

Further Reading Wyman Guin

Books

Living Way Out. New York: Avon Books, 1967. (This volume contains all of Guin's published short fiction with the exception of one short-short.)
The Standing Joy. New York: Avon Books, 1969.

I know nothing about F[loyd] L. Wallace other than that he is a short man of great physical strength who holds a belt in judo and who for reasons I cannot understand gave up writing science fiction two decades ago, did a couple of obscure mystery novels, and then stopped writing altogether. (I can understand giving up writing very easily; what I cannot is giving up writing what you do better than almost anyone to write what can be written equally well by many others. . . . If you're going to stay around you might as well run the full course.) Naturally, I don't need an autobiographical vita to understand all that is necessary within this compass: Wallace made an extraordinary contribution to the genre because he did something that at the time was almost new. He was patient and thorough. When he was done with the exploration of one of his themes, there was almost nothing left to be done with it.

This may sound simple but it is not: most science fiction is written in haste and under economic pressure; it fails to explore the implications of the thematic or technological issues it raises and is frustratingly incomplete. Truncation seems to be the name of this game. Aside from Wallace, I can think quickly of only three other writers who were able within the magazine (short of book-length) format to pull off the miracle of total utilization: Walter M. Miller, Jr., who let nothing go until there was not even a scrap for lesser writers to pounce on (after "The Darfstellar" there was never another actor-in-the-future story); and the team of Henry Kuttner/C. L. Moore, who of course were extraordinary and who, happily enough, need never appear within the focus of a book dedicated to the unjustly forgotten. Wallace, in work like "Tangle Hold," "Mezzerow Loves Company," "Accidental Flight," and the following amazing novella, approached science fiction the way that Captain Donald H. Evans told I Company at Fort Dix to approach the basic training PT test: "All out, so you don't have anything left when you're done. . . . I want you men when the test is over to be able to do nothing but lie on the ground and gasp."

Come to think of it, I suspect for the first time at this very moment, writing this, why Wallace went off into mysteries and got himself a belt in judo.

Wallace, like Wyman Guin, like Robert Sheckley, like Phillip Klass (William Tenn), was a writer brought to full artistic stature by Horace Gold, the editor of *Galaxy* during the 1950s. Gold, as other writers have pointed out, simply brought out the best in writers, older and newer, who submitted to him, and "Delay in Transit" may be as much his triumph as Wallace's.

B.N.M.

Delay in Transit

by F[LOYD] L. WALLACE

"Muscles tense," said Dimanche. "Neural index 1.76, unusually high. Adrenalin squirting through his system. In effect, he's stalking you. Intent: probably assault with a deadly weapon."

"Not interested," said Cassal firmly, his subvocalization inaudible to anyone but Dimanche. "I'm not the victim type. He was standing on the walkway near the brink of the thoroughfare. I'm going back to the habitat hotel and sit tight."

"First you have to get there," Dimanche pointed out. "I mean, is it safe for a stranger to walk through the city?"

"Now that you mention it, no," answered Cassal. He looked around apprehensively. "Where is he?"

"Behind you. At the moment he's pretending interest in a merchandise display."

A native stamped by, eyes brown and incurious. Apparently he was accustomed to the sight of an Earthman standing alone, Adam's apple bobbing up and down silently. It was a Godolphian axiom that all travelers were crazy.

Cassal looked up. Not an air taxi in sight; Godolph shut down at dusk. It would be pure luck if he found a taxi before morning. Of course he *could* walk back to the hotel, but was that such a good idea?

A Godolphian city was peculiar. And, though not intended, it was peculiarly suited to certain kinds of violence. A human pedestrian was at a definite disadvantage.

"Correction," said Dimanche. "Not simple assault. He has murder in mind."

"It still doesn't appeal to me," said Cassal. Striving to look unconcerned, he strolled toward the building side of the walkway and stared into the interior of a small cafe. Warm, bright and dry. Inside, he might find safety for a time.

Damn the man who was following him! It would be easy enough to elude him in a normal city. On Godolph, nothing was normal. In an hour the streets would be brightly lighted—for native eyes. A human would consider it dim.

"Why did he choose me?" asked Cassal plaintively. "There must be something he hopes to gain."

"I'm working on it," said Dimanche. "But remember, I have limitations. At short distances I can scan nervous systems, collect and interpret physiological data. I can't read minds. The best I can do is report what a person says or subvocalizes. If you're really interested in finding out why he wants to kill you, I suggest you turn the problem over to the godawful police."

"Godolph, not godawful," corrected Cassal absently.

That was advice he couldn't follow, good as it seemed. He could give the police no evidence save through Dimanche. There were various reasons, many of them involving the law, for leaving the device called Dimanche out of it. The police would act if they found a body. His own, say, floating face-down on some quiet street. That didn't seem the proper approach, either.

"Weapons?"

"The first thing I searched him for. Nothing very dangerous. A long knife, a hard striking object. Both concealed on his person."

Cassal strangled slightly. Dimanche needed a good stiff course in semantics. A knife was still the most silent of weapons. A man could die from it. His hand strayed toward his pocket. He had a measure of protection himself.

"Report," said Dimanche. "Not necessarily final. Based, perhaps, on tenuous evidence."

"Let's have it anyway."

"His motivation is connected somehow with your being marooned here. For some reason you can't get off this planet."

That was startling information, though not strictly true. A thousand star systems were waiting for him, and a ship to take him to each one.

Of course, the one ship he wanted hadn't come in. Godolph was a transfer point for stars nearer the center of the Galaxy. When he had left Earth, he had known he would have to wait a few days here. He hadn't expected a delay of nearly three weeks. Still, it wasn't unusual. Interstellar schedules over great distances were not as reliable as they might be.

Was this man, whoever and whatever he might be, connected with that delay? According to Dimanche, the man thought he was. He was self-deluded or did he have access to information that Cassal didn't?

Denton Cassal, sales engineer, paused for a mental survey of himself. He was a good engineer and, because he was exceptionally well matched to his instrument, the best salesman that Neuronics, Inc., had. On the basis of these qualifications, he had been selected to make a long journey, the first part of which already lay behind him. He had to go to Tunney 21 to see a man. That man wasn't important to anyone save the company that employed him, and possibly not even to them.

The thug trailing him wouldn't be interested in Cassal himself, his mission, which was a commercial one, nor the man on Tunney. And money wasn't the objective, if Dimanche's analysis was right. What *did* the thug want?

Secrets? Cassal had none, except, in a sense, Dimanche. And that was too well kept on Earth, where the instrument was invented and made, for anyone this far away to have learned about it.

And yet the thug wanted to kill him. Wanted to? Regarded him as good as dead. It might pay him to investigate the matter further, if it didn't involve too much risk.

"Better start moving." That was Dimanche. "He's getting suspicious."

Cassal went slowly along the narrow walkway that bordered each side of that boulevard, the transport tide. It was raining again. It usually was on Godolph, which was a weather-controlled planet where the natives like rain.

He adjusted the controls of the weak force field that repelled the rain. He widened the angle of the field until water slanted through it unhindered. He narrowed it around him until it approached visibility and the drops bounced away. He swore at the miserable climate and the near amphibians who created it.

A few hundred feet away, a Godolphian girl waded out of the transport tide and climbed to the walkway. It was this sort of thing that made life dangerous for a human—Venice revised, brought up to date in a faster-than-light age.

Water. It was a perfect engineering material. Simple, cheap, infinitely flexible. With a minimum of mechanism and at breakneck speed, the ribbon of the transport tide flowed at different levels throughout the city. The Godolphian merely plunged in and was carried swiftly and noiselessly to his destination. Whereas a human— Cassal shivered. If he were found drowned, it would be considered an accident. No investigation would be made. The thug who was trailing him had certainly picked the right place.

The Godolphian girl passed. She wore a sleek brown fur, her own. Cassal was almost positive she muttered a polite "Arf?" as she sloshed by. What she meant by that, he didn't know and didn't intend to find out.

"Follow her," instructed Dimanche. "We've got to investigate our man at closer range."

Obediently, Cassal turned and began walking after the girl. Attractive in an anthropomorphic, seal-like way, even from behind. Not graceful out of her element, though.

The would-be assassin was still looking at merchandise as Cassal retraced his steps. A man, or at least man type. A big fellow, physically quite capable of violence, if size had anything to do with it. The face, though, was out of character. Mild, almost meek. A scientist or scholar. It didn't fit with murder.

"Nothing," said Dimanche disgustedly. "His mind froze when we got close. I could feel his shoulderblades twitching as we passed. Anticipated guilt, of course. Projecting to you the action he plans. That makes the knife definite."

Well beyond the window at which the thug watched and waited, Cassal stopped. Shakily he produced a cigarette and fumbled for a lighter.

"Excellent thinking," commended Dimanche. "He won't attempt anything on this street. Too dangerous. Turn aside at the next deserted intersection and let him follow the glow of your cigarette."

The lighter flared in his hand. "That's one way of finding out," said Cassal. "But wouldn't I be a lot safer if I just concentrated on getting back to the hotel?"

"I'm curious. Turn here."

"Go to hell," said Cassal nervously. Nevertheless, when he came to that intersection, he turned there.

It was a Godolphian equivalent of an alley, narrow and dark, oily slow-moving water gurgling at one side, high cavernous walls looming on the other.

He would have to adjust the curiosity factor of Dimanche. It was all very well to be interested in the man who trailed him, but there was also the problem of coming out of this adventure alive. Dimanche, an electronic instrument, naturally wouldn't consider that.

"Easy," warned Dimanche. "He's at the entrance to the alley, walking fast. He's surprised and pleased that you took this route."

"I'm surprised, too," remarked Cassal. "But I wouldn't say I'm pleased. Not just now."

"Careful. Even subvocalized conversation is distracting." The mechanism concealed within his body was silent for an instant and then continued: "His blood pressure is rising, breathing is faster. At a time like this, he may be ready to verbalize why he wants to murder you. This is critical."

"That's no lie," agreed Cassal bitterly. The lighter was in his hand. He clutched it grimly. It was difficult not to look back. The darkness assumed an even more sinister quality.

"Quiet," said Dimanche. "He's verbalizing about you."

"He's decided I'm a nice fellow after all. He's going to stop and ask me for a light."

"I don't think so," answered Dimanche. "He's whispering: 'Poor devil. I hate to do it. But it's really his life or mine.'"

"He's more right than he knows. Why all this violence, though? Isn't there any clue?"

"None at all," admitted Dimanche. "He's very close. You'd better turn around."

Cassal turned, pressed the stud on the lighter. It should have made him feel more secure, but it didn't. He could see very little.

A dim shadow rushed at him. He jumped away from the water side of the alley, barely in time. He could feel the rush of air as the assailant shot by.

"Hey!" shouted Cassal.

Echoes answered; nothing else did. He had the uncomfortable feeling that no one was going to come to his assistance.

"He wasn't expecting that reaction," explained Dimanche. "That's why he missed. He's turned around and is coming back."

"I'm armed!" shouted Cassal.

"That won't stop him. He doesn't believe you."

Cassal grasped the lighter. That is, it had been a lighter a few seconds before. Now a needle-thin blade had snapped out and projected stiffly. Originally it had been designed as an emergency surgical instrument. A little imagination and a few changes had altered its function, converting it into a compact, efficient stiletto.

"Twenty feet away," advised Dimanche. "He knows you can't see him, but he can see your silhouette by the light from the main thoroughfare. What he doesn't know is that I can detect every move he makes and keep you posted below the level of his hearing."

"Stay on him," growled Cassal nervously. He flattened himself against the wall.

"To the right," whispered Dimanche. "Lunge forward. About five feet. Low."

Sickly, he did so. He didn't care to consider the possible effects of a miscalculation. In the darkness, how far was five feet? Fortunately, his estimate was correct. The rapier encountered yielding resistance, the soggy kind: flesh. The tough blade bent, but did not break. His opponent gasped and broke away.

"Attack!" howled Dimanche against the bone behind his ear.

"You've got him. He can't imagine how you know where he is in the darkness. He's afraid."

Attack he did, slicing about wildly. Some of the thrusts landed; some didn't. The percentage was low, the total amount high. His opponent fell to the ground, gasped and was silent.

Cassal fumbled in his pockets and flipped on a light. The man lay near the water side of the alley. One leg was crumpled under him. He didn't move.

"Heartbeat slow," said Dimanche solemnly. "Breathing barely perceptible."

"Then he's not dead," said Cassal in relief.

Foam flecked from the still lips and ran down the chin. Blood oozed from cuts on the face.

"Respiration none, heartbeat absent," stated Dimanche.

Horrified, Cassal gazed at the body. Self-defense, of course, but would the police believe it? Assuming they did, they'd still have to investigate. The rapier was an illegal concealed weapon. And they would question him until they discovered Dimanche. Regrettable, but what could he do about it?

Suppose he were detained long enough to miss the ship bound for Tunney 21?

Grimly, he laid down the rapier. He might as well get to the bottom of this. Why had the man attacked? What did he want?

"I don't know," replied Dimanche irritably. "I can interpret body data—a live body. I can't work on a piece of meat."

Cassal searched the body thoroughly. Miscellaneous personal articles of no value in identifying the man. A clip with a startling amount of money in it. A small white card with something scribbled on it. A picture of a woman and a small child posed against a background which resembled no world Cassal had ever seen. That was all.

Cassal stood up in bewilderment. Dimanche to the contrary, there seemed to be no connection between this dead man and his own problem of getting to Tunney 21.

Right now, though, he had to dispose of the body. He glanced toward the boulevard. So far no one had been attracted by the violence.

He bent down to retrieve the lighter-rapier. Dimanche shouted at him. Before he could react, someone landed on him. He fell forward, vainly trying to grasp the weapon. Strong fingers felt for his throat as he was forced to the ground.

He threw the attacker off and staggered to his feet. He heard footsteps rushing away. A slight splash followed. Whoever it was, he was escaping by way of water.

Whoever it was. The man he had thought he had slain was no longer in sight.

"Interpret body data, do you?" muttered Cassal. "Liveliest dead man I've ever been strangled by."

"It's just possible there are some breeds of men who can control the basic functions of their body," said Dimanche defensively. "When I checked him, he had no heartbeat."

"Remind me not to accept your next evaluation so completely," grunted Cassal. Nevertheless, he was relieved, in a fashion. He hadn't *wanted* to kill the man. And now there was nothing he'd have to explain to the police.

He needed the cigarette he stuck between his lips. For the second time he attempted to pick up the rapier-lighter. This time he was successful. Smoke swirled into his lungs and quieted his nerves. He squeezed the weapon into the shape of a lighter and put it away.

Something, however, was missing—his wallet.

The thug had relieved him of it in the second round of the scuffle. Persistent fellow. Damned persistent.

It really didn't matter. He fingered the clip he had taken from the supposedly dead body. He had intended to turn it over to the police. Now he might as well keep it to reimburse him for his loss. It contained more money than his wallet had.

Except for the identification tab he always carried in his wallet, it was more than a fair exchange. The identification, a rectangular piece of plastic, was useful in establishing credit, but with the money he now had, he wouldn't need credit. If he did, he could always send for another tab.

A white card fluttered from the clip. He caught it as it fell. Curiously he examined it. Blank except for one crudely printed word, STAB. His unknown assailant certainly had tried.

The old man stared at the door, an obsolete visual projector wobbling precariously on his head. He closed his eyes and the lettering on the door disappeared. Cassal was too far away to see what it had been. The technician opened his eyes and concentrated. Slowly a new sign formed on the door.

TRAVELERS AID BUREAU
Murra Foray, First Counselor

It was a drab sign, but, then, it was a dismal, backward planet. The old technician passed on to the next door and closed his eyes again.

With a sinking feeling, Cassal walked toward the entrance. He needed help and he had to find it in this dingy rathole.

Inside, though, it wasn't dingy and it wasn't a rathole. More like a maze, an approved scientific one. Efficient, though not comfortable. Travelers Aid was busier than he thought it would be. Eventually he managed to squeeze into one of the many small counseling rooms.

A woman appeared on the screen, crisp and cool. "Please answer everything the machine asks. When the tape is complete, I'll be available for consultation."

Cassal wasn't sure he was going to like her. "Is this necessary?" he asked. "It's merely a matter of information."

"We have certain regulations we abide by." The woman smiled frostily. "I can't give you any information until you comply with them."

"Sometimes regulations are silly," said Cassal firmly. "Let me speak to the first counselor."

"You are speaking to her," she said. Her face disappeared from the screen.

Cassal sighed. So far he hadn't made a good impression.

Travelers Aid Bureau, in addition to regulations, was abundantly supplied with official curiosity. When the machine finished with him, Cassal had the feeling he could be recreated from the record it had of him. His individuality had been capsuled into a series of questions and answers. One thing he drew the line at—why he wanted to go to Tunney 21 was his own business.

The first counselor reappeared. Age, indeterminate. Not, he supposed, that anyone would be curious about it. Slightly taller than average, rather on the slender side. Face was broad at the brow, narrow at the chin and her eyes were enigmatic. A dangerous woman.

She glanced down at the data. "Denton Cassal, native of Earth. Destination, Tunney 21." She looked up at him. "Occupation, sales engineer. Isn't that an odd combination?" Her smile was quite superior.

"Not at all. Scientific training as an engineer. Special knowledge of customer relations."

"Special knowledge of a thousand races? How convenient." Her eyebrows arched.

"I think so," he agreed blandly. "Anything else you'd like to know?"

"Sorry. I didn't mean to offend you."

He could believe that or not as he wished. He didn't.

"You refused to answer why you were going to Tunney 21. Perhaps I can guess. They're the best scientists in the Galaxy. You wish to study under them."

Close—but wrong on two counts. They were good scientists, though not necessarily the best. For instance, it was doubtful that they could build Dimanche, even if they had ever thought of it, which was even less likely.

There was, however, one relatively obscure research worker on Tunney 21 that Neuronics wanted on their staff. If the fragments of his studies that had reached Earth across the vast distance meant anything, he could help Neuronics perfect instantaneous radio. The company that could build a radio to span the reaches of the Galaxy with no time lag could set its own price, which could be control of all communications, transport, trade—a galactic monopoly. Cassal's share would be a cut of all that.

His part was simple, on the surface. He was to persuade that researcher to come to Earth, *if he could.* Literally, he had to guess the Tunnesian's price before the Tunnesian himself knew it. In addition, the reputation of Tunnesian scientists being exceeded only by their arrogance, Cassal had to convince him that he wouldn't be working for ignorant Earth savages. The existence of such an instrument as Dimanche was a key factor.

Her voice broke through his thoughts. "Now, then, what's your problem?"

"I was told on Earth I might have to wait a few days on Godolph. I've been here three weeks. I want information on the ship bound for Tunney 21."

"Just a moment." She glanced at something below the angle of the screen. She looked up and her eyes were grave. "*Rickrock C* arrived yesterday. Departed for Tunney early this morning."

"Departed?" He got up and sat down again, swallowing hard. "When will the next ship arrive?"

"Do you know how many stars there are in the Galaxy?" she asked.

He didn't answer.

"That's right," she said. "Billions. Tunney, according to the notation, is near the center of the Galaxy, inside the third ring. You've covered about a third of the distance to it. Local traffic, anything within a thousand light-years, is relatively easy to manage. At longer distances, you take a chance. You've had yours and missed it. Frankly, Cassal, I don't know when another ship bound for Tunney will show up on or near Godolph. Within the next five years— maybe."

He blanched. "How long would it take to get there using local transportation, star-hopping?"

"Take my advice: don't try it. Five years, if you're lucky."

"I don't need that kind of luck."

"I suppose not." She hesitated. "You're determined to go on?" At the emphatic nod, she sighed. "If that's your decision, we'll try to help you. To start things moving, we'll need a print of your identification tab."

"There's something funny about her," Dimanche decided. It was the usual speaking voice of the instrument, no louder than the noise the blood made in coursing through arteries and veins. Cassal could hear it plainly, because it was virtually inside his ear.

Cassal ignored his private voice. "Identification tab? I don't have it with me. In fact, I may have lost it."

She smiled in instant disbelief. "We're not trying to pry into any part of your past you may wish concealed. However, it's much easier for us to help you if you have your identification. Now if you can't *remember* your real name and where you put your identification—" She arose and left the screen. "Just a moment."

He glared uneasily at the spot where the first counselor wasn't. His *real* name!

"Relax," Dimanche suggested. "She didn't mean it as a personal insult."

Presently she returned.

"I have news for you, whoever you are."

"Cassal," he said firmly. "Denton Cassal, sales engineer, Earth. If you don't believe it, send back to—" He stopped. It had taken him four months to get to Godolph, non-stop, plus a six-month wait on Earth for a ship to show up that was bound in the right direction. Over distances such as these, it just wasn't practical to send back to Earth for anything.

"I see you understand." She glanced at the card in her hand. "The spaceport records indicate that when *Rickrock C* took off this morning, there was a Denton Cassal on board, bound for Tunney 21."

"It wasn't I," he said dazedly. He knew who it was, though. The man who had tried to kill him last night. The reason for the attack now became clear. The thug had wanted his identification tab. Worse, he had gotten it.

"No doubt it wasn't," she said wearily. "Outsiders don't seem to understand what galactic travel entails."

Outsiders? Evidently what she called those who lived beyond the second transfer ring. Were those who lived at the edge of the Galaxy, beyond the first ring, called Rimmers? Probably.

She was still speaking: "Ten years to cross the Galaxy, without stopping. At present, no ship is capable of that. Real scheduling is impossible. Populations shift and have to be supplied. A ship is taken off a run for repairs and is never put back on. It's more urgently needed elsewhere. The man who depended on it is left waiting; years pass before he learns it's never coming.

"If we had instantaneous radio, that would help. Confusion

wouldn't vanish overnight, but it would diminish. We wouldn't have to depend on ships for all the news. Reservations could be made ahead of time, credit established, lost identification replaced—"

"I've traveled before," he interrupted stiffly. "I've never had any trouble."

She seemed to be exaggerating the difficulties. True, the center was more congested. Taking each star as the starting point for a limited number of ships and using statistical probability as a guide—why, no man would arrive at his predetermined destination.

But that wasn't the way it worked. Manifestly, you couldn't compare galactic transportation to the erratic paths of air molecules in a giant room. Or could you?

For the average man, anyone who didn't have his own interstellar ship, was the comparison too apt? It might be.

"You've traveled outside, where there are still free planets waiting to be settled. Where a man is welcome, if he's able to work." She paused. "The center is different. Populations are excessive. Inside the third ring, no man is allowed off a ship without an identification tab. They don't encourage immigration."

In effect, that meant no ship bound for the center would take a passenger without identification. No ship owner would run the risk of having a permanent guest on board, someone who couldn't be rid of when his money was gone.

Cassal held his head in his hands. Tunney 21 was inside the third ring.

"Next time," she said, "don't let anyone take your identification."

"I won't," he promised grimly.

The woman looked directly at him. Her eyes were bright. He revised his estimate of her age drastically downward. She couldn't be as old as he. Nothing outward had happened, but she no longer seemed dowdy. Not that he was interested. Still, it might pay him to be friendly to the first counselor.

"We're a philanthropic agency," said Murra Foray. "Your case is special, though—"

"I understand," he said gruffly. "You accept contributions."

She nodded. "If the donor is able to give. We don't ask so much that you'll have to compromise your standard of living." But she named a sum that would force him to do just that if getting to Tunney 21 took any appreciable time.

He stared at her unhappily. "I suppose it's worth it. I can always work, if I have to."

"As a salesman?" she asked. "I'm afraid you'll find it difficult to do business with Godolphians."

Irony wasn't called for at a time like this, he thought reproachfully.

"Not just another salesman," he answered definitely. "I have special knowledge of customer reactions. I can tell exactly—"

He stopped abruptly. Was she baiting him? For what reason? The instrument he called Dimanche was not known to the Galaxy at large. From the business angle, it would be poor policy to hand out that information at random. Aside from that, he needed every advantage he could get. Dimanche was his special advantage.

"Anyway," he finished lamely, "I'm a first class engineer. I can always find something in that line."

"A scientist, maybe," murmured Murra Foray. "But in this part of the Milky Way, an engineer is regarded as merely a technician who hasn't yet gained practical experience." She shook her head. "You'll do better as a salesman."

He got up, glowering. "If that's all—"

"It is. We'll keep you informed. Drop your contribution in the slot provided for that purpose as you leave."

A door, which he hadn't noticed in entering the counseling cubicle, swung open. The agency was efficient.

"Remember," the counselor called out as he left, "identification is hard to work with. Don't accept a crude forgery."

He didn't answer, but it was an idea worth considering. The agency was also eminently practical.

The exit path guided him firmly to an inconspicuous and yet inescapable contribution station. He began to doubt the philanthropic aspect of the bureau.

"I've got it," said Dimanche as Cassal gloomily counted out the sum the first counselor had named.

"Got what?" asked Cassal. He rolled the currency into a neat bundle, attached his name, and dropped it into the chute.

"The woman, Murra Foray, the first counselor. She's a Huntner."

"What's a Huntner?"

"A sub-race of men on the other side of the Galaxy. She was vocalizing about her home planet when I managed to locate her."

"Any other information?"

"None. Electronic guards were sliding into place as soon as I reached her. I got out as fast as I could."

"I see." The significance of that, if any, escaped him. Nevertheless, it sounded depressing.

"What I want to know is," said Dimanche, "why such precautions as electronic guards? What does Travelers Aid have that's so secret?"

Cassal grunted and didn't answer. Dimanche could be annoyingly inquisitive at times.

Cassal had entered one side of a block-square building. He came out on the other side. The agency was larger than he had thought. The old man was staring at a door as Cassal came out. He had apparently changed every sign in the building. His work finished, the technician was removing the visual projector from his head as Cassal came up to him. He turned and peered.

"You stuck here, too?" he asked in the uneven voice of the aged.

"Stuck?" repeated Cassal. "I suppose you can call it that. I'm waiting for my ship." He frowned. He was the one who wanted to ask questions. "Why all the redecoration? I thought Travelers Aid was an old agency. Why did you change so many signs? I could understand it if the agency were new."

The old man winked mysteriously. He opened his mouth and then selor resigned suddenly, in the middle of the night, they say. The new one didn't like the name of the agency, so she ordered it changed."

She would do just that, thought Cassal. "What about this Murra Foray?"

The old man winked mysteriously. He opened his mouth and then seemed overcome with senile fright. Hurriedly he shuffled away.

Cassal gazed after him, baffled. The old man was afraid for his job, afraid of the first counselor. Why he should be, Cassal didn't know. He shrugged and went on. The agency was now in motion in his behalf, but he didn't intend to depend on that alone.

"The girl ahead of you is making unnecessary wriggling motions as she walks," observed Dimanche. "Several men are looking on with approval. I don't understand."

Cassal glanced up. They walked that way back in good old L.A. A pang of homesickness swept through him.

"Shut up," he growled plaintively. "Attend to the business at hand."

"Business? Very well," said Dimanche. "Watch out for the transport tide."

Cassal swerved back from the edge of the water. Murra Foray had been right. Godolphians didn't want or need his skills, at least not on terms that were acceptable to him. The natives didn't have to exert themselves. They lived off the income provided by travelers, with which the planet was abundantly supplied by ship after ship.

Still, that didn't alter his need for money. He walked the streets at random while Dimanche probed.

"Ah!"

"What is it?"

"That man. He crinkles something in his hands. Not enough, he is subvocalizing."

"I know how he feels," commented Cassal.

"Now his throat tightens. He bunches his muscles. 'I know where I can get more,' he tells himself. He is going there."

"A sensible man," declared Cassal. "Follow him."

Boldly the man headed toward a section of the city which Cassal had not previously entered. He believed opportunity lay there. Not for everyone. The shrewd, observant, and the courageous could succeed if— The word that the quarry used was a slang term, unfamiliar to either Cassal or Dimanche. It didn't matter as long as it led to money.

Cassal stretched his stride and managed to keep the man in sight. He skipped nimbly over the narrow walkways that curved through the great buildings. The section grew dingier as they proceeded. Not slums; not the showplace city frequented by travelers, either.

Abruptly the man turned into a building. He was out of sight when Cassal reached the structure.

He stood at the entrance and stared in disappointment. "Opportunities Inc.," Dimanche quoted softly in his ear. "Science, thrills, chance. What does that mean?"

"It means that we followed a gravity ghost!"

"What's a gravity ghost?"

"An unexplained phenomenon," said Cassal nastily. "It affects the instruments of spaceships, giving the illusion of a massive dark body that isn't there."

"But you're not a pilot. I don't understand."

"You're not a very good pilot yourself. We followed the man to a gambling joint."

"Gambling," mused Dimanche. "Well, isn't it an opportunity of a sort? Someone inside is thinking of the money he's winning."

"The owner, no doubt."

Dimanche was silent, investigating. "It is the owner," he confirmed finally. "Why not go in, anyway. It's raining. And they serve drinks." Left unstated was the admission that Dimanche was curious, as usual.

Cassal went in and ordered a drink. It was a variable place, depending on the spectator—bright, cheerful, and harmonious if he were winning, garish and depressingly vulgar if he were not. At the moment Cassal belonged to neither group. He reserved judgment.

An assortment of gaming devices were in operation. One in particular seemed interesting. It involved the counting of electrons passing through an aperture, based on probability.

"Not that," whispered Dimanche. "It's rigged."

"But it's not necessary," Cassal murmured. "Pure chance alone is good enough."

"They don't take chances, pure or adulterated. Look around. How many Godolphians do you see?"

Cassal looked. Natives were not even there as servants. Strictly a clip joint, working travelers.

Unconsciously, he nodded. "That does it. It's not the kind of opportunity I had in mind."

"Don't be hasty," objected Dimanche. "Certain devices I can't control. There may be others in which my knowledge will help you. Stroll around and sample some games."

Cassal equipped himself with a supply of coins and sauntered through the establishment, disbursing them so as to give himself the widest possible acquaintance with the layout.

"That one," instructed Dimanche.

It received a coin. In return, it rewarded him with a large shower of change. The money spilled to the floor with a satisfying clatter. An audience gathered rapidly, ostensibly to help him pick up the coins.

"There was a circuit in it," explained Dimanche. "I gave it a shot of electrons and it paid out."

"Let's try it again," suggested Cassal.

"Let's not," Dimanche said regretfully. "Look at the man on your right."

Cassal did so. He jammed the money back in his pocket and stood up. Hastily, he began thrusting the money back into the machine. A large and very unconcerned man watched him.

"You get the idea," said Dimanche. "It paid off two months ago. It wasn't scheduled for another this year." Dimanche scrutinized the man in a multitude of ways while Cassal continued play. "He's satisfied," was the report at last. "He doesn't detect any sign of crookedness."

"Crookedness?"

"On your part, that is. In the ethics of a gambling house, what's done to insure profit is merely prudence."

They moved on to other games, though Cassal lost his briefly acquired enthusiasm. The possibility of winning seemed to grow more remote.

"Hold it," said Dimanche. "Let's look into this."

"Let me give *you* some advice," said Cassal. "This is one thing we can't win at. Every race in the Galaxy has a game like this. Pieces of plastic with values printed on them are distributed. The trick is to get certain arbitrarily selected sets of values in the plastics dealt to you. It seems simple, but against a skilled player a beginner can't win."

"Every race in the Galaxy," mused Dimanche. "What do men call it?"

"Cards," said Cassal, "though there are many varieties within that general classification." He launched into a detailed exposition of the subject. If it were something he was familiar with, all right, but a foreign deck and strange rules—

Nevertheless, Dimanche was interested. They stayed and observed. The dealer was clumsy. His great hands enfolded the cards. Not a Godolphian nor quite human, he was an odd type, difficult to place. Physically burly, he wore a garment chiefly remarkable for its ill-fitting appearance. A hard round hat jammed closely over his skull completed the outfit. He was dressed in a manner that, somewhere in the Universe, was evidently considered the height of fashion.

"It doesn't seem bad," commented Cassal. "There might be a chance."

"Look around," said Dimanche. "Everyone thinks that. It's the classic struggle, person against person and everyone against the house. Naturally, the house doesn't lose."

"Then why are we wasting our time?"

"Because I've got an idea," said Dimanche. "Sit down and take a hand."

"Make up your mind. You said the house doesn't lose."

"The house hasn't played against us. Sit down. You get eight cards, with the option of two more. I'll tell you what to do."

Cassal waited until a disconsolate player relinquished his seat and stalked moodily away. He played a few hands and bet small sums in accordance with Dimanche's instructions. He held his own and won insignificant amounts while learning.

It was simple. Nine orders, or suits, of twenty-seven cards each. Each suit would build a different equation. The lowest hand was a quadratic. A cubic would beat it. All he had to do was remember his math, guess at what he didn't remember, and draw the right cards.

"What's the highest possible hand?" asked Dimanche. There was a note of abstraction in his voice, as if he were paying more attention to something else.

Cassal peeked at the cards that were face-down on the table. He shoved some money into the betting square in front of him and didn't answer.

"You had it last time," said Dimanche. "A three dimensional encephalocurve. A time modulated brainwave. If you had bet right, you could have owned the house by now."

"I did? Why didn't you tell me?"

"Because you had it three successive times. The probabilities against that are astronomical. I've got to find out what's happening before you start betting recklessly."

"It's not the dealer," declared Cassal. "Look at those hands."

They were huge hands, more suitable, seemingly, for crushing the life from some alien beast than the delicate manipulation of cards. Cassal continued to play, betting brilliantly by the only standard that mattered: he won.

One player dropped out and was replaced by a recruit from the surrounding crowd. Cassal ordered a drink. The waiter was placing it in his hand when Dimanche made a discovery.

"I've got it!"

A shout from Dimanche was roughly equivalent to a noiseless kick in the head. Cassal dropped the drink. The player next to him scowled but said nothing. The dealer blinked and went on dealing.

"What have you got?" asked Cassal, wiping up the mess and trying to keep track of the cards.

"How he fixes the deck," explained Dimanche in a lower and less painful tone. "Clever."

Muttering, Cassal shoved a bet in front of him.

"Look at that hat," said Dimanche.

"Ridiculous, isn't it? But I see no reason to gloat because I have better taste."

"That's not what I meant. It's pulled down low over his knobby ears and touches his jacket. His jacket rubs against his trousers, which in turn come in contact with the stool on which he sits."

"True," agreed Cassal, increasing his wager. "But except for his physique, I don't see anything unusual."

"It's a circuit, a visual projector broken down into components. The hat is a command circuit which makes contact, via his clothing, with the broadcasting unit built into the chair. The existence of a visual projector is completely concealed."

Cassal bit his lip and squinted at his cards. "Interesting. What does it have to do with anything?"

"The deck," exclaimed Dimanche excitedly. "The backs are regular, printed with an intricate design. The front is a special plastic, susceptible to the influence of the visual projector. He doesn't need manual dexterity. He can make any value appear on any card he wants. It will stay there until he changes it."

Cassal picked up the cards. "I've got a Loreenaroo equation. Can he change that to anything else?"

"He can, but he doesn't work that way. He decides before he deals who's going to get what. He concentrates on each card as he deals it. He can change a hand after a player gets it, but it wouldn't look good."

"It wouldn't." Cassal wistfully watched the dealer rake in his wager. His winnings were gone, plus. The newcomer to the game won.

He started to get up. "Sit down," whispered Dimanche. "We're just beginning. Now that we know what he does and how he does it, we're going to take him."

The next hand started in the familiar pattern, two cards of fairly good possibilities, a bet, and then another card. Cassal watched the dealer closely. His clumsiness was only superficial. At no time were the faces of the cards visible. The real skill was unobservable, of course—the swift bookkeeping that went on in his mind. A duplication in the hands of the players, for instance, would be ruinous.

Cassal received the last card. "Bet high," said Dimanche. With trepidation, Cassal shoved the money into the betting area.

The dealer glanced at his hand and started to sit down. Abruptly he stood up again. He scratched his cheek and stared puzzledly at the players around him. Gently he lowered himself onto the stool. The contact was even briefer. He stood up in indecision. An impatient murmur arose. He dealt himself a card, looked at it, and paid off all the way around. The players buzzed with curiosity.

"What happened?" asked Cassal as the next hand started.

"I induced a short in the circuit," said Dimanche. "He couldn't sit down to change the last card he got. He took a chance, as he had to, and dealt himself a card, anyway."

"But he paid off without asking to see what we had."

"It was the only thing he could do," explained Dimanche. "He had duplicate cards."

The dealer was scowling. He didn't seem quite so much at ease. The cards were dealt and the betting proceeded almost as usual. True, the dealer was nervous. He couldn't sit down and stay down. He was sweating. Again he paid off. Cassal won heavily and he was not the only one.

The crowd around them grew almost in a rush. There is an indefinable sense that tells one gambler when another is winning. This time the dealer stood up. His leg contacted the stool occasionally. He jerked it away each time he dealt to himself. At the last card he hesitated. It was amazing how much he could sweat. He lifted a corner of the cards. Without indicating what he had drawn, determinedly and deliberately he sat down. The chair broke. The dealer grinned weakly as a waiter brought him another stool.

"They still think it may be a defective circuit," whispered Dimanche.

The dealer sat down and sprang up from the new chair in one motion. He gazed bitterly at the players and paid them.

"He had a blank hand," explained Dimanche. "He made contact with the broadcasting circuit long enough to erase, but not long enough to put anything in its place."

The dealer adjusted his coat. "I have a nervous disability," he declared thickly. "If you'll pardon me for a few minutes while I take a treatment—"

"Probably going to consult with the manager," observed Cassal.

"He is the manager. He's talking with the owner."

"Keep track of him."

A blonde, pretty, perhaps even Earth-type human, smiled and wriggled closer to Cassal. He smiled back.

"Don't fall for it," warned Dimanche. "She's an undercover agent for the house."

Cassal looked her over carefully. "Not much under cover."

"But if she should discover—"

"Don't be stupid. She'll never guess you exist. There's a small lump behind my ear and a small round tube cleverly concealed elsewhere."

"All right," sighed Dimanche resignedly. "I suppose people will always be a mystery to me."

The dealer reappeared, followed by an unobtrusive man who carried a new stool. The dealer looked subtly different, though he was the same person. It took a close inspection to determine what the difference was. His clothing was new, unrumpled, unmarked by perspiration. During his brief absence, he had been furnished with new visual projector equipment, and it had been thoroughly checked out. The house intended to locate the source of the disturbance.

Mentally, Cassal counted his assets. He was solvent again, but in other ways his position was not so good.

"Maybe," he suggested, "we should leave. With no further interference from us, they might believe defective equipment is the cause of their losses."

"Maybe," replied Dimanche, "you think the crowd around us is composed solely of patrons?"

"I see," said Cassal soberly.

He stretched his legs. The crowd pressed closer, uncommonly aggressive and ill-tempered for mere spectators. He decided against leaving.

"Let's resume play." The dealer-manager smiled blandly at each player. He didn't suspect any one person—yet.

"He might be using an honest deck," said Cassal hopefully.

"They don't have that kind," answered Dimanche. He added absently: "During his conference with the owner, he was given authority to handle the situation in any way he sees fit."

Bad, but not too bad. At least Cassal was opposing someone who had authority to let him keep his winnings, *if he could be convinced*. The dealer deliberately sat down on the stool. Testing. He could endure the charge that trickled through him. The bland smile spread into a triumphant one.

"While he was gone, he took a sedative," analyzed Dimanche. "He also had the strength of the broadcasting circuit reduced. He thinks that will do it."

"Sedatives wear off," said Cassal. "By the time he knows it's me, see that it has worn off. Mess him up."

The game went on. The situation was too much for the others. They played poorly and bet atrociously, on purpose. One by one they lost and dropped out. They wanted badly to win, but they wanted to live even more.

The joint was jumping, and so was the dealer again. Sweat rolled down his face and there were tears in his eyes. So much liquid began to erode his fixed smile. He kept replenishing it from some inner source of determination.

Cassal looked up. The crowd had drawn back, or had been forced back by hirelings who mingled with them. He was alone with the dealer at the table. Money was piled high around him. It was more than he needed, more than he wanted.

"I suggest one last hand," said the dealer-manager, grimacing. It sounded a little stronger than a suggestion.

Cassal nodded.

"For a substantial sum," said the dealer, naming it.

Miraculously, it was an amount that equaled everything Cassal had. Again Cassal nodded.

"Pressure," muttered Cassal to Dimanche. "The sedative has worn off. He's back at the level at which he started. Fry him if you have to."

The cards came out slowly. The dealer was jittering as he dealt. Soft music was lacking, but not the motions that normally accompanied it. Cassal couldn't believe that cards could be so bad. Somehow the dealer was rising to the occasion. Rising and sitting.

"There's a nerve in your body," Cassal began conversationally, "which, if it were overloaded, would cause you to drop dead."

The dealer didn't examine his cards. He didn't have to. "In that event, someone would be arrested for murder," he said. "You."

That was the wrong tack; the humanoid had too much courage. Cassal passed his hand over his eyes. "You can't do this to men, but, strictly speaking, the dealer's not human. Try suggestion on him. Make him change the cards. Play him like a piano. Pizzicato on the nerve strings."

Dimanche didn't answer; presumably he was busy scrambling the circuits.

The dealer stretched out his hand. It never reached the cards. Danger: Dimanche at work. The smile dropped from his face. What remained was pure anguish. He was too dry for tears. Smoke curled up faintly from his jacket.

"Hot, isn't it?" asked Cassal. "It might be cooler if you took off your cap."

The cap tinkled to the floor. The mechanism in it was destroyed. What the cards were, they were. Now they couldn't be changed.

"That's better," said Cassal.

He glanced at his hand. In the interim, it had changed slightly. Dimanche had got there.

The dealer examined his cards one by one. His face changed color. He sat utterly still on a cool stool.

"You win," he said hopelessly.

"Let's see what you have."

The dealer-manager roused himself. "You won. That's good enough for you, isn't it?"

Cassal shrugged. "You have Bank of the Galaxy service here. I'll deposit my money with them *before* you pick up your cards."

The dealer nodded unhappily and summoned an assistant. The crowd, which had anticipated violence, slowly began to drift away.

"What did you do?" asked Cassal silently.

"Men have no shame," sighed Dimanche. "Some humanoids do. The dealer was one who did. I forced him to project onto his cards something that wasn't a suit at all."

"Embarrassing if that got out," agreed Cassal. "What did you project?"

Dimanche told him. Cassal blushed, which was unusual for a man.

The dealer-manager returned and the transaction was completed. His money was safe in the Bank of the Galaxy.

"Hereafter, you're not welcome," said the dealer morosely. "Don't come back."

Cassal picked up the cards without looking at them. "And no accidents after I leave," he said, extending the cards face-down. The manager took them and trembled.

"He's an honorable humanoid, in his own way," whispered Dimanche. "I think you're safe."

It was time to leave. "One question," Cassal called back. "What do you call this game?"

Automatically the dealer started to answer. "Why everyone knows . . ." He sat down, his mouth open.

It was more than time to leave.

Outside, he hailed an air taxi. No point in tempting the management.

"Look," said Dimanche as the cab rose from the surface of the transport tide.

A technician with a visual projector was at work on the sign in front of the gaming house. Huge words took shape: WARNING—NO TELEPATHS ALLOWED.

There were no such things anywhere, but now there were rumors of them.

Arriving at the habitat wing of the hotel, Cassal went directly to his room. He awaited the delivery of the equipment he had ordered and checked through it thoroughly. Satisfied that everything was there, he estimated the size of the room. Too small for his purpose.

He picked up the intercom and dialed Services. "Put a Life Stage Cordon around my suite," he said briskly.

The face opposite his went blank. "But you're an Earthman. I thought—"

"I know more about my own requirements than your Life Stage Bureau. Earthmen do have life stages. You know the penalty if you refuse that service."

There were some races who went without sleep for five months and then had to make up for it. Others grew vestigial wings for brief periods and had to fly with them or die; reduced gravity would suffice for that. Still others—

But the one common feature was always a critical time in which certain conditions were necessary. Insofar as there was a universal law, from one end of the Galaxy to the other, this was it: The habitat hotel had to furnish appropriate conditions for the maintenance of any life-form that requested it.

The Godolphian disappeared from the screen. When he came back, he seemed disturbed.

"You spoke of a suite. I find that you're listed as occupying one room."

"I am. It's too small. Convert the rooms around me into a suite."

"That's very expensive."

"I'm aware of that. Check the Bank of the Galaxy for my credit rating."

He watched the process take place. Service would be amazingly good from now on.

"Your suite will be converted in about two hours. The Life Stage Cordon will begin as soon after that as you want. If you tell me how long you'll need it, I can make arrangements now."

"About ten hours is all I'll need." Cassal rubbed his jaw reflectively. "One more thing. Put a perpetual service at the spaceport. If a ship comes in bound for Tunney 21 or the vicinity of it, get accommodations on it for me. And hold it until I get ready, no matter what it costs."

He flipped off the intercom and promptly went to sleep. Hours later, he was awakened by a faint hum. The Life Stage Cordon had just been snapped safely around his newly created suite.

"Now what?" asked Dimanche.

"I need an identification tab."

"You do. And forgeries are expensive and generally crude, as that Huntner woman, Murra Foray, observed."

Cassal glanced at the equipment. "Expensive, yes. Not crude when we do it."

"*We* forge it?" Dimanche was incredulous.

"That's what I said. Consider it this way. I've seen my tab a countless number of times. If I tried to draw it as I remember it, it would be inept and wouldn't pass. Nevertheless, that memory is in my mind, recorded in neuronic chains, exact and accurate." He paused significantly. "You have access to that memory."

"At least partially. But what good does that do?"

"Visual projector and plastic which will take the imprint. I think hard about the identification as I remember it. You record and feed it back to me while I concentrate on projecting it on the plastic. After we get it down, we change the chemical composition of the plastic. It will then pass everything except destructive analysis, and they don't often do that."

Dimanche was silent. "Ingenious," was its comment. "Part of that we can manage, the official engraving, even the electron stamp. That, however, is gross detail. The print of the brain area is beyond our capacity. We can put down what you remember, and you remember what you saw. You didn't see fine enough, though. The general area will be recognizable, but not the fine structure, nor the charges stored there nor their interrelationship."

"But we've got to do it," Cassal insisted, pacing about nervously.

"With more equipment to probe—"

"Not a chance. I got one Life Stage Cordon on a bluff. If I ask for another, they'll look it up and refuse."

"All right," said Dimanche, humming. The mechanical attempt at music made Cassal's head ache. "I've got an idea. Think about the identification tab."

Cassal thought.

"Enough," said Dimanche. "Now poke yourself."

"Where?"

"Everywhere," replied Dimanche irritably. "One place at a time."

Cassal did so, though it soon became monotonous.

Dimanche stopped him. "Just above your right knee."

"What above my right knee?"

"The principal access to that part of your brain we're concerned with," said Dimanche. "We can't photomeasure your brain the way it was originally done, but we can investigate it remotely. The results will be simplified, naturally. Something like a scale model as compared to the orignial. A more apt comparison might be that of a relief map to an actual locality."

"Investigate it remotely?" muttered Cassal. A horrible suspicion touched his consciousness. He jerked away from that touch. "What does that mean?"

"What it sounds like. Stimulus and response. From that I can construct an accurate chart of the proper portion of your brain. Our probing instruments will be crude out of necessity, but effective."

"I've already visualized those probing instruments," said Cassal worriedly. "Maybe we'd better work first on the official engraving and the electron stamp, while I'm still fresh. I have a feeling . . ."

"Excellent suggestion," said Dimanche.

Cassal gathered the articles slowly. His lighter would burn and it would also cut. He needed a heavy object to pound with. A violent irritant for the nerve endings. Something to freeze his flesh . . .

Dimanche interrupted: "There are also a few glands we've got to pick up. See if there's a stimi in the room."

"Stimi? Oh yes, a stimulator. Never use the damned things." But he was going to. The next few hours weren't going to be pleasant. Nor dull, either.

Life could be difficult in Godolph.

As soon as the Life Stage Cordon came down, Cassal called for a doctor. The native looked at him professionally.

"Is this a part of the Earth life process?" he asked incredulously. Gingerly, he touched the swollen and lacerated leg.

Cassel nodded wearily. "A matter of life and death," he croaked.

"If it is, then it is," said the doctor, shaking his head. "I, for one, am glad to be a Godolphian."

"To each his own habitat," Cassal quoted the motto of the hotel.

Godolphians were clumsy, good-natured caricatures of seals. There was nothing wrong with their medicine, however. In a matter of minutes he was feeling better. By the time the doctor left, the swelling had subsided and the open wounds were fast closing.

Eagerly, he examined the identification tab. As far as he could tell, it was perfect. What the scanner would reveal was, of course, another matter. He had to check that as best he could without exposing himself.

Services came up to the suite right after he laid the intercom down. A machine was placed over his head and the identification slipped into the slot. The code on the tab was noted; the machine hunted and found the corresponding brain area. Structure was mapped, impulses recorded, scrambled, converted into a ray of light which danced over a film.

The identification tab was similarly recorded. There was now a means of comparison.

Fingerprints could be duplicated—that is, if the race in question had fingers. Every intelligence, however much it differed from its neighbors, had a brain, and tampering with that brain was easily detected. Each identification tab carried a psychometric number which corresponded to the total personality. Alteration of any part of the brain could only subtract from personality index.

The technician removed the identification and gave it to Cassal. "Where shall I send the strips?"

"You don't," said Cassal. "I have a private message to go with them."

"But that will invalidate the process."

"I know. This isn't a formal contract."

Removing the two strips and handing them to Cassal, the technician wheeled the machine away. After due thought, Cassal composed the message.

Travelers Aid Bureau
Murra Foray, first counselor:
   If you were considering another identification tab for me, don't. As you can see, I've located the missing item.

He attached the message to the strips and dropped them into the communication chute.

He was wiping his whiskers away when the answer came. Hastily he finished and wrapped himself, noting but not approving the amused glint in her eyes as she watched. His morals were his own, wherever he went.

"Denton Cassal," she said. "A wonderful job. The two strips were in register within one per cent. The best previous forgery I've seen was six per cent, and that was merely a lucky accident. It couldn't be duplicated. Let me congratulate you."

His dignity was professional. "I wish you weren't so fond of that word 'forgery.' I told you I mislaid the tab. As soon as I found it, I sent you proof. I want to get to Tunney 21. I'm willing to do anything I can to speed up the process."

Her laughter tinkled. "You don't *have* to tell me how you did it or where you got it. I'm inclined to think you made it. You understand that I'm not concerned with legality as such. From time to time the agency has to furnish missing documents. If there's a better way than we have, I'd like to know it."

He sighed and shook his head. For some reason, his heart was beating fast. He wanted to say more, but there was nothing to say. When he failed to respond, she leaned toward him. "Perhaps you'll discuss this with me. At greater length."

"At the agency?"

She looked at him in surprise. "Have you been sleeping? The agency is closed for the day. The first counselor can't work all the time, you know."

Sleeping? He grimaced at the remembrance of the self-administered beating. No, he hadn't been sleeping. He brushed the thought aside and boldly named a place. Dinner was acceptable.

Dimanche waited until the screen was dark. The words were carefully chosen.

"Did you notice," he asked, "that there was no apparent change in clothing and makeup, yet she seemed younger, more attractive?"

"I didn't think you could trace her that far."

"I can't. I looked at her through your eyes."

"Don't trust my reaction," advised Cassal. "It's likely to be subjective."

"I don't," answered Dimanche. "It is."

Cassal hummed thoughtfully. Dimanche was a business neurological instrument. It didn't follow that it was an expert in human psychology.

Cassal stared at the woman coming toward him. Center-of-the-Galaxy fashion. Decadent, of course, or maybe ultra-civilized. As an Outsider, he wasn't sure which. Whatever it was, it did to the human body what should have been done long ago.

And this body wasn't exactly human. The subtle skirt of proportions betrayed it as an offshoot or deviation from the human race. Some of the new subraces stacked up against the original stock much in the same way Cro-Magnons did against Neanderthals, in beauty, at least.

Dimanche spoke a single syllable and subsided, an event Cassal didn't notice. His consciousness was focused on another discovery: the woman was Murra Foray.

He knew vaguely that the first counselor was not necessarily what she had seemed that first time at the agency. That she was capable of such a metamorphosis was hard to believe, though pleasant to accept. His attitude must have shown on his face.

"Please," said Murra Foray. "I'm a Huntner. We're adept at camouflage."

"Huntner," he repeated blankly. "I knew that. But what's a Huntner?"

She wrinkled her lovely nose at the question. "I didn't expect you to ask that. I won't answer it now." She came closer. "I thought you'd ask which was the camouflage—the person you see here, or the one at the Bureau?"

He never remembered the reply he made. It must have been satisfactory, for she smiled and drew her fragile wrap closer. The reservations were waiting.

Dimanche seized the opportunity to speak. "There's something phony about her. I don't understand it and I don't like it."

"You," said Cassal, "are a machine. You don't have to like it."

"That's what I mean. You *have* to like it. You have no choice."

Murra Foray looked back questioningly. Cassal hurried to her side.

The evening passed swiftly. Food that he ate and didn't taste. Music he heard and didn't listen to. Geometric light fugues that were seen and not observed. Liquor that he drank—and here the sequence ended, in the complicated chemistry of Godolphian stimulants.

Cassal reacted to that smooth liquid, though his physical reactions were not slowed. Certain mental centers were depressed, others left wide open, subject to acceleration at whatever speed he demanded.

Murra Foray, in his eyes at least, might look like a dream, the kind men have and never talk about. She was, however, interested solely in her work, or so it seemed.

"Godolph is a nice place," she said, toying with a drink, "if you like rain. The natives seem happy enough. But the Galaxy is big and there are lots of strange planets in it, each of which seems ideal to those who are adapted to it. I don't have to tell you what happens when people travel. They get stranded. It's not the time spent in actual flight that's important; it's waiting for the right ship to show up and then having all the necessary documents. Believe me, that can be important, as you found out."

He nodded. He had.

"That's the origin of Travelers Aid Bureau," she continued. "A loose organization, propagated mainly by example. Sometimes it's called Star Travelers Aid. It may have other names. The aim, however, is always the same: to see that stranded persons get where they want to go."

She looked at him wistfully, appealingly. "That's why I'm interested in your method of creating identification tabs. It's the thing most commonly lost. Stolen, if you prefer the truth."

She seemed to anticipate his question. "How can anyone use another's identification? It can be done under certain circumstances. By neural lobotomy, a portion of one brain may be made to match, more or less exactly, the code area of another brain. The person operated on suffers a certain loss of function, of course. How great that loss is depends on the degree of similarity between the two brain areas before the operation took place."

She ought to know, and he was inclined to believe her. Still, it didn't sound feasible.

"You haven't accounted for the psychometric index," he said.

"I thought you'd see it. That's diminished, too."

Logical enough, though not a pretty picture. A genius could always be made into an average man or lowered to the level of an idiot. There was no operation, however, that could raise an idiot to the level of a genius.

The scramble for the precious identification tabs went on, from the higher to the lower, a game of musical chairs with grim overtones.

She smiled gravely. "You haven't answered my implied question."

The company that employed him wasn't anxious to let the secret of Dimanche get out. They didn't sell the instrument; they made it for their own use. It was an advantage over their competitors they intended to keep. Even on his recommendation, they wouldn't sell to the agency.

Moreover, it wouldn't help Travelers Aid Bureau if they did. Since she was first counselor, it was probable that she'd be the one to use it. She couldn't make identification for anyone except herself, and then only if she developed exceptional skill.

The alternative was to surgery it in and out of whoever needed it. When that happened, secrecy was gone. Travelers couldn't be trusted.

He shook his head. "It's an appealing idea, but I'm afraid I can't help you."

"Meaning you won't."

This was intriguing. Now it was the agency, not he, who wanted help.

"Don't overplay it," cautioned Dimanche, who had been consistently silent.

She leaned forward attentively. He experienced an uneasy moment. Was it possible she had noticed his private conversation? Of course not. Yet—

"Please," she said, and the tone allayed his fears. "There's an emergency situation and I've got to attend to it. Will you go with me?" She smiled understandingly at his quizzical expression. "Travelers Aid is always having emergencies."

She was rising. "It's too late to go to the Bureau. My place has a number of machines with which I keep in touch with the spaceport."

"I wonder," said Dimanche puzzledly. "She doesn't subvocalize at all. I haven't been able to get a line on her. I'm certain she didn't receive any sort of call. Be careful.

"This might be a trick."

"Interesting," said Cassal. He wasn't in the mood to discuss it.

Her habitation was luxurious, though Cassal wasn't impressed. Luxury was found everywhere in the Universe. Huntner women weren't. He watched as she adjusted the machines grouped at one side of the room. She spoke in a low voice; he couldn't distinguish words. She actuated levers, pressed buttons: impedimenta of communication.

At last she finished. "I'm tired. Will you wait till I change?" Inarticulately, he nodded.

"I think her 'emergency' was a fake," said Dimanche flatly as soon as she left. "I'm positive she wasn't operating the communicator. She merely went through the motions."

"Motions," murmured Cassal dreamily, leaning back. "And what motions."

"I've been watching her," said Dimanche. "She frightens me."

"I've been watching her, too. Maybe in a different way."

"Get out of here while you can," warned Dimanche. "She's dangerous."

Momentarily, Cassal considered it. Dimanche had never failed him. He ought to follow that advice. And yet there was another explanation.

"Look," said Cassal. "A machine is a machine. But among humans there are men and women. What seems dangerous to you may be merely a pattern of normal behavior . . ." He broke off. Murra Foray had entered.

Strictly from the other side of the Galaxy, which she was. A woman can be slender and still be womanly beautiful, without being obvious about it. Not that Murra disdained the obvious, technically. But he could see through technicalities.

The tendons in his hands ached and his mouth was dry, though not with fear. An urgent ringing pounded in his ears. He shook it out of his head and got up.

She came to him.

The ringing was still in his ears. It wasn't a figment of imagination; it was a real voice—that of Dimanche, howling:

"Huntner! It's a word variant. In their language it means Hunter. *She can hear me!*"

"Hear you?" repeated Cassal vacantly.

She was kissing him.

"A descendant of carnivores. An audiosensitive. She's been listening to you and me all the time."

"Of course I have, ever since the first interview at the bureau," said Murra. "In the beginning I couldn't see what value it was, but you convinced me." She laid her hand gently over his eyes. "I hate to do this to you, dear, but I've got to have Dimanche."

She had been smothering him with caresses. Now, deliberately, she began smothering him in actuality.

Cassal had thought he was an athlete. For an Earthman, he was. Murra Foray, however, was a Huntner, which meant hunter—a descendant of incredibly strong carnivores.

He didn't have a chance. He knew that when he couldn't budge her hands and he fell into the airless blackness of space.

Alone and naked, Cassal awakened. He wished he hadn't. He turned over and, though he tried hard not to, promptly woke up again. His body was willing to sleep, but his mind was panicked and disturbed. About what, he wasn't sure.

He sat up shakily and held his roaring head in his hands. He ran aching fingers through his hair. He stopped. The lump behind his ear was gone.

"Dimanche!" he called, and looked at his abdomen.

There was a thin scar, healing visibly before his eyes.

"Dimanche!" he cried again. "Dimanche!"

There was no answer. Dimanche was no longer with him.

He staggered to his feet and stared at the wall. She'd been kind enough to return him to his own rooms. At length he gathered enough strength to rummage through his belongings. Nothing was missing. Money, identification—all were there.

He could go to the police. He grimaced as he thought of it. The neighborly Godolphian police were hardly a match for the Huntner; she'd fake them out of their skins.

He couldn't prove she'd taken Dimanche. Nothing else normally considered valuable was missing. Besides, there might even be a local prohibition against Dimanche. Not by name, of course; but they could dig up an ancient ordinance—invasion of privacy or something like that. Anything would do if it gave them an opportunity to confiscate the device for intensive study.

For the police to believe his story was the worst that could happen. They might locate Dimanche, but he'd never get it.

He smiled bitterly and the effort hurt. "Dear," she had called him as she had strangled and beaten him into unconsciousness. Afterward singing, very likely, as she had sliced the little instrument out of him.

He could picture her not very remote ancestors springing from cover and overtaking a fleeing herd—
No use pursuing that line of thought.
Why did she want Dimanche? She had hinted that the agency wasn't always concerned with legality as such. He could believe her. If she wanted it for making identification tabs, she'd soon find that it was useless. Not that that was much comfort—she wasn't likely to return Dimanche after she'd made that discovery.

For that matter, what was the purpose of Travelers Aid Bureau? It was a front for another kind of activity. Philanthropy had nothing to do with it.
If he still had possession of Dimanche, he'd be able to find out. Everything seemed to hinge on that. With it, he was nearly a superman, able to hold his own in practically all situations—anything that didn't involve a Huntner woman, that is.
Without it—well, Tunney 21 was still far away. Even if he should manage to get there without it, his mission on the planet was certain to fail.
He dismissed the idea of trying to recover it immediately from Murra Foray. She was an audio-sensitive. At twenty feet, unaided, she could hear a heartbeat, the internal noise muscles made in sliding over each other. With Dimanche, she could hear electrons rustling. As an antagonist she was altogether too formidable.

He began pulling on his clothing, wincing as he did so. The alternative was to make another Dimanche. *If* he could. It would be a tough job even for a neuronic expert familiar with the process. He wasn't that expert, but it still had to be done.
The new instrument would have to be better than the original. Maybe not such a slick machine, but more comprehensive. More wallop. He grinned as he thought hopefully about giving Murra Foray a surprise.
Ignoring his aches and pains, he went right to work. With money not a factor, it was an easy matter to line up the best electronic and neuron concerns on Godolph. Two were put on a standby basis. When he gave them plans, they were to rush construction at all possible speed.
Each concern was to build a part of the new instrument. Neither part was of value without the other. The slow-thinking Godolphians weren't likely to make the necessary mental connection between the seemingly unrelated projects.
He retired to his suite and began to draw diagrams. It was harder than he thought. He knew the principles, but the actual details were far more complicated than he remembered.

Functionally, the Dimanche instrument was divided into three main phases. There was a brain and memory unit that operated much as the human counterpart did. Unlike the human brain, however, it had no body to control, hence more of it was available for thought processes. Entirely neuronic in construction, it was far smaller than an electronic brain of the same capacity.

The second function was electronic, akin to radar. Instead of material objects, it traced and recorded distant nerve impulses. It could count the heartbeat, measure the rate of respiration, was even capable of approximate analysis of the contents of the bloodstream. Properly focused on the nerves of tongue, lips or larynx, it transmitted that data back to the neuronic brain, which then reconstructed it into speech. Lip reading, after a fashion, carried to the ultimate.

Finally, there was the voice of Dimanche, a speaker under the control of the neuronic brain.

For convenience of installation in the body, Dimanche was packaged in two units. The larger package was usually surgeried into the abdomen. The small one, containing the speaker, was attached to the skull just behind the ear. It worked by bone conduction, allowing silent communication between operator and instrument. A real convenience.

It wasn't enough to know this, as Cassal did. He'd talked to the company experts, had seen the symbolical drawings, the plans for an improved version. He needed something better than the best though, that had been planned.

The drawback was this: *Dimanche was powered directly by the nervous system of the body in which it was housed.* Against Murra Foray, he'd be overmatched. She was stronger than he physically, probably also in the production of nervous energy.

One solution was to make available to the new instrument a larger fraction of the neural currents of the body. That was dangerous—a slight miscalculation and the user was dead. Yet he had to have an instrument that would overpower her.

Cassal rubbed his eyes wearily. How could he find some way of supplying additional power?

Abruptly, Cassal sat up. That was the way, of course—an auxiliary power pack that need not be surgeried into his body, extra power that he would use only in emergencies.

Neuronics, Inc., had never done this, had never thought that such an instrument would ever be necessary. They didn't need to overpower their customers. They merely wanted advance information via subvocalized thoughts.

It was easier for Cassal to conceive this idea than to engineer it. At the end of the first day, he knew it would be a slow process.

Twice he postponed deadlines to the manufacturing concerns he'd engaged. He locked himself in his rooms and took Anti-Sleep against the doctor's vigorous protests. In one week he had the necessary drawings, crude but legible. An expert would have to make innumerable corrections, but the intent was plain.

One week. During that time Murra Foray would be growing hourly more proficient in the use of Dimanche.

Cassal followed the neuronics expert groggily, seventy-two hours sleep still clogging his reactions. Not that he hadn't needed sleep after that week. The Godolphian showed him proudly through the shops, though he wasn't at all interested in their achievements. The only noteworthy aspect was the grand scale of their architecture.

"We did it, though I don't think we'd have the job if we'd known how hard it was going to be," the neuronics expert chattered. "It works exactly as you specified. We had to make substitutions, of course, but you understand that was inevitable."

He glanced anxiously as Cassal, who nodded. That was to be expected. Components that were common on Earth wouldn't necessarily be available here. Still, any expert worth his pay could always make the proper combinations and achieve the same results.

Inside the lab, Cassal frowned. "I thought you were keeping my work separate. What is this planetary drive doing here?"

The Godolphian spread his broad hands and looked hurt. "Planetary drive?" He tried to laugh. "This is the instrument you ordered!"

Cassal started. It was supposed to fit under a flap of skin behind his ear. A Three World saurian couldn't carry it.

He turned savagely on the expert. "I told you it had to be small."

"But it is. I quote your orders exactly: 'I'm not familiar with your system of measurement, but make it tiny, very tiny. Figure the size you think it will have to be and cut it in half. And than cut *that* in half.' This is the fraction remaining."

It certainly was. Cassal glanced at the Godolphian's hands. Excellent for swimming. No wonder they built on a grand scale. Broad, blunt, webbed hands weren't exactly suited for precision work.

Valueless. Completely valueless. He knew now what he would find at the other lab. He shook his head in dismay, personally saw to it that the instrument was destroyed. He paid for the work and retrieved the plans.

Back in his rooms again, he sat and thought. It was still the only solution. If the Godolphians couldn't do it, he'd have to find some race that could. He grabbed the intercom and jangled it savagely. In half an hour he had a dozen leads.

The best seemed to be the Spirella. A small, insectlike race, about three feet tall, they were supposed to have excellent manual dexterity, and were technically advanced. They sounded as if they were acquainted with the necessary fields. Three lightyears away, they could be reached by readily available local transportation within the day. Their idea of what was small was likely to coincide with his.

He didn't bother to pack. The suite would remain his headquarters. Home was where his enemies were.

He made a mental correction—enemy.

He rubbed his sensitive ear, grateful for the discomfort. His stomach was sore, but it wouldn't be for long. The Spirella had made the new instrument just as he had wanted it. They had built an even better auxiliary power unit than he had specified. He fingered the flat cases in his pocket. In an emergency, he could draw on these, whereas Murra Foray would be limited to the energy in her nervous system.

What he had now was hardly the same instrument. A Military version of it, perhaps. It didn't seem right to use the same name. Call it something staunch and crisp, suggestive of raw power. Manche. As good a name as any. Manche against Dimanche. Cassal against a queen.

He swung confidently along the walkway beside the transport tide. It was raining. He decided to test the new instrument. The Godolphian across the way bent double and wondered why his knees wouldn't work. They had suddenly became swollen and painful to move. Maybe it was the climate.

And maybe it wasn't, thought Cassal. Eventually the pain would leave, but he hadn't meant to be so rough on the native. He'd have to watch how he used Manche.

He scouted the vicinity of Travelers Aid Bureau, keeping at least one building between him and possible detection. Purely precautionary. There was no indication that Murra Foray had spotted him. For a Huntner, she wasn't very alert, apparently.

He sent Manche out on exploration at minimum strength. The electronic guards which Dimanche had spoken of were still in place. Manche went through easily and didn't disturb an electron. Behind the guards there was no trace of the first counselor.

He went closer. Still no warning of danger. The same old technician shuffled in front of the entrance. A horrible thought hit him. It was easy enough to verify. Another "reorganization" *had* taken place. The new sign read:

STAR TRAVELERS AID BUREAU
STAB *Your Hour*
of Need
Delly Mortinbras, first counselor

Cassal leaned against the building, unable to understand what it was that frightened and bewildered him. Then it gradually became, if not clear, at least not quite so muddy.

STAB was the word that had been printed on the card in the money clip that his assailant in the alley had left behind. Cassal had naturally interpreted it as an order to the thug. It wasn't, of course.

The first time Cassal had visited the Travelers Aid Bureau, it had been in the process of reorganization. The only purpose of the reorganization, he realized now, had been to change the name so he wouldn't translate the word on the slip into the original initials of the Bureau.

Now it probably didn't matter any more whether or not he knew, so the name had been changed back to Star Travelers Aid Bureau— STAB.

That, he saw bitterly, was why Murra Foray had been so positive that the identification tab he'd made with the aid of Dimanche had been a forgery.

She had known the man who robbed Cassal of the original one, perhaps had even helped him plan the theft.

That didn't make sense to Cassal. Yet it had to. He'd suspected the organization of being a racket, but it obviously wasn't. By whatever name it was called, it actually was dedicated to helping the stranded traveler. The question was—which travelers?

There must be agency operatives at the spaceport, checking every likely prospect who arrived, finding out where they were going, whether their papers were in order. Then, just as had happened to Cassal, the prospect was robbed of his papers so somebody stranded here could go on to that destination!

The shabby, aging technician finished changing the last door sign and hobbled over to Cassal. He peered through the rain and darkness.

"You stuck here, too?" he quavered.

"No," said Cassal with dignity, shaky dignity. "I'm not stuck. I'm here because I want to be."

"You're crazy," declared the old man. "I remember—"

Cassal didn't wait to find out what it was he remembered. An impossible land, perhaps, a planet which swings in perfect orbit around an ideal sun. A continent which reared a purple mountain range to hold up a honey sky. People with whom anyone could relax easily and without worry or anxiety. In short, his own native world from which, at night, all the constellations were familiar.

Somehow, Cassal managed to get back to his suite, tumbled wearily onto his bed. The showdown wasn't going to take place.

Everyone connected with the agency—including Murra Foray—

had been "stuck here" for one reason or another: no identification tab, no money, whatever it was. That was the staff of the Bureau, a pack of desperate castaways. The "philanthropy" extended to them and nobody else. They grabbed their tabs and money from the likeliest travelers, leaving them marooned here—and they in turn had to join the Bureau and use the same methods to continue their journeys through the Galaxy.

It was an endless belt of stranded travelers robbing and stranding other travelers, who then had to rob and strand still others, and so on and on . . .

Cassal didn't have a chance of catching up with Murra Foray. She had used the time—and Dimanche—to create her own identification tab and escape. She was going back to Kettikat, home of the Huntners, must already be light-years away.

Or was she? The signs on the Bureau had just been changed. Perhaps the ship was still in the spaceport, or cruising along below the speed of light. He shrugged defeatedly. It would do him no good; he could never get on board.

He got up suddenly on one elbow. He couldn't, but Manche could! Unlike his old instrument, it could operate at tremendous distances, its power no longer dependent only on his limited nervous energy.

With calculated fury, he let Manche strike out into space.

"There you are!" exclaimed Murra Foray. "I thought you could do it."

"Did you?" he asked coldly. "Where are you now?"

"Leaving the atmosphere, if you can call the stuff around this planet an atmosphere."

"It's not the atmosphere that's bad," he said as nastily as he could. "It's the philanthropy."

"Please don't feel that way," she appealed. "Huntners are rather unusual people, I admit, but sometimes even we need help. I had to have Dimanche and I took it."

"At the risk of killing me."

Her amusement was strange; it held a sort of sadness. "I didn't hurt you. I couldn't. You were too cute, like a—well, the animal native to Kettikat that would be called a teddy bear on Earth. A cute, lovable teddy bear."

"Teddy bear," he repeated, really stung now. "Careful. This one may have claws."

"Long claws? Long enough to reach from here to Kettikat?" She was laughing, but it sounded thin and wistful.

Manche struck out at Cassal's unspoken command. The laughter was canceled.

"Now you've done it," said Dimanche. "She's out cold."

There was no reason for remorse; it was strange that he felt it. His throat was dry.

"So you, too, can communicate with me. Through Manche, of course. I built a wonderful instrument, didn't I?"

"A fearful one," said Dimanche sternly. "She's unconscious."

"I heard you the first time." Cassal hesitated. "Is she dead?"

Dimanche investigated. "Of course not. A little thing like that wouldn't hurt her. Her nerve system is marvelous. I think it could carry current for a city. Beautiful!"

"I'm aware of the beauty," said Cassal.

An awkward silence followed. Dimanche broke it. "Now that I know the facts, I'm proud to be her chosen instrument. Her need was greater than yours."

Cassal growled, "As first counselor, she had access to every—"

"Don't interrupt with your half truths," said Dimanche. "Huntners *are* special; their brain structure, too. Not necessarily better, just different. Only the auditory and visual centers of their brains resemble that of man. You can guess the results of even superficial tampering with those parts of her mind. And stolen identification would involve lobotomy."

He could imagine? Cassal shook his head. No, he couldn't. A blinded and deaf Murra Foray would not go back to the home of the Huntners. According to her racial conditioning, a sightless young tiger should creep away and die.

Again there was silence. "No, she's not pretending unconsciousness," announced Dimanche. "For a moment I thought—but never mind."

The conversation was lasting longer than he expected. The ship must be obsolete and slow. There were still a few things he wanted to find out, if there was time.

"When are you going on Drive?" he asked.

"We've been on it for some time," answered Dimanche.

"Repeat that!" said Cassal, stunned.

"I said that we've been on faster-than-light drive for some time. Is there anything wrong with that?"

Nothing wrong with that at all. Theoretically, there was only one means of communicating with a ship hurtling along faster than light, and that way hadn't been invented.

Hadn't been until he had put together the instrument he called Manche.

Unwittingly, he had created far more than he intended. He ought to have felt elated.

Dimanche interrupted his thoughts. "I suppose you know what she thinks of you."

"She made it plain enough," said Cassal wearily. "A teddy bear. A brainless, childish toy."

"Among the Huntners, women are vigorous and aggressive," said Dimanche. The voice grew weaker as the ship, already light-years away, slid into unfathomable distances. "Where words are concerned, morals are very strict. For instance, 'dear' is never used unless the person means it. Huntner men are weak and not overburdened with intelligence."

The voice was barely audible, but it continued: "The principal romantic figure in the dreams of women . . ." Dimanche failed altogether.

"Manche!" cried Cassal.

Manche responded with everything it had. ". . . is the teddy bear."

The elation that had been missing, and the triumph, came now. It was no time for hesitation, and Cassal didn't hesitate. Their actions had been directed against each other, but their emotions, which each had tried to ignore, were real and strong.

The gravitor dropped him to the ground floor. In a few minutes, Cassal was at the Travelers Aid Bureau.

Correction. Now it was Star Travelers Aid Bureau.

And, though no one but himself knew it, even that was wrong. Quickly he found the old technician.

"There's been a reorganization," said Cassal bluntly. "I want the signs changed."

The old man drew himself up. "Who are you?"

"I've just elected myself," said Cassal. "I'm the new first counselor."

He hoped no one would be foolish enough to challenge him. He wanted an organization that could function immediately, not a hospital full of cripples.

The old man thought about it. He was merely a menial, but he had been with the bureau for a long time. He was nobody, nothing, but he could recognize power when it was near him. He wiped his eyes and shambled out into the fine cold rain. Swiftly the new signs went up.

STAR TRAVELERS AID BUREAU
S.T.A. WITH US
DENTON CASSAL, FIRST COUNSELOR

Cassal sat at the control center. Every question cubicle was visible at a glance. In addition there was a special panel, direct from the spaceport, which recorded essential data about every newly arrived traveler. He could think of a few minor improvements, but he wouldn't have time to put them into effect. He'd mention them to his assistant, a man with a fine, logical mind. Not really first-rate, of course, but well suited to his secondary position. Every member quickly rose or sank to his proper level in this organization, and this one had, without a struggle.

Business was dull. The last few ships had brought travelers who were bound for unimaginably dreary destinations, nothing he need be concerned with.

He thought about the instrument. It was the addition of power that made the difference. Dimanche plus power equaled Manche, and Manche raised the user far above the level of other men. There was little to fear.

But essentially the real value of Manche lay in this—it was a beginning. Through it, he had communicated with a ship traveling far faster than light. The only one instrument capable of that was instantaneous radio. Actually it wasn't radio, but the old name had stuck to it.

Manche was really a very primitive model of instantaneous radio. It was crude; all first steps were. Limited in range, it was practically valueless for that purpose now. Eventually the range would be extended. Hitch a neuronic manufactured brain to human one, add the power of a tiny atomic battery, and Manche was created.

The last step was his share of the invention. Or maybe the credit belonged to Murra Foray. If she hadn't stolen Dimanche, it never would have been necessary to put together the new instrument.

The stern lines on his face relaxed. Murra Foray. He wondered about the marriage customs of the Huntners. He hoped marriage was a custom on Kettikat.

Cassal leaned back; officially, his mission was complete. There was no longer any need to go to Tunney 21. The scientist he was sent to bring back might as well remain there in obscure arrogance. Cassal knew he should return to Earth immediately. But the Galaxy was wide and there were lots of places to go.

Only one he was interested in, though—Kettikat, as far from the center of the Galaxy as Earth, but in the opposite direction, incredibly far away in terms of trouble and transportation. It would be difficult even for a man who had the services of Manche.

Cassal glanced at the board. Someone wanted to go to Zombo.

"Delly," he called to his assistant. "Try 13. This may be what you want to get back to your own planet."

Delly Mortinbras nodded gratefully and cut in.

Cassal continued scanning. There was more to it than he imagined, though he was learning fast. It wasn't enough to have identification, money, and a destination. The right ship might come in with standing room only. Someone had to be "persuaded" that Godolph was a cozy little place, as good as any for an unscheduled stopover.

It wouldn't change appreciably during his lifetime. There were too many billions of stars. First he had to perfect it, isolate from dependence on the human element, and then there would come the installation. A slow process, even with Murra to help him.

Someday he would go back to Earth. He should be welcome. The information he was sending back to his former employers, Neuronics, Inc., would more than compensate them for the loss of Dimanche.

Suddenly he was alert. A report had just come in.

Once upon a time, he thought tenderly, scanning the report, there was a teddy bear that could reach to Kettikat. With claws—but he didn't think they would be needed.

Further Reading   F[loyd] L. Wallace

Books:

Address: Centauri. New York: Gnome Press, 1955.

Stories:

"Accidental Flight." *Galaxy Science Fiction*, April 1952. (*Time Waits for Winthrop*, ed. Frederik Pohl.)

"Big Ancestor." *Galaxy Science Fiction*, November 1954. (*Five-Odd*, ed. Groff Conklin.)

"Bolden's Pets." *Galaxy Science Fiction*, October 1955. (*Great Science Fiction About Doctors*, ed. Groff Conklin and Noah Fabricant.)

"End As a World." *Galaxy Science Fiction*, September 1955. (*The Third Galaxy Reader*, ed. H. L. Gold.)

"Growing Season." *Worlds of If*, July 1959. (*The Frozen Planet and Four Other SF Novellas from Worlds of If.*)

"The Impossible Voyage Home." *Galaxy Science Fiction*, August 1954. (*Science Fiction Adventures in Mutation*, ed. Groff Conklin.)

"Mezzerow Loves Company." *Galaxy Science Fiction*, June 1956. (*World That Couldn't Be*, ed. H. L. Gold.)

"Student Body." *Galaxy Science Fiction*, March 1953. (*Spectrum 5*, ed. Kingsley Amis and Robert Conquest.)

"Tangle Hold." *Galaxy Science Fiction*, June 1953. (*Five Galaxy Short Novels*, ed. H. L. Gold.)